Book One: City Of Orés

THE RIDERS OF APOCALYPSE SERIES
Book One: City of Orés

Copyright © 2007 Anthony L. Isom

Genre: Fantasy
First Edition

Dedication

To: Grandfather George Walker, from whence this immense writing talent came. Thank God for such brilliant blood. God bless you, Grandpa Walker.

To: God "Jesu" Almighty, He who has been my strength and ever-present co-writer on this project. To You be the glory and I love You more than anything.

To: Colton Stollenmaier, my surrogate brother in our Lord Jesus Christ. Thanks for your support in everything. God bless you.

A NOTE FROM THE AUTHOR

Friends, family and strangers, lovers of stories, whether short and long, I hope that you will immediately become enamored with the characters of this particular tale. Everyone to whom I've explained the most basic of details, this story seems either folly or impossible. The strangest thing about this entire process has been the fact that it started with the character of Triaphor. His name was the second name I wrote down, only because Tahiti, his master's name, was in the preceding line.

The fact of the matter is this: Triaphor is the most important character in the entire book. As you continue to read on, you may begin to wonder why? Though it is well explained, you must understand something. Triaphor, never for one moment, thinks that he is as central to his people's survival as he becomes. You will start out with an insecure little pipsqueak teenager and end up with a confident, trusting and loyal young adult.

There are several key points that I wish to divulge upon throughout this notary. The first of these is the fact that we begin this novel with young people who are "correct". That is to say, in comparison with the elders of the City of Orés, the youth of this miniscule town are more righteous in their opinion, for it is indeed fact. By this, I'm telling every reader, whether young or old, to listen to the voices of our young people. This world will soon be inhabited by us and the elders had best set a pretty good example for us, for if not, all of their worst fears shall come to fruition. Scared yet? Read on.

Next, I would like to point out that Tahiti, the only elder left loyal to Jesu, is the guide for our youthful friends in Orés. This is key to us as youngsters in this world. You don't always have the answers. You never will, so stop trying. The fact of the matter is that we need an elder that we can look up to with the utmost respect to be that guide for our lives. Only then, through prayer and consultation, can we really begin to see what God has in store for our lives. The elders were placed upon this Earth for such a purpose. As a young person, utilize this to your advantage.

And now, I will stress my last point, though many more could be made. Trust in God. This seems a theme most redundant among people who know what I'm talking about. But even to you who understand, it doesn't make it any easier. I'm here to tell you that the people of Orés thought the same thing. If you learn nothing else from this novel, at least take this away with you (if you read past this statement, that is), trust in God and He will keep you content, no matter what you're going through. Don't believe me? Read the story, try it for yourself and then contact me. Your life shall never be the same again.

As for the novel, I want you all, whether Christian, Atheist, Jewish, Buddhist or anything you feel like being, to enjoy this story. It is a fantastic story filled with good versus evil, love triumphing over all and of course, trusting in more than just yourself. It is good to have a company of people that can give you hope when you're feeling down and vice-versa. It uplifts your spirit. I hope that the following characters: Triaphor, Jewel, Tahiti, King Ric, Sultan Salzahirz, Councilor Autôw, Aléshai and Kyliõn really feed you and lead you to better knowledge and wisdom in your own life. As for our villains… just enjoy their names.

God Bless,
Anthony L. Isom '07

Prologue
Two Rival Cities

A long time ago in an ancient world called Névorn, two cities refused to settle their dispute. For many years, this war had raged between the city of Orés and the residents of Tortroc. The fact that everyone in Orés had a relative of an elderly age in the city of Tortroc didn't really make the situation any easier.

The city of Orés, City of the Young as many called it, was vibrant and full of life. The people of Orés consistently kept their city under maintenance until its walls were completely defensible. Almost no one in Névorn could take Orés under their control. Orés was ruled by King Ric, one whom most considered foolish, yet he had protected Orés thus far. Princess Jewel, his daughter, the wisest of all the women in Orés, jointly ruled the kingdom with her father. Though her young opinion was often thwarted, it was something that gave the people hope.

Dwelling within the city of Orés as well were the Prophets of Jesu. These prophets had been living in Orés since it was founded. They were the born protectors of Névorn. They had been blessed with powers from the Great God Jesu, the One & Only. For centuries, it was the Prophets of Jesu that gave the people hope for a brighter future. Each prophet also contributed to The Prophecy of Névorn. Whatever was prophesied by Jesu through one of his servants was written down. This task had finally been completed when Trílautûs, a prophet who lived until he was 2,007 years old, received a vision, spelling out how the Apocalypse of Névorn was to occur. The current prophet's name was Tahiti, an elderly sort of fellow whose leadership was well respected.

Tortroc was a city filled with the crooked elders of the people from Orés. They named the city Tortroc after Mount Tortroc, on which the city sat. The elders had built a massive temple dedicated to the goddess Sornsé. The young people of Orés, they who had built a temple to Jesu, considered Sornsé a demon and the ruler of utter evil. Jesu was believed to be the God of fair rule and justice amongst the people, the One and Only God. The elders had argued that Sornsé was righteous above both gods; therefore they wanted to build a temple to her honor in Orés. Upon this declaration, the elders were run out of the city by the young citizens of Orés. They fled to Mount Tortroc. There, Datos, leader of the rebellious elders, was chosen as ruler.

An agreement was made between the two cities that none would attack the other, no matter what strong hatred there was, because they were blood relatives. The elders were the first to break the pact. King Ric drove them back to Tortroc. Prophet Tahiti, the only elder that had remained loyal to Jesu, placed a curse on the temple of Sornsé and the gate of Tortroc. The elders were turned into giant venomous spiders. Until a Chosen One of Prophecy, named Lalrola, came and spoke the words on these buildings in nearest vicinity of these places, they were to remain alive and well.

But the Lalrola's task was even bigger than this. No one knew when he/she would come, nor did they know the full responsibility that would befall this person. All the inhabitants of Orés, as well as others of Névorn, knew was the fact that the Lalrola would bring them hope.

They would need hope, for soon a great evil would spread over the whole of Névorn. It had been prophesied, but no one knew the disastrous proportions of the calamity that would soon come upon them.

In the year 3015, a boy was born to the house of Biora. Biora's husband, Niron, had died years ago. The boy was named Triaphor, which means "Forbidden Lovechild". Biora noticed that strange things happened wherever she went with Triaphor. The infant attracted the attention of all in Névorn. Perhaps it was because of the fact that he was the first dark-skinned baby the citizens of Orés had ever seen, for they were of a fair complexion. Biora sent for Tahiti to inspect the activities of Triaphor. The elderly prophet moved in with them and noticed what Biora had.

Therefore, when Triaphor was 5 years of age, Tahiti took him away & was training him to become a faithful and powerful prophet. The boy learned quickly and his powers grew faster than Tahiti could teach them. Tahiti, having been a prophet for over 700 years, had seen many things, but never did he see anything as remarkable as Triaphor's ascension to what was known as *The Order of Prophecy*. The prophet did deep research and discovered that Triaphor could possibly be someone of great importance to the history of Névorn. He would have the daunting ask of training this boy to live up to this significance.

Currently, Triaphor was 16 years old & a successful young prophet protégé. Tahiti had been with Triaphor for eleven long years, teaching the boy many things, from government and philosophy to industry and religion. The two had grown to love each other like father and son. Tahiti had held back the information he'd discovered about Triaphor's impending impact. Through his method of training, though, he schooled the boy on all he need know.

"Master Tahiti!" Triaphor called.

"Yes, my son?" asked Tahiti.

"I've returned from the post office."

"Excellent!"

Tahiti stood from his chair in his cozy home. He took the mail from Triaphor's hands. He looked over his letters. One of them was from Sésad, Keeper of the Golden Tree. Tahiti hastily opened the letter and read it. A look of disdain appeared upon his face. Triaphor began to worry.

"What is it master?" he asked.

"Sit down, my son." Tahiti said.

Triaphor sat in a chair directly across from his master's big recliner. As Tahiti seated himself, age seemed to be taking him. But Triaphor knew better. He had learned that Jesu could empower even the oldest of his prophets.

"Triaphor, have you ever heard of the Land of Apocalypse?" Tahiti asked.

"Most certainly," Triaphor told him, "According to the legends, there are Four notorious horsemen from Apocalypse. There's the white horse and his Rider is War. He goes around conquering all the lands he passes. There's the red horse and his Rider is Pestilence. He carries a huge sword with him not to kill, but to wound all in his path. The third is the black horse and his Rider is Famine. He carries a morning star and a massive mace that easily crushes the strongest of gates. He also carries a pair of balances in his hands. The fourth is the ashen horse and his Rider is Hades. He causes death to happen wherever he passes. These Riders are toughest when riding all together. They also dwell in a shadowy castle known as the Fortress of Daréngir. "

"These Riders are unleashed from Apocalypse," Tahiti said, "And are ready to come here. They may join allegiance with the elders of Mount Tortroc."

Triaphor began to fear what may happen if these Riders passed through Orés. It was easy to run off the elders, but the Riders of Apocalypse were different. Their power was unlike any in Névorn. Many had tried, but none had been able to successfully stop the Riders of the Apocalypse. Most believed that no one could kill them. There were some, like the Prophets of Jesu, who had faith that these beasts would not rule forever.

"When are they passing through?" Triaphor asked.

"Apocalypse is a long way away from here." Tahiti assured, "But the horsemen ride fast. But they also have stops to make and the place they seek is not easily found. It's no telling when the Riders themselves will appear in this region of the world. But when they arrive, we must stop at nothing to keep them from joining Tortroc. Meanwhile I will continually teach you to trust in Jesu. He is the only one who will be able to stop these monsters from destroying Orés."

Triaphor became less worried once his master told him this. Tahiti was a very kind and loving person and he had so much faith that no one could stand in his path. He knew that in order to get this powerful, he would have to listen to every word from his master. For one day, he would be the only prophet around to protect Orés from the Apocalypse Riders and the elders of Tortroc.

Triaphor continued to grow quickly in wit and power among the people. Soon it was said that Tahiti and Triaphor alone protected the city. The two prophets denied such a claim. And even if such a thing were true, it would've been Jesu working through them. This they knew, but it was difficult to convince the masses of such a thing.

Now, you see, these Prophets of Jesu were required to attend monthly meetings at the castle just like council members. Today would be Triaphor's first time going with Tahiti. Tahiti had finally passed him to be a full-fledged prophet. Once Tahiti died, Triaphor would be the only prophet left to protect Orés. It had taken years, but the elderly prophet had, at last, made the decision that Triaphor was mature enough to be the next foolproof Prophet of Jesu.

The two walked into the castle and the double doors to the throne room immediately opened. The lord of the city, King Ric, sat upon the throne. In his younger days, he had seen many wars. He had even been to the border of the Land of Apocalypse itself. Though by his age you could not tell. His hair, still enflamed in red, had not a gray or white strand in it. Wrinkles on his face were non-existent, though he and Tahiti were of the same era. Almost ten years difference stood between them.

"Welcome to the court, young Triaphor!" Ric exclaimed.

"Thank you." Triaphor bowed.

As they spoke, someone came striding down the stairs. Triaphor's eyes widened as he saw her. She was so beautiful. She had black curly hair that ran slightly past her shoulders and her bodily curves were perfect. No one on Névorn possessed such beauty as this woman. Her robes were magnificent as they were a gorgeous river green with purple sleeve tips. The sleeves were long on her arms and the robes flowed from her body with splendor.

"Aw, Triaphor, there is someone I wish you to meet." Ric said.

As the woman stepped off the last stair and walked to them, Ric spoke.

"This is my 15 year-old daughter, Princess Jewel."

"It is," Triaphor said, "a pleasure for me to meet you."

"And you as well, young prophet." Jewel replied.

Little did Ric know, but Triaphor had already met the young princess. He and she had kept this a secret, for Ric didn't need to know that his daughter had been fraternizing with the prophet before it was time for her to meet him. In Orés, there was an appointed time for everything.

Shivers ran down Triaphor's spine. As they all sat for the meeting, Triaphor listened not to one word. Tahiti would consistently look over at Triaphor, yet he said nothing. But he knew what Triaphor was thinking and what he wanted. Tahiti tried pinching Triaphor a couple of times to get his attention. Yet after each pinch, Triaphor would only pretend to pay attention for a minute and return to Jewel.

Tahiti wondered if this was right. He would have to confront Triaphor about it later, when they had time.

***************************   ***************************

Breaking through clouds of white, the kingdom finally appeared in their sight. A city of splendor was this, Skyland as it was called. It was ruled by the Tiki people and their king, Asta, was a cruel and torturous tyrant. They had finally found the city so greatly talked about. For many long months they had searched among the sky.

The Three Horsemen rode swiftly to the castle of the king. Asta, a hairy, rather nasty looking man who looked as if he hadn't had a bath a day in his life sat upon the throne. As the Three walked to the throne, Asta bowed. He knew that they were so powerful that no one could surpass them if they tried.

"Asta, king of Skyland," Hades spoke, "A proposition from our master you must answer. For seven years, you've had the chance to decide. Now the decision must be final."

"May I remind you," said Famine, "You might want to do what we expect, for we alone have the advantage of power."

"Great Riders from Apocalypse," Asta replied, "I shall gather my armies together. We fly upon Orés at once."

"Excellent," Pestilence said.

The Three left the palace of King Asta. Now it was time to depart. Their master's plans would astound the little city in the valley. Tortroc's power would grow, as their alliances were some of the strongest military powers because of their advantages.

The Lords Of Ardenôs never used horses, for there was no need for them. They used dragons. The Red Dragons of Ardenôs were the fastest flying creatures in all of Névorn except for their cousins, the Bakrôns of Bélgôrith. They could storm a city better than any other beast of burden could. With their speed and agility combined with the mind power of the riders, they would break Orés to its knees.

Glory and honor would be theirs. Asta was sure of this. Orés was a city of beauty, its grandeur outmatching any kingdom ever to rise and fall. Orés had been built since the beginning of the world and long had it stood. It had seen the rise and fall of many nations, but would see it no more. Once Asta and Datos joined alliances against them, the young people of Orés and all those loyal to Jesu would perish.

"Death to them all." Asta whispered as the dragons were ready to depart.

The Three watched as the Lords Of The Sky lifted off and flew down to Orés. They turned and rode the opposite direction. They reached the Staircase of Clouds within minutes. They quickly made their way down the stairway. Their next destination was very important to their master's plan. It must be accomplished.

****************************   *****************************

Triaphor sat under an apple tree beside the castle. The area surrounding the tree had to be the most gorgeous part of Orés. He had loved sitting under the tree since he was a little boy. Sometimes he would just come here to think. He remembered spilling tears here one day. It was the day his mother, Biora, had died. She was a wonderful woman. There was no other like her. The cause of her death was never explained to him, but he always knew that one day, her murderer would pay dearly for it.

As Triaphor looked up in the horizon, he saw a figure approach. This figure wore long robes that flowed down to the ground. As he saw the hourglass shape of her body, he knew it was the princess. She sat down beside him.

"Your favorite spot too huh?" Jewel asked.

"Since I was five." Triaphor replied.

"I've always loved the peace that dwells here," Jewel said, "Serenity could have never been placed any more conveniently than this."

The two sat in silence for a while. Jewel could not help but stare at him. He was so endearing, yet in his wonderful features, she saw something else. Something she had seen in only one other many years ago. She had loved him very much.

"Power and glory," Jewel broke the silence, "was once given to the great kings of Orés. It was they who began the city. Every king restored the city as much as possible. Strong defenses we've always maintained. Yet, somehow I feel that in these days, Orés may die."

"How so?" Triaphor asked.

"The strongest forces of the world now join together to destroy us. But there is one reason why we may not defeat them." Jewel said.

"What reason is that?" Triaphor questioned.

"Lack of love and care." Jewel responded.

Triaphor was confused.

"How does love and care mingle with the affairs of war?" Triaphor asked.

"Take this tree for instance," Jewel pointed up, "If it were not for loving and caring hands that built it and maintained it, the tree would not stand today. Same for this city. For centuries, king after king has shown love and care for the city. But now, my father has stopped the tradition and soon the city may fall. If we do not begin to show pride in our city, we shall no longer have a city to show pride in."

"Good point," Triaphor said, "Do you show such love and care in all you do?"

"I must." Jewel told him.

The two sat in silence once more. Triaphor was amazed at her wisdom. He had traveled many places with Tahiti and had seen many beautiful women. He had even kissed many of these women and had not found in them the qualities he found in Jewel.

Triaphor had known Jewel for a long time. They had practically grown up together secretly. Tahiti had taken her from the castle day by day to keep the two reacquainted with one another for he felt that they would one day be the ones who would decide the fate of Orés. For what seemed to be an eternity, Triaphor had longed to openly love Jewel but knew that Tahiti would disapprove, as well as her father. But today was different. The cares of the world at large no longer mattered to Triaphor.

He leaned over and closed his eyes. The two kissed under the apple tree that meant so much to both of them. The kiss was a release of so many emotions for Triaphor. He could not only feel the excellence of the kiss, but the love and care behind everything that Jewel had done in her lifetime. He also felt the love and care she had for him.

"Many years ago, as I was growing up," Jewel began, "My father got tutors for me. Many was the number of these tutors and most of them were old. I looked up to them for their wisdom. But once, my eyes carried to one young tutor of mine. He was five years older than I. We began to fall in love and dated for many years. As soon as talk of marriage began, war broke out. He, my father, who was at the time Prince Ric of Orés, and the armies, tracked down the Riders of Apocalypse. Only the border was reached and a great battle they fought at the gate. But the leader of these Riders, War, who rode a white horse and a crown upon his head, came and destroyed my fiancé. Terrible was the news of defeat. I closed my mind to love for many years. My father has tried to get me to marry princes from far lands, but only one man has ever crossed my path and surpassed that of my tutor."

"Who might that be?" Triaphor asked, half knowing the answer.

"The one I've kissed." Jewel got up.

She walked back to the castle. He watched her as she walked away in all her beauty. The river green robe flowed with such magnificence. He stared off into the distance knowing that Jesu had brought together their union.

That night, Triaphor stared up at her window, knowing that the light was on for a reason. Jewel was singing a song to herself. It was an old song that appeared in many of the legends. It was the song one sang when they had found love.

Triaphor called up to her.

"Jewel!"

Jewel turned and looked out of her window.

"What are you doing here?"

"I heard your beautiful voice." Triaphor replied.

Jewel threw down a rope to him. He climbed to her window. He crawled in. He hugged Jewel. Then he kissed her.

"Answer me." Jewel said.

"I just wanted to let you know something." Triaphor said.

"Well," Jewel started, "out with it.

Triaphor took out a necklace. It was dazzling in the light. The emblem on it was the emblem of the Golden Tree. The Golden Tree lied past the Forest of Death in the Field of Gold. This was the most honored emblem in all of Orés. The inhabitants of what was known as The Golden Kingdom were former allies of Orés. They would've been still, save for the fact that their king before this one refused to fight in Apocalypse with them. Ever since the rise of this new ruler, no one had extended forth an invitation for friendship.

"A gift made from the fires of the Golden Kingdom itself." Triaphor said, "I love you."

Jewel could only stare at it. Triaphor put the necklace around her neck for her. He began to kiss her. They landed on her bed. Before clothing was removed, they stopped. Jewel wanted to keep going, but she knew she would be in deep trouble if she lay with a man to whom she wasn't married. Triaphor got up and left by the window. He blew her a kiss before he walked to Tahiti's cottage.

Tahiti sat in his chair, awaiting the door's close.

"You've been out late," he said.

"I'm sorry," Triaphor said, "I've had business to take care of."

"I hope that thy business is not regrettable."

Triaphor looked at his master strangely. Tahiti had never been so suspicious of him before.

"My father, I haven't done anything wrong." Triaphor told him.

"If you have not, then is love permittable?" Tahiti asked.

"Is not love essential?" Triaphor returned.

"Our duty is to protect the people in the name of Jesu," Tahiti explained, "Relationships aren't allowed for us because they stand in our way of protecting the people. If we are too busy protecting our relationship, we tend to forget about the people we've been given to protect. Hence creatures like Belwin, Prophet of Evil come forth."

Triaphor remembered the horror stories of Belwin. The former Prophet of Jesu had been trained by Sõnércus, Tahiti's old master. Many people felt that together, Belwin and Tahiti would be greater even than Sõnércus had been. But Belwin's pride came first and filled him with hatred for Tahiti's growing fame. Soon after Sõnércus' death, the young man delved into black magic. As the Dark Spirits filled him, he left Orés with his wife and was never seen again.

"There is room for both." Triaphor argued.

"Yes," Tahiti agreed, "But can you separate the two? Can you maintain your relationship and protect the city as well?"

"Not easily." Triaphor's head lowered.

"Then why put so much stress on your soul?" Tahiti asked compassionately.

"It has been destined by Jesu," Triaphor said, "I have kissed many girls. I've had relationships with many women. Yet none compare in beauty or in wisdom to Jewel. She is in her own league. She is elite. She is above all women. She is the one for me. In my heart, Jesu has confirmed this."

Tahiti knew that Triaphor was right. He had proven his point. Jesu had given Triaphor remarkable powers. Tahiti saw something in Triaphor that he hadn't seen in any of his students that he had taught in his many years.

The two prophets went to bed that night thinking on these things. Tahiti knew that soon he would be gone. Triaphor had to know now that he would be the only prophet left. He would have to know how to handle it. Soon Tahiti would be gone forever.

The morning sun rose and set in the sky. The colors of blue and lavender combined together to form the perfect sunrise. On such a vibrant morning, King Ric stood in his throne room, listening to what he considered to be the biggest mass of pig swallow he'd ever heard. His daughter, Jewel, Princess of Orés, was in love.

"And a prophet of Jesu at that!" Ric fussed.

"What is so wrong with that?" Jewel asked.

"You must marry a prince if you are to marry, my daughter." Ric explained.

"But I don't love a prince, my father," Jewel said, "I love a prophet. He has the qualities that no prince would ever have. Princes are cocky, arrogant sons of mindless queens and political-seeking kings. But prophets are children of none alive and they have wisdom and the highest belief standard in all the world."

"But what's so special about *this* prophet?" Ric asked his daughter.

"*This* prophet…" Jewel was about to explain when Tahiti and Triaphor entered the throne room.

"Your majesty!" Tahiti exclaimed, "I need to speak to you at once!"

"Then we must go into the antechamber." Ric said.

Ric and Tahiti made their way to the antechamber. Jewel sat down on the throne and stared into the floor. Triaphor walked over to her. Jewel had a look of dismay on her face. Urgency seemed to flood her soul.

"What's wrong?" Triaphor asked.

"Soon," Jewel began, "Tahiti shall be gone. You will then be the only one left."

"What?" Triaphor was shocked.

Jewel looked up at her lover. She could feel that he didn't know the truth about himself. How was he going to fully protect Orés when he didn't know the task ahead of him?

"You have special powers, Triaphor," Jewel said, "You are the Lalrola spoken of in Prophecy."

Jewel had somewhat of a prophetic sense of mind. Not always could she interpret things the way a prophet could, but every once in a blue moon, she would pick up on things and begin to prophesy. Most of the time, her predictions were truth, for Jesu worked through her.

But this time…no way! How could this be? Triaphor would've never guessed that he was the Lalrola. The Lalrola was meant to be the one to break the curse of the elders in Tortroc. This also meant that soon the Apocalypse was to befall them. The Lalrola was only to be born in a time when the Apocalypse was nearing Névorn. Horrid thoughts ran through Triaphor's mind as he remembered his studies of The Prophecy and its remarks on such things.

"If I'm Lalrola," Triaphor spoke, "I hope that I may perform my tasks that Jesu has set aside for me."

He didn't really want to accept this fact, but he knew that he must. Jewel smiled. She stood from the throne and walked past him. She then walked up the stairs. Entranced by her beauty, Triaphor followed her up the stairs. They wound up in Jewel's room.

Jewel allowed Triaphor to sit in a chair. She then sat in his lap. Triaphor removed his outer garment and began to kiss her. As the two sat and kissed, Triaphor could feel everything that Jewel was thinking. Every intricate detail and vision of her mind came forth and eradicated all his thought processes. He then knew that he must be the Lalrola, for only a person with that much power could feel this way.

The kissing lasted for a while until Triaphor felt a disturbance. Someone was at the gate. An intruder. The size that filled his mind was of monstrous proportions. It swamped him to where he could think of nothing else.

"Jewel," Triaphor became serious, "Hand me my garment and let us get to the gate!"

"Why?" Jewel asked.

"The Lords of the Sky are here!" he shouted as he donned his outer garment out of the door.

Triaphor grabbed his sword as Jewel prepared for battle. The two ran towards the gate with archers at their backs. As they reached the top of the gate, they saw them.

The Lords of the Sky upon the Red Dragons of Ardenôs were lined up, ready for battle. Tahiti rode out on his horse to the gate with speed.

"Pôrl min mantha!" Tahiti spoke, "Cover the city from the Lords of Ardenôs!"

An invisible shield instantly cloaked the city from the sight of the Lords Of The Sky. Asta was quite upset. Now he would have to listen closely to the orders of the leader to know what to do.

"Archers!" Triaphor shouted, "Rally behind Tahiti!"

All archers not on the wall began formation behind Tahiti.

"Swordsmen!" Triaphor shouted once more, "Rally behind Tahiti!"

The swordsmen did as the archers had done.

"Cavalry!" Triaphor shouted with a final breath, "Rally behind Tahiti!"

The entire army, save for the archers perched on the wall, had united behind Tahiti. Tahiti was to lead them in war against the Lords Of The Sky. Triaphor glanced at Jewel. The Lords Of The Sky were powerful. Not many walled cities had the defenses with which to fight them. But Triaphor's faith in Jesu assured him that the One & Only would decide their fate.

"Archers on the wall!" Triaphor commanded, "Set arrows!"

The archers nocked the arrows on their bows. Asta looked around to his fellow comrades. His general came up to him.

"Your Majesty," he said, "What are we to do?"

"Get the battering ram ready and steady the men!" Asta told him.

The Lords Of The Sky were terrified. They couldn't defeat their enemies if they weren't able to be seen.

"Jewel," Triaphor whispered, "Make sure their arrows are lighted."

"Why do you not shout the command?" Jewel asked.

"The city's been shielded," Triaphor informed, "They can only hear us. I've a little surprise for them."

The arrows were lit on every archer's bow. The archers aimed their arrows at the dragons. The people could be defeated, but the dragons were what made it difficult.

"Fire!" Triaphor commanded.

"Steady!!!" Asta demanded his men.

The arrows came from the wall of Orés with force. Dragons were pierced in their heads. Many of them were killed. The men without dragons to ride upon went to the battering ram to help carry it.

"Volley!" Triaphor shouted.

More arrows came through the nothingness. More dragons were pierced. Men and beast were massacred by the numberless arrows that streamed from the bows of Orés.

"Tahiti!" Triaphor yelled, "Pôrl min mantha du ayantas! (Uncover the city from their sight!)"

"Uncover the city from their sight!" Tahiti shouted.

Suddenly Asta and the Lords Of Ardenôs could see the city.

"Send forth the battering ram!!!" Asta commanded.

The men holding the battering ram ran forth with strength. The dragons lifted off into the sky. They all followed the pace of the battering ram, which was going pretty fast for its size.

Tahiti stood with the army of Orés behind him.

"Send these foul skinks back to the abyss!" he commanded the army.

The battering ram reached the gate.

"Open the gate!" Tahiti shouted.

The gate swung wide open. Arrows whizzed around as the foot soldiers who had lost their dragons came straddling into the gate. Blood filled the streets quickly. The Lords Of Ardenôs swooped down upon their dragons.

"Fire!!!" Triaphor demanded.

The archers began a stream of arrows at the dragons. Every rider lost his dragon. They jumped from their dragons and began fighting. Triaphor and Jewel fought side by side as the fools tried to salvage their attack.

Tahiti rode quickly throughout the city, killing all in his path. Eventually Asta called a retreat and the men ran out of the city to the mountain.

"Archers on the wall!" Triaphor, who had made it to the floor of the city, cried, "Kill as many as possible!"

The archers shot two volleys and killed many. And after ridding the army of Ardenôs of their attack force, there were still hundreds of men running to Tortroc.

"We've achieved victory!" Jewel exclaimed.

"Not yet," Tahiti told her, "The Three Riders that have been unleashed must pass through first."

Tahiti, Triaphor, Jewel, King Ric and his counselors stood in the throne room. They were discussing what their next move would be. Tahiti had kept silent the whole time as people threw out numberless ideas on what to do.

"Perhaps," Jewel said, "the best thing to do would be to wait until the words of the Prophecy are fulfilled. The mountain must glow red before we can attack Tortroc. Meanwhile, let's renew our allegiance with The Golden Kingdom that we once had. That is our only chance of survival."

The people agreed with what was being said. Jewel once again proved her wisdom. Tahiti had already spoken to Triaphor over what should be done when he left this world. Triaphor had not wanted to hear it, but as the Riders neared the city, he could feel death breathing down his very neck.

All they had to do now was wait.

The Three Riders of Apocalypse looked upon Orés. The City of the Prophets. The City of the Kings. The City of the Warriors. Majestic glory had been granted unto the city's location. The high walls and the splendorous gates were a sight to see. Soon Orés would be known as the City of the Dead. They had come for one purpose alone.

"I shall handle him," Hades spoke.

Tahiti felt them. They were here. They had charged through the gate. Someone had to stop them. Tahiti rode out on his horse in front of their path. They charged onward with strength. They stopped when they saw Tahiti.

"Back to the fires of death from which you came!" Tahiti shouted.

The Riders just stood there, knowing that Tahiti would be foolish to take on the three of them. Then the Ashen Rider, Hades, stepped forward on his horse. His deep eyes shone through the hood of his Ashen Cloak. He glared at Tahiti with hatred filling his eyes.

"No one can defeat me," Hades said.

Black clouds began to form above the city. They were steadfastly heading towards Tahiti. When they had just begun to cover the very head of the Ashen Rider, Tahiti spoke.

"Pak pôrthi clu cin dôrta!"

The clouds rolled back a little. Hades commanded them to come forth once more. They came on headstrong this time. As Tahiti spoke the words again, he knew he could not defeat the Ashen Rider.

Triaphor and Jewel held each other as they watched the inevitable. The city was capsized by the aura surrounding them at that moment. The Ashen Rider's power was renowned in the land. No one had defeated him. Yet.

Hades reached for a knife. He grasped it in preparation of throwing it.

"No one shall conquer me."

He threw the knife into Tahiti's chest. Tahiti screamed in pain. His body began to immediately burn. His skin was flaying from his body. The nerves within his soul roared with immense heat and the sound of his scream filled the citizens of Orés with horror.

Tahiti fell from his horse. Triaphor's eyes widened. He drew his sword. Before he could advance out to save Tahiti, Jewel grabbed him.

"No!!" Jewel exclaimed, "You cannot defeat him!"

The Ashen Rider disembarked from his horse. He viewed Tahiti's body. A mark was burned onto Tahiti's head. The symbol of the Apocalypse. A giant *A* with a sword behind it had appeared upon Tahiti's forehead.

Hades got upon his horse at once and the Three Riders rode out of the city. Hades eyed Triaphor as they galloped away. Triaphor dropped his sword on the ground and ran to Tahiti's rescue. Tahiti was already fading fast. The power of the Ashen Rider had soaked throughout his veins and consumed his soul with death.

The entire city stood and watched as Triaphor wept over his master.

A long processional was led by a red coffin out of the front gate of Orés. Triaphor and Jewel stood in front of the line nearest the coffin. Triaphor's eyes burned from the crying he had been doing all night long. His sockets, now dry, were anticipating the return of tears.

The processional reached the Grove of Prophets and stopped. The coffin was set upon a wooden truss that would soon be let into the ground. All men, women and children bowed their head low in sadness of Tahiti's death. Triaphor and Jewel were hooded in black.

"Great was Tahiti," a priest proclaimed, "And great shall be the memory of him."

Tahiti was immediately lowered into the ground. Triaphor began to cry once more. He felt a comforting hand reach across and grasp his side. He was greatly loved by Jewel and she alone could comfort him.

The hole was covered as the processional began to leave. As Triaphor and Jewel walked away back to the castle, Jewel's lips burned to inquire of Triaphor something that was pressing on her soul.

"I have an important question."

"What?"

"Well," Jewel began, "I was wondering if you would like to stay with me in the castle. Forever."

"Is that legal?" Triaphor asked.

"Marriage is always legal." Jewel said.

Triaphor was astonished. He loved Jewel. He accepted the offer, but they would first have to take care of certain issues. They couldn't possibly be married with peace now that the Riders had joined up with Tortroc and Ardenôs. Nothing would permit it. The three kingdoms had to be stopped.

The castle was filled with buzzing noise as many counselors screamed their opinion on what should be done next.

"Fulfill the Prophecy!" some shouted.

"We cannot wait that long!" others shouted.

"Nothing can stop the Riders if Tahiti couldn't!!" still others shouted.

Triaphor, Jewel, and Ric looked around in irritation. They couldn't believe that with the Dark Alliance so close to them, they were arguing over what to do. After a servant made sure that the throne room was quiet, Triaphor rose to speak.

"Nothing can be done about the Dark Alliance until the mountain glows red as fire as the Prophecy states." Triaphor said, "But there is one thing that I was told to do as Tahiti was nearing death. We must renew the alliance we once had with The Golden Kingdom. It's our only chance of survival. Once the Dark Alliance gets the hint that we're not just sitting here, waiting for destruction, then they won't attack the city as much."

The counselors nodded their head in approval to this. They had no choice.

"Now we must decide who shall go with thee." Ric said.

"I have already decided this," Triaphor said, "A battalion of soldiers, Jewel, and myself are going to The Golden Tree."

"My daughter will not go with you on this journey!" Ric shouted.

Jewel stood quickly.

"Father I must!" she shouted back.

"There is no reason for you to go, you might never return!" King Ric bellowed.

"There must be a representative of the city bearing the emblem of the city present when Sésad and I meet." Triaphor explained.

"You bear the emblem on your robe and your staff." Ric pointed out.

"They already know that the prophets are loyal, but they must know that all of Orés is loyal, else we shall fall at the hands of the Dark Alliance." Triaphor continued, "Trust in Jesu. He will make sure that Jewel is safe."

"Jesu!" Ric cried, "Jesu is not to be trusted. If He could not protect his own prophet from death, what makes you think that He'll protect us?!"

At this, Triaphor turned to Ric with anger in his eyes. They pierced into the very soul of the king.

"From this day forth, thou art cursed," Triaphor punished, "You shall not come outside of three yards of this castle or you will be killed by intruding neighbors and Jewel shall be queen in thy stead. You must not venture from here until this curse is uplifted from thee."

Ric sat in silence and he spoke not another word the whole time.

The counselors agreed with Triaphor's proposition. The battalion was readied. Triaphor and Jewel prepared themselves for battle. They knew that in the Forest of Death, trouble would come, but no one would stop them. Not even the evil demoness Sornsé.

*************************   *************************

The Riders made their way into the castle of Datos, king of Tortroc. When they arrived in the large throne room they saw many men from both kingdoms. Asta and his fellow men from Ardenôs looked bruised and battered.

"Great Riders of Apocalypse," Datos said, "Welcome to Tortroc. It is a pleasure to finally meet you."

The Riders said nothing. As they all stood there, Asta began to tell his story of how he and his men were utterly defeated by the city of Orés. Hades almost wanted to laugh. They must've looked pathetic. Losing to such a small city must've been a sight to see.

Suddenly, in their midst, there appeared the evil goddess Sornsé. Everyone in the whole court except for the Three Riders, bowed in obeisance to her. The Riders showed obeisance to no one. No one except for their leader, War, but many times not even then. Hades had begged to differ that he was below the White Rider, even though it had been proven up to date that War was more powerful.

"I have seen the plans of Orés this day." Sornsé spoke, "They ride to The Golden Tree to ask assistance of them. The young prophet goes with them. A plan I've conceived in my head."

"What plan is that?" Hades spoke.

"Lord Hades, you have an arrow for death, do you not?" Sornsé asked.

Hades nodded his head, merely because he liked the sound of being called a lord.

"Excellent!" Sornsé exclaimed.

The Dark Alliance prepared everything for the plan that Sornsé had outlaid to them. Triaphor, the Lalrola, would now die and be buried beside his master. Then Orés would be left hopeless. Without their victor, the cursed spiders would finally rule the world alongside the Riders.

****************************   ******************************

The battalion was camped upon a hill that overlooked the Forest of Death. Many didn't want to go in there, but it was their allegiance to Triaphor and trust in Jesu that made them anxious to ride once more. Triaphor gave the soldiers a sense of hope, even if the War Council despised him. Jesu was their God and He had provided such a warrior as Triaphor to take the place of the wise Tahiti.

Nightfall fell as Triaphor and Jewel sat near a tent looking up at the stars. Their iridescence glowed with elegance. Triaphor wished that Tahiti was here with him. He remembered the days he was taught astrology, learning of only one God, the one, true God, Jesu.

"Look, my love," Triaphor spoke, "Behold the beauteous star Talsûrõn."

Jewel looked into the night. She saw exactly what Triaphor had pointed out. No one who was observing the sky tonight would miss it. Not only was it glowing as bright as a beacon, but Talsûrõn looked as giant as a moon.

"Did you ever know the story of Talsûrõn?" Jewel asked her lover.

"Yea," the young man responded, "Would you like to hear it, my love?"

"Surely you jest?"

"I do no such thing."

The two laughed lightly.

"Alright then," Triaphor started, "I shall tell you. Talsûrõn, as you know, is one of the brightest stars in Jesu's glorious galaxy. But what many do not know is that thousands of years ago, there were people who inhabited it."

"People?" Jewel inquired, "What did they look like?"

"It is hard to describe them," Triaphor continued, "Most legends agree that they were people of many different colors, but they all glowed as bright as the star itself. Now Talsûrõn was one of the first stars created by Jesu, therefore they were tender to His heart. But, for some strange reason, He permitted the Riders of the Apocalypse to travel to Talsûrõn and view its flawless beauty. Now, the people of Talsûrõn knew that the Riders of the Apocalypse were coming, so they prepared themselves. This was not good enough. There was an ancient order of female warriors that resided on Talsûrõn known as *The Order of The MorningStar Talsûrõn.* As soon as they were wiped out, Talsûrõn had no choice but to surrender. The Riders tortured those pour souls. Hades created a murky river, much like the River of Hades that lies before the Fortress of Daréngir, and threw all babies into it. And if a nursing mother was found, the child was cut from her belly and thrown into the river along with the others."

"How awful!" Jewel exclaimed, "And have they been punished for such a crime?"

"A curse," Triaphor stated, "has been placed upon them. According to the Prophecy, when Talsûrõn shines directly after dusk settles—meaning that the sun has set—then there shall rise from Névorn, a leader who shall rebuild the MorningStar Talsûrõn. She will kill one of the Riders before the Apocalypse."

Jewel shuddered under Triaphor's arm. He could feel fear rushing into her as she began to realize how dangerous and dreadful these Riders really were. Sweat poured from her body.

He kissed her for comfort. Then he took her face in his hands and looked deeply into her eyes.

"What lies ahead may shock you," Triaphor said.

"What do you mean?" Jewel asked.

"The way things must transpire," Triaphor replied, "You must be ready to fight without me."

"But I don't want to have to bare this road without you here…"

Jewel felt devastated. How many more fiancé's was she going to have to go through before she finally found the right one. Perhaps she could talk him out of going.

"Triaphor…" Jewel began but was interrupted by the all-knowing Triaphor.

"Jewel," Triaphor said, "If I could, I would stay, but my mission as Lalrola calls for much more than you realize. Many think its only a position filled for the one who is to uplift the curse and destroy the elderly Spiders of Tortroc, but it means so much more than that. The Riders want to take over the world of Névorn and I've been born and assigned to stop them. Its my duty."

"But why must you die?" Jewel's big blue eyes gazed into his.

"This I know not, but I'll be sure to tell thee when I find out." He kissed her softly.

Then the two departed to their tents to rest. As Triaphor stepped into his tent, a figure robed in blue stood before him. His cautiousness caused him to draw his sword.

"Put thy sword away, great Lalrola," the voice said.

Triaphor knew that voice. He had heard it so many times.

"Who are you?" Triaphor asked.

"One you lost," the man said. He removed his hood and Triaphor knew that it was indeed Tahiti.

"How…" Triaphor started.

"There is no time for questions," Tahiti interrupted, "Sornsé has much planned for you in the forest. Be careful. Seeing that you are the Lalrola, you may begin to become smug in your abilities. But you must remember that thy full strength has not yet been put upon you. You will make it to The Golden Tree as long as you listen to my instruction. You will become great one day. But remember that day has not yet come."

"Yes master." Triaphor said.

Tahiti disappeared from Triaphor's sight. As Triaphor slept that night, he felt as if he were snuggling into the arms of Jesu. Jesu would be with them and He would make sure that nothing harmed them. He would be the one to stop the Dark Alliance from conquering the world.

The sun rose into the sky as the camp had already begun to awake. The battalion of soldiers began to pack for what might be their last moment to live. They all were assembled, waiting for the two leaders to ride to the front.

"Men of Orés!" Triaphor shouted, "Jesu is with us! He has assured me that this day we shall not lose one man to this beastly forest. No one shall perish in the hands of Sornsé this day. Rise up and stand! Rise up and fight! Rise up, for victory is yours!"

The men shouted as Triaphor and Jewel led them into the forest. A journey this would be for them all. They would have to trust in Jesu in order to win and in order to strike against the evil forces that surrounded their city.

The group trudged through the forest cautiously but quickly. As they moved onward a voice spoke to them. It was Sornsé.

"Can you not move quicker than that?"

No one responded.

"A challenge I extend unto thee. You shall have three attacks that you must destroy before you reach the edge of the forest."

"Bring them on!" Triaphor shouted back.

The battalion still continued moving, but they slowed their pace, readying themselves for anything.

"First challenge," Sornsé spoke, "Three arrows from any direction. Find them."

Triaphor and Jewel readied themselves. Everyone else was commanded to stand down. Jewel drew her sword. Triaphor readied his staff. An arrow whizzed from a tree closest to Jewel. She cleaved the arrow in two.

Another arrow came from a tree closest to the captain of the battalion. The captain cut the arrow down. The last arrow came from the sky. Triaphor struck it down with his staff and then stomped upon it with his cast iron boot.

"Very good," Sornsé congratulated, "Now an army of seven comes at you. Second challenge."

"Archers, surround us all!" Triaphor commanded.

The archers circled the entire battalion. Triaphor waited to give the command. He heard drums. He knew they were from a different land than what was on the eastern side of Névorn. As they drew close, the archers nocked their arrows on the bows.

The men came into sight. They were beastly creatures. They had obviously been through much torture. They were once men but you couldn't tell by their look.

"Fire!!!" Triaphor shouted.

Arrows pierced the seven and they fell immediately. Triaphor knew that the last challenge wouldn't be so easy.

"Excellent," Sornsé praised, "The third and final challenge is this. Five arrows from any given area and an army of twenty comes at you."

The army of twenty came at them quickly. Swordsmen fought the ghastly men. Heads were flying everywhere. Two arrows whizzed at Triaphor and he took them down. Triaphor turned and cleaved a head from a soldier's body.

Three arrows whizzed at Jewel and she struck them out of her way. She charged at a soldier and pierced his stomach. Blood spurted from his mouth onto her face. She shook her head to remove the blood. All put away their swords.

"Let's move!" Triaphor shouted as he sensed something horrible ready to happen. The battalion began to run to the edge of the forest. As they neared it, a light appeared at the edge of the forest. Sornsé intended on stopping them.

"Halt!" Triaphor commanded.

The battalion stopped.

"You can't stop us!"

"You will not make it to the Tree!" Sornsé screamed.

Fire came from her mouth as she screeched at them.

Triaphor lifted his staff and returned the fire back to her saying,

"Pan thôrl tag ai faan!"

Sornsé screamed in reply and the power of Tahiti took over. His voice emanated from the sky as he spoke.

"You shall not defeat *me*!!"

Sornsé yelled out her fury. Chains appeared around her wrists and ankles. She wafted away into the sky, disbanded for centuries. She would no longer be trouble to Orés' people.

"All we need to do now is destroy her temple in Tortroc and she is finished." Tahiti explained.

Triaphor, Jewel, and the battalion trudged out of the forest. They did a head count and discovered that they had not lost one man. Many men left believing more in Jesu and knowing that they could trust Him to do anything.

They moved onward to The Golden Tree. They could see it from where they were. It wouldn't be long before the treaty with The Golden Kingdom was renewed.

The company stood before The Golden Tree and looked upon it with wonder. Triaphor had heard many stories of this tree and the kingdom that it belonged to. He had always begged Tahiti to let him see it, but the prophet refused. The Golden Kingdom hadn't been upon Névorn for very long. It had only been in existence for about 1,500 years. The legends spoke of how The Golden Kingdom was made up of those who rebelled against the evil Sorcerer Eléctrasûmõn. This kingdom was located in Dimensia[2] of the planet (for Névorn was divided into 3 dimensions). Now Triaphor had finally glimpsed the celebrated tree.

From behind the tree there came a man dressed in golden robes. He had long brown hair that flowed slightly past his shoulders. He also had a small beard that was attached to his chin. This must've been...

"Sésad," he extended his hand to Triaphor, "Keeper of The Golden Tree. What business have ye with The Golden Kingdom?"

"I," Triaphor spoke, "am Triaphor, the Lalrola of Prophecy, Prophet of Jesu residing in the city of Orés."

"And I," Jewel bowed, "am Jewel, Princess of Orés. Our mission to thee today is to renew the treaty that was made in the days of our ancestors."

"Do I have your word that no matter what," Sésad asked, "you will keep the treaty alive?"

"That is why I have come." Jewel replied.

"The treaty is sure!" Sésad exclaimed.

Jewel was happy that the treaty with The Golden Kingdom had finally been renewed. It had been a long time since anyone from Orés had come forth to even communicate with the Keeper of The Golden Tree.

"Well then," Sésad began, " I suppose that we'd better..." As he was speaking, his eyes looked into the distance and saw the unthinkable.

Triaphor felt something. He looked up into the sky. They were here.

"Behold, the Lords of Ardenôs!" Triaphor shouted.

Everyone in the battalion drew their weapons. Archers fired several torrents at the riders of Ardenôs. Jewel and Triaphor fought off the beasts of burden as best they could. The Lords of Ardenôs landed and began to fight back.

Sésad threw several knives at the dragon riders. Swords clashed down in the Valley of Gold as the battalion from Orés tried to fight off the Lords of Ardenôs as best they could. Triaphor had been killing many.

The commander of this army landed in front of Triaphor. Triaphor prepared his sword. He began to dodge the dragon's head as he looked for a vulnerable spot. He stuck the sword in the dragon's mouth. As he did so, an arrow came flying from the rider. Triaphor could see the Ashen Rider's face as the arrow came at him.

Black clouds formed above them all. The arrow hit Triaphor in the chest and Triaphor roared in pain. Blood poured from his mouth. Jewel ran to his assistance. Triaphor hit the ground and his skin began to fry as Tahiti's had. Before his eyes closed and before the mark appeared upon his head, Jewel held him in her arms. He felt one tear drop onto his forehead where the mark appeared. Then he faded away. His carcass lie there, barely recognizable.

In rage, Jewel rose with her sword in her hand. She cut off the head of the gagging dragon. She charged after the rider as he ran to catch up with the other riders. She took out a knife and threw it at his back. The rider fell at the edge of the Forest of Death. Jewel dislodged the knife from his back.

Sésad picked up Triaphor and took him into his cottage. He lay him upon a bed. Jewel sat by his bedside all night. He had always been there for her when no one else had. She began to call herself a jinx. If any man whom she loved wanted to live, they'd have to leave her. She couldn't understand why all her loves were perishing so quickly. Right when the time for marriage was near, the soul was lost.

She stood and looked into the sky. She could see the Ashen Rider's face embedded into the stars. Half-crazed and overwhelmed by emotion, she shot an arrow at the sky and nothing happened. The image of the Ashen Rider only laughed at her. She fell to the ground, weeping. How could this be?

"The Age of Death has come," she heard a voice say from the door.

She stood and with tearstained eyes she looked upon Sésad. She ran to him and hugged him. His muscular arms wrapped around her petite body as she clasped him. She cried upon his massive shoulders.

"Great, was he not?" Sésad asked.

Jewel simply nodded as the tears streamed down her face.

"Many times they are," Sésad continued, "Now I know not much of love, but this I do know… Triaphor loved you more than any *I've* ever seen and I know that if he can, he shall return with haste to continue his love for you."

That night she stood there in Sésad's arms, weeping for the lost.

The sun shone through the window into the chair on which she had fallen asleep. She awoke and looked upon the bed that Triaphor had been laid upon. As she looked, she was astonished. She screamed, for the bed was neat, made up, but there was no one there.

Sésad rushed into the room and looked upon the bed. He knew what was going on.

"What happened?" Jewel screamed.

"He has passed," Sésad spoke, "Passed into a land that no one alive has ever seen. He has passed into the White Temple of Jesu."

"What?" Jewel was confused.

"All prophets go there when they die and when Névorn is at its end, it is where we shall go as well." Sésad said, "But you must go. Go back to Orés. For behold the Mountain of Tortroc glows with an audacious red. It is time."

Jewel knew he was speaking the truth. But she didn't know if she could do it alone.

"When you go back to Orés," Sésad continued, "You must take these with you. They shall be of great assistance to you."

He handed her two knives. They had the symbol of The Golden Tree upon it. Jewel prepared the battalion quickly. Sésad stood and watched. Though she felt as if she could not lead her people into battle, the Keeper saw something different. What he witnessed was overwhelming talent. The soldiers, every single one of them, listened intently as she spoke. Though they'd lost their newest prophetic leader, this did not phase them, for they knew—somehow—that they could depend upon the princess. Sésad walked up to Jewel as she embarked her horse.

"Remember," Sésad said, "Jesu is always with you."

Jewel nodded and the battalion moved on. They trekked around the Forest of Death and Sésad could see them no more. He wished them the very best luck. He walked back behind the tree and returned to his own land.

Chapter 5 – Lalrola's Power

White!!! All around was white!! The young prophet awoke from his elongated slumber and glanced around with a cautious gaze. Perhaps the death dart had not totally done its job. Was this what Skyland looked like? He knew Ardenôs was gorgeous, but he did not expect it to be so… grandiose. The door to the spacious cubicle opened and in walked an unexpected face. Though it was a very familiar one, Triaphor did not know what to think about this place any longer.

"Welcome!" Tahiti exclaimed, "to the White Temple of Jesu."

Triaphor side-glanced Tahiti. As he sat up, he then realized that he was unclothed. After such a revelation, he then recognized what Tahiti had just mentioned.

"White Temple?" Triaphor was astonished.

"Yes," Tahiti said, "Dost thou not remember it from thy studies?"

Oh, he remembered them. He had long dreamed of escaping the tortures of the world of Névorn just to be a part of a perfect society where everything was centered around Jesu. Before he could think to speak another word…

"We must bring in thy robes." Tahiti said, "Servants! Clothes!"

The servants brought forth such robes that not even royalty donned. His tunic was of a solid white that was so bright that Triaphor had trouble seeing to put it on. Then, the servants brought his outer garment, which was silver and seemed to be made from the finest silk. As Triaphor walked around the room, it shimmered in the light. The final article of clothing was a robe of a magnificent scarlet. Such a wine press red Triaphor had not seen in his entire life.

"This is what the Lalrola is fit to wear. Combat clothing shall be given when it is time for you to depart."

"Depart?" Triaphor asked.

"Oh yes. You did not possibly think that you would be staying forever did you?" Tahiti inquired.

Triaphor gave a deadening stare. If Tahiti had been younger then he would've been a bit more frightened, but assuring himself that Triaphor should've known it somewhere in his heart kept Tahiti from the slightest shiver.

******************************   ******************************

Council meetings were beginning to become a routine annoyance. Every week, Jewel hated to see the day come for council meetings. This week she'd made it back just in time for it and decided that it was time to take action. No more would these meetings be filled with meaningless debates.

"Silence!" Jewel shouted, "The next action this city shall take will be under my command and mine alone. No one, not even you father, shall stand in my way, for it is the Prophecy that needs fulfilling."

"What is thy plan, daughter?" Ric asked.

"To take back the mountain as ours and raze the temple of Sornsé!" Jewel stated.

"Then may ye go forth with thy plans," Ric encouraged. He had not wanted to be one subject to his daughter's anger. Her glare was worse than her stab. He'd already experienced what it was like to try and stop her. It had ended up in her choosing Triaphor anyway.

Jewel left the throne room and began to make plans as to how she would take Tortroc and burn it to the ground. The elders would now pay for their treachery that they had committed. No worshiper of Sornsé would be left alive.

***************************   ***************************

Triaphor had been up for hours now, just viewing the splendor of the White Temple. It was not only enormous, but it was so peaceful in comparison to anything he'd ever seen. He passed a family having lunch and it seemed much more serene than he'd remembered Névorn ever being. He paused in his walk. As he noticed the family, he looked up and saw a tree. He smiled as a tear rolled down his cheek. This same apple tree was his mother's death tree and his first kiss with Jewel.

"Triaphor!" he heard Tahiti call.

He looked up and saw his master running at a nippy pace. He grabbed Triaphor by the arm and they raced away, Triaphor almost tripping over his long robe.

"Where are we going?" Triaphor asked.

"The White Rotunda," Tahiti said, "There you shall meet all the prophets that have lived in Orés since its beginning."

As they walked into the White Rotunda, Triaphor was astonished. The balcony from which he and his former master stood was indeed the best view in the house. Triaphor felt powerful as his eyes beamed down upon the elderly prophets. Centuries of Orés' most influential people lie in this one room. What an honor for any man to sight.

"Look," Tahiti pointed to the balcony across from them, "There is my former master, Prophet Sōnércus, standing with his former master, the great and wise Prophet Trílautûs. Long have they waited for this day."

They definitely must've. Trílautûs was the prophet who, long ago, finished the *Prophecy of Névorn* when receiving the vision of all the events prior and during the Apocalypse.

As Triaphor walked through the door onto the balcony, the prophets didn't say one word. They only gazed at the boy with wonder and whispered amongst each other. Soon majestic beings with robes almost as bright in luminescence as Triaphor's stepped forward on a balcony directly in the center of the globe. His waving gesture silenced the crowd and whisked them to their seats. He stepped forward to speak.

"Friends and family," he began, "Entering is the mighty Jesu."

The trumpets and horns sounded as they all rose and bowed on one knee in acknowledgement. As Triaphor slightly lifted his head, his eyes saw a marvelous light that filled the whole room. Different from the Jesu he'd expected, a look of confusion crossed his face.

"You cannot see him because thy mission is not yet complete." Tahiti spoke.

Jesu looked to the balcony in which Triaphor and Tahiti were prostrate. Triaphor could feel his eyes burning into his mind, reading all of his thoughts.

"Arise," he bellowed, "Son of Biora."

Triaphor, in humility, rose to his feet. Head still bowed, he awaited the next phrase.

"Look boldly into my eyes."

Triaphor's head slowly ascended until his pupils glared into that of his Creator. A sigh of relief and fear washed over the Lalrola as His gaze deepened.

"That is only the beginning of thy bravery, O young one…" Jesu said.

The remainder of the prophets at that time arose and applauded him. Triaphor began to feel the weight of his responsibilities. All the prophets' hopes and dreams rested upon his shoulders. Soon their power would as well.

The speaker for Jesu arose from the seat he had taken.

"We will all celebrate for 48 hours over the greatness and wonder that must occur within the near future. Then we shall begin the process by which we place our powers upon Triaphor, Son of Biora."

The prophets within the rotunda approved with another round of applause. This time there could be heard shouts of joy erupting throughout the room. Triaphor knew it would only be a matter of time before he would become the most powerful created being to ever walk the face of Névorn. He was their savior. He would become the one thing that could actually have a chance at stopping the Riders from Apocalypse. But he found within himself a welling sensation of pleasure in the White Temple. So much so, that he began to feel ungrateful for his opportunity to be the Lalrola, this elaborately dressed human who could, with just the snap of his fingers, do almost anything his mind desired.

Triaphor knew that this would take some getting used to.

Chapter 6 – Prophetic Fulfillment

The sun arose on this grand morn like any other day. But this day, there was one key difference. A lone figure within the city walked to the gates and headed up the stairs. There she confronted Autôw, the General of the Army.

"Your Highness," he bowed.

"Look well upon the mountains, Autôw" Jewel said, "For this day will they be stained in blood."

She descended the wall and prepared for battle. As she walked back to the palace, she wondered if she might ever see Triaphor again as she had seen Tahiti. But a more ponderous question that filled her mind was would she be able to feel the passion that had so strongly urged her to ask for him in marriage.

***************************   ***************************

Lalrola. That's what he was now. In full power could he claim the name that his ancestors had so long desired. Tahiti had called him into a private conference room. He wasn't sure he was going to like what he had to say. He had made up his mind that he wouldn't. He just couldn't go back to a world so intrinsically saturated with sin.

Triaphor reached the double doors to the conference room and they separated for him. He seated himself across from Tahiti. As he positioned himself comfortably in the seat, Tahiti prepared to speak.

"You cannot stay here," Tahiti announced.

"I knew it. That is why I've so purposed in my mind…"

"…that you will stay? Yes, I know." Tahiti interrupted.

"You felt it…"

"Our people are in suffering," Tahiti proclaimed, "Jewel cannot lead the armies alone and you cannot deny the Prophecy. You must do it or someone else will replace you. There are over 300,000,000 prophets in The White Temple. Jesu will choose whom He deems worthy. You MUST fulfill the Prophecy."

"Jewel is well capable of defeating the elders in Tortroc." Triaphor looked Tahiti square in the eyes.

"The war is much bigger than that and you know it. The Riders of the Apocalypse have been there since their betrayal of Orés. Once the elders of the city decided to follow Sornsé, the only hope that we had left was that of The Golden Kingdom. They live in a completely different dimension, as if it were another world. Our list of allies is dead, save for The Golden Kingdom. Therefore, Jesu has appointed you to assist our people in The War of the Apocalypse. He saw you as the only prophet capable of such power without mingling it with corrupted injustice." Tahiti slammed, not backing down.

This meant that the young prophet was even stronger than the mighty Trílautûs. Many claimed that he was the greatest of all the prophets. But when talk of the Lalrola began from Tahiti, the people then realized that this Chosen One of Prophecy would be even greater in might and mind than Trílautûs. Fitting that his name was Triaphor, the boy thought.

Triaphor knew the truth. He knew that Jesu had wanted him to do nearly the impossible. No one had ever obtained such power since Névorn's origin. As his mind had been made up, he felt an inward passion to get back, just to take Jewel back to the

Temple with him. Maybe they could have children together and become like the little family under the tree in the park.

"It's her isn't it…" Tahiti knew his thoughts.

"I want her here, but is there no way to salvage her without ravaging Névorn to total destruction?" Triaphor asked, knowing the answer to the question.

"You must be realistic with yourself before you begin to involve anyone else into this situation," Tahiti began, "Before you can even begin to factor Jewel into the equation, you must first place yourself into the whole of the spectrum. Then and only then will you be able to live as you have with Jewel by your side.

Jesu has confirmed that you must marry the princess."

"So it is true…" Triaphor was astonished.

"Yes! That is why you must go. Jesu has set up this position so that you, Triaphor, Son of Biora, may not only assist in the defeat of Tortroc's elders by removing the curse but ridding the world of Névorn of the fowl stench that the Riders have caused for so long. This is not something to be taken lightly. Only when you have defeated the Riders can you live peaceably with Jewel. Until then, war will constantly ravage your life because you are the Lalrola and we are soon to be only *some* of the people who know of this. The Riders, the moment you touch, will know that the Invocation of Power has indeed been performed. You cannot escape this for the rest of your life unless you…"

"…fulfill the mission." Triaphor finished.

It had taken him his entire muster and might to say just those three words. He could not feel the importance of the mission until he realized that Jewel and he would not be happy until the Riders were completely and thoroughly destroyed.

"Some people aren't as fortunate as I," Triaphor spoke, "I have all the power in the world. My power even exceeds that of the greatest mentors, scholars, and prophets the entire history of Névorn has ever known. But… my decision is final."

Tahiti sat up, anticipation beaming in his eyes, hoping Triaphor was not really going to forsake a mission of such significance.

"I must continue on the path of Jesu," Triaphor said, "I must now depart, for the time of fulfillment is near. You, I shall see once more when I return. Goodbye my master."

"Farewell, my young novice." Tahiti bid him.

Triaphor got up and walked out of the room. Tahiti watched as Lalrola's train on his robe finally made it around the corner. The last trace of his beloved apprentice was now gone. He felt a hand on his shoulder. It could've been no other. He knew that Jesu stood there, comforting him.

******************************   *******************************

"The battle lines are set, my lord," the commander reported.

"Good work, commander," Datos, the leader of the arachnid nation, proclaimed.

Hades, Pestilence, & Famine stood alongside Datos. They looked down upon the City of the Prophets. They knew that they could easily conquer this scrawny city with just their power. It should be even easier to destroy with such an immense army.

The Dark Alliance watched and waited ever so patiently as the Army of Orés advanced.

At the head of the proceeding army, Jewel was filled with resentment. These spiders had plagued her people long enough. It was time to strike back. Death and destruction would come to the traitors of Jesu's name. As she walked, she heard a voice talking to her inside of her head.

"Jewel," the voice said, "Be looking for me in a scarlet robe. I shall come upon a pure white horse. You must look for me to ride upon the mountain from Orés. Then you and I shall destroy Sornsé's temple. Search your feelings and become bold. It is within the depths of your soul. When this is over, you and I shall rule Orés alongside your father, but you must be strong, if not for me, for yourself. May Jesu be with you, love."

She could not speak.

The army emerged the mount and reached the gate of the city of Tortroc. Assembled there was Datos, Three of the Four Riders and the entirety of the elders encamped within the city.

Cowards!

Thought Jewel.

"Fools of Orés!" Datos shouted from atop, "This day wilt thy blood be spilt upon such holy ground!"

"From this day forth!" Jewel shouted back, "All men shall know the strength possessed by the warriors of Orés! You and your Dark Alliance of death, pestilence, and destruction shall know the meaning of what each of those Riders represent! May Jesu punish you for your deeds! From this day forth, you will never again afflict our people, the rightful owners of Orés and the city upon the mountain! To change our world is what we seek after and change our world we will!! Forward, men of Orés!!! TAKE BACK WHAT'S OURS!!!! "

As the last phrase broke from Jewel's lips, so did her sword from her sheath. The entire force of the Army of Orés stormed the gate. For all their effort, it would not break. Jewel and a force of horsemen broke a hole into a side of the wall and there crawled through and opened the gate. As Datos watched, he marveled at such strength in a woman.

The army charged Tortroc with vigor and Datos gave the command. The armies clashed into each other, killing with a wild sense of adrenaline. Jewel's heart sped as she chopped off legs of spiders and watched their towering figures crash to the ground.

Haphazardly, the battle raged onward. Arachnids falling by the hundreds, Jewel ran from spider to spider, slaying each one, but tiring as she went. Her frail body could only keep this up for a while. It was much worse than any wild dance she had ever done. She looked up and as she looked to see if the voice had yet arrived, she saw an astonishing number. Over 1,000,000 spiders were descending from the summit of Mount Tortroc.

As Datos turned to see this, it brought hope to he and his ever-tiring men. They assaulted Jewel and her army with new strength. Losing ground as she was being pushed back, Jewel was fighting off as many of the spiders as possible. She wasn't killing as many as before. All she was doing now was keeping up her guard. Datos' attempt had been to enervate her strength, she now realized. She sheathed her sword into the spider that she was fighting and left it, running back towards the gate.

"Archers!" she shouted as she ran past them, "Follow me!!"

As they were backing up, Autôw took out a horn and blew it. The ground began to shake as the battle paused. Spiders began to look around, confused as to what was making the ground shake so heavily. Fortunately, the general had perfectly timed his cavalry attack.

ELEPHANTS!!!! An entire troupe of 10,000 elephants and 40,000 foot soldiers joined the battlefront. Again Orés regained the lead position.

"FIRE!!!" Jewel shouted to her archers.

A volley of arrows directly battered the Elders' infantry.

The Dark Alliance tried to resume their small chance at the victory, but the harder they pushed, Jewel made sure that her troops were thrusting tougher blows to the elders.

Jewel then turned her attention to the Temple of Sornsé. A battalion of soldiers had tried to penetrate the source of war. The Three Riders, Hades, Famine, & Pestilence were single handedly holding them off! Just as Hades was about to kill the commander of the battalion, Jewel ran to save him…

But she was too late.

Lalrola had arrived.

"Triaphor!!" Jewel shouted.

"What?" Hades looked back in distraction. Just as he did so, Jewel nocked an arrow and aimed for the morbid creature.

HIT!!

Hades fell from his horse and Triaphor stomped upon the ground with his boot and the hillside rumbled as an earthquake erupted all around the temple. Disrupting the fighting that had been going on, he knew he had one of the biggest affects on this battle that anyone could have.

Hades began to speak magic and Triaphor looked at him. He took his staff and struck the morose Rider with it. He then gestured his hand towards Hades and lifted him into the air, throwing him into his two gruesome comrades.

When the Three realized that only by riding in the formation of Four that they had been originally created for, could they defeat Triaphor now, they headed for Apocalypse. Jewel started after them.

" Let them go!" Triaphor said, "We have no time to lose."

"Bring him," Triaphor continued, pointing at the commander of the battalion, which had scattered to other parts of the battle.

Jewel helped up the commander and then they, along with Triaphor, entered the Temple of Sornsé. In here, Triaphor knew the fate of both cities would be decided by his power alone.

As the battle raged on outside, malevolent ceremonies filled the walls of the Temple of Sornsé. Within the confinements of the temple, priests and prophets of the iniquitous demoness worshiped her as a goddess and prayed for deliverance from the followers of Jesu. Around the corner were the three warriors from Orés.

"Alright," Triaphor said, "On the count of three."

On three, they all charged the scene.

"You're under arrest!" Triaphor shouted.

"By whose orders?" the apparent leader asked.

Triaphor snapped his fingers. An entire troupe of Jesu's prophets appeared in front of them. The prophets and priests of Sornsé were instantly killed. Triaphor snapped once more. The prophets were gone.

"Excellent work!" Jewel congratulated.

Triaphor walked over to her. Right there, in the middle of the temple, the two lovers stood, locked in a kiss. The bloody worn commander sat upon the floor and looked upon the temple in wonder. A beautiful place it was. What a perfect place in which to die. Here he'd be happy to see his last.

As the two were kissing, they heard a solid thud. Triaphor let Jewel go and rushed to his aid. There was still some life left. Triaphor waved his hand over the commander. The commander sat up.

"You may live a little longer, my friend." Triaphor informed.

"What's next?" Jewel asked.

"We have to look for an inscription on a wall in the next room."

"Why?"

"It is how we lift the curse and destroy the elders." Triaphor explained.

The three began walking down the hall. As they trudged the long hallway, Jewel caught up to Triaphor, who was speed walking, and asked,

"What of the elders? If we lift the curse, they'll just be men…"

"Without weapons plus…" Triaphor added, "There's a catch."

"What's that?" Jewel asked.

"If we break the curse now, the elders will die. Since they were old when they left us and were to eternally live past the normal life expectancy under the curse, they're technically dead. When we break the curse, they die."

Jewel kept silent. A disturbing thought was this. Such power Triaphor seemed to possess now, yet it seemed that with all this power in his hands, he was the same Triaphor that she had seen fall into her arms and die. But what would his power do to him in time, she wondered.

The three reached the door to the room.

"Don't touch anything!" Triaphor warned.

The door opened and they entered a shrine. In this shrine, there stood several artifacts from the old kingdoms that once sat upon this mountain. Before Tortroc was built, several cities of great importance stood upon Mount Tortroc and were owned by the kings of Orés. But when the elders rebelled, a whole new chapter of life was written for Tortroc.

Triaphor and Jewel found the wall on which the inscription was written. They began to browse over it.

"It's hard to make out." Triaphor noted.

"Is there anything you can do about it?" Jewel inquired.

"I'll try."

He spoke a couple of words and the wall began to shine. Suddenly, the two could see the adjacent chamber. Triaphor realized he'd spoken the command for transparency. After going through several of these rituals and finally giving up on the wall altogether, he sat in a big, old throne chair.

He was Lalrola. He had ultimate power. None could kill him. None could or would ever possess, steal, or acquire his power. Yet and still, he couldn't even make an inscription on a wall be made large enough or clear enough for one to read. How was the Prophecy to be fulfilled now?

Jewel walked over to him. Garbed in armor, sweat, and caked up blood from her wounds, she sat upon his lap. There she began playing with his hair and they began to kiss. Just as they had started, the whole temple shook.

Triaphor pushed Jewel to the floor and stood. The commander had touched a statue of Sornsé.

"DON'T TOUCH ANYTHING!!!!" he shouted.

The walls around them began falling. Jewel got up and ran to the commander and picked him up. Triaphor grabbed Jewel, who had taken the commander in her arms, and waved his hand. With a poof of smoke, the three had disappeared.

The three exited the temple, appearing at the front door, and as they did, the entire temple went up in flames. Several of the spiders turned to see the commotion and came towards them to attack. Triaphor didn't know if they'd last too much longer against these spiders. Already was more of the army beginning to fall. Orés was sinking into submission.

Jewel didn't know what she would do. Her father was locked up in the palace until his curse was lifted and the spiders were rapidly defeating the army. How would she save Orés and her father from death? She heard a voice whisper to her.

She remembered the knives. Sésad had given her knives with which to call upon the Golden Kingdom. She dropped her sword and grasped the two knives. The ground gyrated. As she fell to the ground, her eyes beheld a glorious sight. Sésad was leading his troops through the gate. The Golden Kingdom was known for their magnificent cavalry. In fact, the entirety of their army consisted of horsemen.

Datos, seeing the new arrivals, rushed to the gate to destroy it before any could enter. Jewel rose from the ground and sped towards him. As she began to speculate that she was too late, a powerful beam of light struck the gate and it stood upright. No matter what Datos did to try to destroy it now, he could not. Jewel leaped and landed in front of the Lord of the Arachnids.

Triaphor, the one holding up the gate, ran to it and began to scan it for the same words that had been written on the temple wall. Once found, he shouted.

"Crap!"

The writing was still the same size as before. As he sat there, he thought to himself about why he didn't just stay at the White Temple. Life would've been so much easier there. No worries, no trials, no suffering. Only peace, love, and happiness, and all a man ever wanted in life and more.

"*Cujus latus perforatum.*"

Someone whispered.

It was Tahiti! Triaphor spoke the words. The inscription became much larger. He took his robe and covered it so that the light would not shine so brightly upon it. As he began reading the inscription, Jewel was warding off the attack of Datos.

Her two knives worked wonders. But for some reason, she could not get past Datos' defenses. He was a strong and powerful spider warrior. Another spider came to his aid. Jewel began to defend herself against both of them. They spun a web up into her face. She cut it down before it could reach its destination.

"Ajahûm saítos pérfos,
 Spidros coûrus bôrkinus."

The last words of the curse had just been spoken.

Jewel had grown ever tired of the runaround these spiders were giving her. She began to circle around Datos and his fellow warrior. Datos spit web at her. Jewel cut it down with one quick swish of her left knife. She dodged an arrow passing her head as she twirled to cut down the legs of Datos and his companion. She saw the moment; the opportunity she'd been waiting for. She threw her two knives into the chests of Datos and his cohort. She let her arms rest at her side, for she noticed something.

At that moment, the curse was lifted. The arachnid army all began transforming back into the old men they had rebelled as. Triaphor came to her side and glared into the eyes of Datos. They walked up to him as he began to speak his last.

"How foolish were we! To think that we could fight the prophets of Jesu. To think that we could defeat Orés, the city ordained by the great Jesu Himself. How evil we've been! Now may the servants of Sornsé perish forever!"

As the last word was spoken, the bodies of the old fools who had ruled atop Tortroc for half a century began to disintegrate. When the bodies had fully consumed into ashes upon the mountain within the city, every weapon that Orés had used fell onto the ground. Triaphor bowed his head and wept.

"Aisté pertisto. Jesu, bless their bodies," he spoke.

Jewel gathered the army together and commanded a servant to go prepare a welcome party for the soldiers. The army of Orés, with Jewel and Triaphor as leaders, marched back to the city triumphant. The reign of terror by the insidious creatures atop Mount Tortroc was now ended. A temple and library would now be built in place of the city. The temple in honor of Jesu and the library in honor of the great wisdom of the elders upon Tortroc even in the days they worshiped the evil goddess Sornsé.

A parade awaited the young couple that arrived with the army triumphant. Ric stared out of his window as the soldiers headed to the castle. They walked in the front gate and into the courtroom. The king was encompassed in his kingdom's defenses as a priest of Jesu came forward.

"May Jewel, daughter of King Ric, princess and warrior of the kingdom of Orés, please step forward."

As Jewel stepped forward in dignity, yet surprise, she bowed before the priest and then stood.

"May Triaphor, son of Biora, triumphant prophet & Lalrola of Prophecy of the kingdom of Orés, please step forward," the priest reiterated.

Triaphor did as instructed. The priest faced them and blessed them saying,

"On this day shalt thou know the full joys of the life of a married couple."

Back turned to the crowd, apparent shock and surprise arose on the face of Jewel as she thought back on how many other times this could've happened. Before she could compose herself, Triaphor had embraced her in his arms and looked at her.

"I love you."

The couple locked in a frenzy of kisses. On this day had many been shown the power and glory of Jesu. He'd helped the kingdom of Orés defeat the massive armies of Tortroc and now their name would be known throughout the ages. Jewel and Triaphor had finally, after many years of frantic searching for a new love, now found eternal love. All problems had whisked away forever, but one small imbalance loomed over all kingdoms. Soon, a kingdom would crush all others with its power and before it was too late, salvation would be found in one small city. A City within the East. A City of Triumph. A City of Love. A City of Glory. The City of Orés.

The plains of the empire were beautiful. The grasses short and wide with a luminescent plush green look and feel. The extensive lands of the Empire of Orés had become central to the survival of many kingdoms. They'd clung to each other for such a long time after the destruction of Tortroc that they couldn't be separated. Many of these fortified cities were beauteous to the eyes. No kingdom in the world, not even those in the south, could compare in splendor. Ever since the Four Riders of Apocalypse had been safely locked away inside of their land by the powers of Lalrola, who worked for Jesu, Orés had flourished into an empire of vast cities and wondrous sites.

One such city was the city of Tortroc, now renamed Menoléon, meaning Place of Wisdom. Menoléon contained many splendorous buildings that many men wished that they could behold. The Library of Marûan contained many copies of the Prophecy and its originators' books. Triaphor had published Tahiti's book called, <u>The Discoveries</u>, telling many tales of he and his crazy adventures. The book had been dedicated to Triaphor, so the boy put the book to a publication and set it in the library amongst other great scholarly works, such as <u>Lalrola Rises</u> and <u>Fairest of the Ladies</u>, which spoke of prophetic things and ancient paintings. The former had been written by the great Trílautûs. The Temple of Jesu, a second of its kind, was the center of worship for the citizens of Orés. A law required that all men must worship Jesu on only one day of the week. On the seventh and last day of the week, Jesu must be honored. On any other day, other gods may be recognized as such, but on the seventh day, Jesu, the One & Only, was to be worshiped. Triaphor preferred to live his life in daily service to Jesu and expected others to do the same, though the law did not specify one to do so.

Many other buildings spanned this city, but amongst these tall magnificent buildings sat a couple that were kissing. Triaphor, who'd been happily married to Jewel ever since the war with Tortroc had ended, began to feel a disturbance. He heard voices inside his head. All were swarming around him. Suddenly, he fell into a trance.

He was riding throughout the Empire of Orés, looking for shelter. But, wherever he went, the cities were no longer there. Then he finally went to the capital city, Orés, and saw a horrible sight. The entire city was on fire. The army was trying to defend the city, but none could save it. King Ric rode upon his horse to try and destroy Hades, the Rider of Death, and was immediately stricken by Hades' power.

A sharp pain rapped Triaphor in the side as he came out of the trance and fell back upon his shoulders. Under the palm tree did Jewel stare upon her husband in wonder. Never had this happened before. It took a moment for Triaphor to process what just happened and what he saw.

"What's wrong?" Jewel asked.

"I had a vision," Triaphor answered.

"Of what sort?"

"Prophetic."

Jewel stared once more. Dare she even ask? Before she could get a chance to, trumpets sounded. In Orés down below, an entire caravan of camels, horses, cattle, & merchants came strolling into the city. They both knew that these were ambassadors from the southern kingdom of Iristaniq. Their kingdom contained buildings of an arabesque style. But the strange thing was…

"Jewel," Triaphor spoke, "Let us go and meet them. Remember that your father cannot leave the castle until his curse is lifted. We must go and welcome them warmly to Orés, the capital city of the Empire."

Jewel followed Triaphor's lead and they went down into the city to meet the caravan from Iristaniq. As they walked through the city, Jewel started thinking.

"Triaphor," she got his attention, "Why are *they* here? Ever since my father was Prince of Orés, they've been our mortal enemies."

"I'll explain later," Triaphor spoke hurriedly, "They're in a desperate situation. Be prepared for anything."

Jewel wasn't exactly sure what was wrong with Triaphor today, but lately he'd been acting extremely uptight. Did she make the wrong choice? Was he really the right one?

Stop that! Jewel thought. She couldn't doubt him. He had to be the one. Why would Jesu allow such a perfect union to turn sour? Or did Jesu have that kind of control?

The king of the great land of Iristaniq, Sultan Salzahirz, walked up to Triaphor and bowed. He realized in front of whom he was standing just by the iridescence of his countenance.

"Great Lalrola," Salzahirz rose, "Trouble dost the land of Iristaniq face. Once again, the Riders..."

"May," Triaphor interrupted, "we not discuss this out in the streets. It is not only common courtesy for you to not discuss such things in front of the common people, but it is also the custom of the Empire to talk to the king and the War Council of such things, not the prophet residing in that land. If you had stayed in contact with the Empire in the first place, you would've known that."

"But you are Prince Triaphor of the Empire of Orés as well, are you not?" Salzahirz asked.

"You know the rules," Triaphor responded, "You know the law, so why dost thou continue to try my patience? Have I not informed you as to what you need do? Are you willing to save your people or have you come here on some other errand?"

Triaphor's words were shrewd, but quick in point.

Salzahirz was speechless. The young prophet was no fool and he spoke more truth than any middle aged man might even think. Salzahirz and his entourage were led into the castle.

As King Ric looked over the glorious things that had been brought to him from the great southern land, the War Council continued to debate amongst themselves as to what to do with these once upon a time friends. Many of the councilors had been there when Iristaniq turned and killed thousands of innocent soldiers just so that the wrath of the Riders was not brought upon them. What good did that do them now? The leader of the War Council, Councilor Autôw, rose from his seat.

"Your majesty," he spoke, "The War Council has now made its decision."

The courtroom was silenced. All eyes glared at Autôw, for he was known as a shrewd man and sharp in wisdom. But sometimes the councilor could become a bit judgmental. Triaphor's eyes gazed at him intently, ready to shoot down any silly remarks the councilor often made.

"We as a body have firmly decided that Salzahirz and his entourage cannot be allowed to stay in our lands."

The courtroom went up in a buzz. Triaphor saw this coming. He felt a soft brush up against his ear.

"I thought you promised them homeland security and everything." Jewel said.

"I did," Triaphor responded, "Didn't I ever teach you at night to be patient? Time will reveal all. It works for everything."

Jewel sat back against Triaphor's chest and leaned her head on his shoulder. She always hated the length of the council meetings.

"Dost thou have reasoning for such a bold statement?" King Ric asked. Salzahirz's smile grew. Perhaps the king would persuade them. The two kings had been princely pals. Ric would never let him down. He hoped.

"What reason should we let them stay?" Autôw asked in return, "What favors have they done for us? *Would* they do the same for us? That is indeed the question. When in our time of need, they did the last thing we expected. They turned on us and sent us running down the streets naked and bleeding. *I* led the armies under your command that day, Your Majesty. And every single member of this War Council stood and witnessed the betrayal of the evil of Salzahirz and his band of Iristaniqan men. **PAIN!!! SUFFERING!!! DEATH!!!** were the only words we knew! And now, they bring new words into the vocabulary… **PEACE!!! LOVE!!! FORGIVENESS!!!** Well, we offer none of these. To think that this pompous king sits in our midst and I have not yet cleaved him in two surprises me!"

Autôw unleashed his sword and struck a pose. The courtroom was filled with horror. Triaphor lunged from his seat, knocking Jewel to the floor. He grabbed his staff and spoke.

"You will stand down and not harm the sultan!!"

Autôw put away his sword.

"Just a demonstration." He laughed.

Triaphor passed his rod to Jewel as she sat in his seat. Triaphor walked around as he spoke.

"So how do we know Iristaniq won't betray us again?" he asked the courtroom, "We didn't know the first time, so how shall…"

"Surely, prophet, thou didst not rise from thy seat in such a steady pace just to repeat the words which I've just finished speaking?"

"No, Autôw my old fool, if thou didst learn patience as a child, you might've known that which I was about to say."

"Continue," King Ric permitted.

"Thank you," Triaphor said, "But we cannot hold a grudge against the kingdom. They are under desperate need for protection. Our pride and prejudice against them cannot cause them to be destroyed. We will be at fault more than they will when the Day of Judgment comes, for we have held anger against them in their time of need."

"But," Autôw stood, "hast thou considered that the Riders of Apocalypse could be using them for the sole purpose of tricking us into harboring them as insiders and then therefore have that much of an easier attack?"

"If such a thing is," Triaphor spoke, "Then I as prophet of this kingdom will decide what is best under such circumstances."

"But where were you during Tortroc?" spoke Autôw, "Late, that's what you were. And we almost lost the battle and would've been slaves to them if you had showed up any later!! I demand that we execute every single one of these bastards before the Riders' plan succeeds!!! And after that I demand that we call for a new prophet for this city. This one's too faulty!! Send us one like Tahiti!!!"

The courtroom went up in a buzz. The entire room was filled with angry shouts and expletives were being tossed around like hotcakes.

Ric looked on in horror. He got eyes from Triaphor. They were eyes of pain. A tear fell to the ground and as it struck the floor, smoke arose in the middle of the courtroom. The courtroom silenced.

Triaphor was gone. He had completely vanished. Jewel arose from her seat and spoke.

"No!!!" Jewel said, "Its not going to happen like this!! I shall make the decision for the city!"

"My daughter!!" Ric yelled.

"Don't bellow at me father, for your decisions only curse the city further!! The one decision I made for this city won us the Battle of Tortroc!"

"Barely…" muttered Autôw.

"SILENCE FOOL!!!" barked Jewel.

Councilor Autôw sat, realizing that the only foolproof decision could be made from the princess. The War Council allowed her to speak.

"We will foster thee, O Salzahirz of Iristaniq," Jewel spoke, "On one condition can you stay. You must pay a sum of 10% of your goods that you reap while you dwell here. And I promise you, that if you decide to betray us once more, I will be at your door, providing you with what these councilor's wished to give you…sevenfold! Now be at peace."

The council session was dismissed. Jewel was the first to open the double-doors to the castle. She knew where Triaphor was. It was one of his favorite spots ever since the city had been built.

"Driver!" she shouted, "Take me to Menoléon!"

Triaphor sat on his bed in the couple's house. The vision. It continued to haunt him. How could this possibly be? The burning down of Orés. After all the work that had been put into it and now the city did not even want him. He felt useless. Tears strolled down his eyes.

Jewel walked into the bedroom and sat upon the silky white sheets.

"I know how you feel."

"No you don't." Triaphor answered back.

"What?"

"No you don't!!!" Triaphor snapped. He arose from the bed and began to throw things around. He destroyed all of their precious things, including the lamp that had been made of pure crystal. He cleaved the chandelier from its position upon the ceiling. When the room was in a complete raucous, he ripped his clothing and fell to his knees, tears swelling in his eyes.

Jewel arose, frightened, yet still in love, and ran to her husband on the floor. She began kissing him and he threw her to the ground. He arose and she followed him. As Triaphor went to the kitchen and was about ready to thrust his sword into himself, Jewel kicked the sword from his hands. He fell to his knees. Jewel met him there.

"Why?!?" Triaphor cried, "Have I not achieved enough for these people?"

"Even if they don't want you, you must stay." Jewel said, "For not only does the Prophecy depend on such, but so do I. I can't move. This city belongs to me as much as it does my father. You must stay. I love you and so does my father. Neither one of us wish you to go. We are in charge of the city and we will decide when it is time for a new prophet. As long as you're around, no other prophet will do."

Triaphor's tears overwhelmed him.

"I just hope that I can be of assistance now… for you will need it."

"What do you mean?"

"I must go." Triaphor jumped.

"What???????" Jewel screamed.

Triaphor ran to the stable and saddled his horse. Jewel was hot in pursuit.

"Where are you going?" Jewel begged.

"I must go to the Library of Rémitron in the northern city of Maesõrn. There's much there that I must find out. I'll be back. Remember, by nightfall a week from today. If I'm not back…"

"But you must be." Jewel shouted.

"Jewel," Triaphor leapt from the horse, "We will not always be together."

"But you promised…"

Triaphor kissed her. He picked her up and led her to the bedroom. Crushing the glass and the crystal from the destructed objects, he laid her down and she removed the rest of his cloak. The afternoon flowed smoothly. Triaphor stroked her and caressed her body softly into the afternoon. Late into the evening did he consume her body with his. Many positions did they lay in. Once again their thoughts connected as well as their bodies.

Triaphor awoke and his wife was not beside him. He looked up and the night lights in the sky shone through the window and shed light onto a figure. Jewel stood by the window and Triaphor watched as a tear fell to the floor.

He arose from the bed and went to her. He caressed her soft cheek and wiped the tears from her eyes. He wrapped his arms around her waist.

"Why do you have to go?" Jewel asked.

"I have to discover what to do next." Triaphor explained, "Jesu hasn't spoken to me in days except through dream and vision and Tahiti will not respond to anything I say or do. I've literally spent long days and nights in the Temple of Jesu, pouring out my heart, begging Him not to take the city. His answer is the same. Prophecy must happen. I must know what is to be done next. How are we going to protect our people and Salzahirz' caravan? More of his kingdom should be arriving sometime midweek. And I don't even know when the city shall be taken. All I know is a week from now by nightfall, the Riders will begin escapades on the cities in every region. Baby, I must know more. Be strong. For me."

He kissed her, adorned himself in a robe and left on his horse. Jewel watched as he disappeared into the night. The tears returned again. She could feel his arms wrapping around her as he left. The tears flowed down her eyes all night long. No one could soothe her now but his presence.

He continually rode onward and onward. He crossed the river and the desert on foot. The horse had to be left behind at a small city along the way. His mouth dried up and his strength left him. He used what little powers from being Lalrola as much as he could. He collapsed upon the desert floor.

***************************   ****************************

Jewel walked the next morning to the castle early before the sunrise. She walked over to the throne and sat upon it. In the dark she sat as the dawn began to rise in the horizon. She looked in the distance and wondered where Triaphor might be by this point. A light appeared. It was her father. He always awoke early to light up the castle halls with his lantern.

The funny thing was, she didn't hear the door open. She looked up and saw a hooded figure, clothed in gold. She noticed that he was of a ghostlike appearance. It was Sésad, the Keeper of The Golden Tree. He cried for help.

"Death! Pestilence!! Famine!!! War!!!!" he said.

No more words were spoken. Only these four were repeated with more urgency in his voice as he spoke. As Sésad disappeared, Jewel glimpsed the Golden City. The Four Riders purged the city clean. The city was ravaged and wrecked. None could save the city it seemed, yet here the Keeper of The Golden Tree called for help.

She felt a cold hand on her shoulder. Was it a Rider? Jewel arose and turned to face him. She was startled beyond belief.

*************************   ***************************

Maesõrn was an absolutely gorgeous city. Some of Névorn's best infrastructures enveloped Maesõrn. Triaphor could even appreciate the city being half knocked out. He awoke with a massive headache. He had been stripped of the upper part of his robes and as he glanced across the room, there sat, at a small desk, a very beautiful young lady. She looked to be about 19 years of age and very asleep. Triaphor tried to move, but the internal pain transfused throughout the entirety of his torso. As he groaned in pain, the young girl awoke. She looked upon the young man with great lust. Her eyes beamed with thoughts that virgin girls were not supposed to think within their father's house. So he thought.

"My nephew!" shouted a man who walked into the room.

"Hey daddy," the girl stood and kissed her father on the cheek.

Triaphor was very confused. These people lived in Maesõrn, one of the most Northern cities in Névorn, and they were his skin tone. Dark-complexioned people only lived in the southern kingdoms of Névorn, which is what made Triaphor an almost stranger amongst his people, save for the fact his mother had been living in Orés for longer than anyone could remember. And nephew? What was that all about?

"Aléshai, leave the room please," the man, his *supposed* uncle, told the daughter.

"Yes, father." Aléshai walked away and closed the door on her way out.

Aléshai. She'd obviously lived up to her name. The various cultures that enveloped the world of Névorn concluded that this name meant *Obedient* and *Trustworthy*. The first meaning had already been proved.

"Triaphor, you won't remember me, for you were five the last time I saw you. How you've grown!" his uncle said, "But I'm your mother's brother. I'm your Uncle Belwin. We moved here after Tahiti agreed to take custody of you. We've made much money being here and we're now the richest of all the merchants in the land. We even surpass some of the politicians financially. Not many people have ever done that. So…"

"Hold on…" Triaphor stopped him, "Why did Tahiti *agree* to take custody of me?"

"As much as I hate to say it," Belwin explained, "We didn't want you. We thought you'd be confused and we didn't know how to control the extraordinary things you did as a child. Tahiti explained what it was and knew that he could help you hone in on your *power*, as he called it."

Triaphor looked upon Belwin strangely. Something seemed unnerving about the entirety of this situation. Irony was not something that Triaphor believed in, simply because he knew of the powers that both Jesu and Sornsé, now deceased, possessed. Plus, *Belwin*. Where had he heard this name before?

To think that if he'd stayed with them, he would've never met Jewel and never had the problems he'd have trying to protect Orés from the never-ending perils it went through. But then his childhood would've been even stranger than his life had become. He began to wish that he'd died with his mother and father. At least that way he'd be free from all this mess. *But somehow*, he thought, *I'd probably end up being Lalrola anyway.*

As Triaphor lie there, pondering over his life and the man that stood before him, Belwin continued.

"When we found you in the desert, we had just been coming back from a vacation in a trip down south. When we finally got you here, we recognized your mother in your features. How strange it is to behold her child once more."

Belwin paused. Triaphor spoke.

"So… how long have I been here?"

"I'd say at least three days."

Triaphor sat up in speed. He sank to the bed quicker than he'd risen. As his body roared with pain, he began to think of Jewel. What was he going to do? She was probably in danger at this time. He'd told her what to do, so she should be ok. He felt someone trying to pry within the inner boundaries of his mind. Knowing that the Riders couldn't possibly find him here so quickly after their release from Apocalypse, he knew from whence the disturbance came. His uncle was peering into his heart. How could he do that unless…

"Uncle Belwin," Triaphor looked up.

"Yes, my son?" Belwin asked.

"Is there any way you could possibly send a messenger to The Empire Of Orés? Send it straight to the palace. Inquire nothing of them. If I'm right… they're being watched. Jewel will understand. Just pass along this message… 'Safety & Comfort. Jesu always watches. Here I lie in hands of blood.'"

"Done." Belwin confirmed.

Triaphor's uncle left the room to do what he instructed. Triaphor hoped that Jewel had made it out of the city or that he'd interpreted the vision wrong and that Orés had not yet been moved upon. There weren't very many cities between Apocalypse and Orés, so the Riders could've very easily have passed through by now.

Jesu. Let them be safe. Triaphor thought.

Pain raptured his body as he lie there. He didn't know how long he'd stay alive, but before he collapsed into deep sleep, he dreamed. He looked into the sky and saw Tahiti. He stood above Triaphor, comforting him. The pain was slightly relieved as the boy fell into submission. The pang had taken its toll. His mind disappeared into the shadows. He felt weightless. His nerves functioned no more.

Chapter 9 – The Golden Kingdom

Jewel turned to see who the person was that had tapped her on the shoulder. She recognized not his face, but realized that his complexion was of a southern glow. With deep glaring eyes she commanded him.

"Speak."

"Safety & Comfort. Jesu always watches. Here I lie in hands of blood."

Jewel understood.

"Be on your way. But in your return say this, 'Pray to Jesu. May He speedily come to thee with a message. To the Golden City will He send you. There you must go. Love shall not go untested.'"

The servant departed unto Maesõrn with the message that had just been given him. Jewel watched as he departed into the horizon. Soon the Council would be meeting and she'd have to discuss the new plan of operations. Salzahirz's men would be arriving soon and she'd have no time then to explain to the Council what she'd seen.

****************************   ****************************

Triaphor lie in his bed, sound asleep. Aléshai watched him and looked upon him with a longing heart. She knew that if her father could feel her mind, she would have been an outcast amongst her family. As Triaphor's lids opened, Aléshai was the first thing he beheld that day. If no one else could, he could see what was in her eyes.

"You can't for two reasons…" he began.

"Shouldn't there be three?" Aléshai questioned.

"Besides the fact that it's morally incorrect," Triaphor continued, "There are two reasons why you and I cannot. One, you are my blood first cousin. Two, I…"

"…have found another love." Aléshai finished, "But for your own sake, I must mean more than just your cousin would mean to you."

"What do you speak of?" Triaphor asked.

"A long time ago, even before you were born," Aléshai begun, "My father, Belwin, was known as Belwin The Prophet, for he and Tahiti had been taught by the same master."

That's where I've heard of Belwin before. Triaphor thought. *He was the one who..*

"Belwin was the first to be married amongst all the prophets of history. He was considered by the city weaker than Tahiti for doing so. Therefore, as Tahiti, a younger and seemingly wiser prophet, soaked up all the glory, my father, Belwin, was losing respect rapidly. So, one day, his sister, Biora, said that she was having a child. Tahiti kept this a secret from Belwin, for no one knew what Tahiti and Biora had with each other."

"What do you mean by that?"

"Let me finish," Aléshai continued, "You see, Belwin had not been very protective or loving of his sister as a brother should be after Biora's husband, Niron, died. So your mother felt she should turn to someone else for she was barren. Well, she did, but this someone was not lawful to commit such a sin. No one, not even Belwin, knew, for your mother kept it a great secret. But one day, Jesu came to Tahiti and spoke unto him saying, 'For the greatness of your sin, I will take away what means most to you.' By this,

Tahiti knew that Biora would soon die. When the elders began to betray Orés, it was my father, Belwin, who convinced them that Sornsé was the right goddess. Therefore, Tahiti, along with King Ric, who at that time was Prince of Orés, fought the elders up the forbidden mountain. Then, Tahiti, after Biora bore his child, cursed the mountain and named it Tortroc. The only one who could break the spell set upon its gate and temple would be the Lalrola. As the baby of the prophet began to grow, Biora slowly began to die.

Finally, one night, when Tahiti and Biora were sleeping together and the five-year-old toddler lie sound asleep in his room, Biora was taken. Tahiti never saw her again and assumed her dead. Jesu came to him and said, 'Belwin is the master of evil. He has taken Biora and burned her body as a sacrifice in the southern kingdom of Iristaniq. Go. Punish him for his crime. Take Ric and his soldiers with you, for trouble awaits you there.' Well, as Tahiti took charge of part of the army and Ric the other, the toddler was left at the palace under charge of the servants. Then Iristaniq, to whom Ric and Tahiti was surely an ally, betrayed the Kingdom of Orés and became a mortal enemy. Belwin, along with his new bride, escaped for their lives to the city of Maesörn and there began making a living for themselves. They bred one daughter, whose name was Aléshai.

Aléshai, being only five years younger than her cousin, had the ability to watch his life and feel his pain. Jesu hid this ability from Aléshai's parents, for they were wicked. Therefore, she has watched him travel many places, fight many faces and has now told him where he came from. My looks upon thee have been truly of love for thy soul, not for any lust for sexual passion. Jewel loves you in a different way, but you mean more to me than anyone will ever mean to you."

Tears strolled down Triaphor's eyes as he stared into hers. The shock of really knowing that Tahiti and even Jesu had kept his real story a secret from him penetrated the very depths of his soul. Finally, his mother's murderer had been revealed. But now he knew that he was definitely running out of time to keep Orés from falling. He needed to hurry. Aléshai read his mind.

"I know what you have come for." Aléshai spoke, "And I will help you fulfill it. Now follow me."

She helped him arise from the bed and dressed him. Then she called for a servant and departed in a carriage to the Library of Rémitron. The Belwin Manor, as it was known to the city, overlooked the entirety of Maesörn. As the carriage passed through the gate, it began its descent into the city square.

****************************   ******************************

Jewel knew what had to be done immediately. She had already rounded up the entire kingdom. They were leaving Orés for good now. The Empire, intact, would be left behind to sit and ruin as age took its toll. All of the work that had been put into building and in return saving the city from destruction was not useless but Jewel could not help but feel such.

The winds from the oceans blew. The wind only blew from the ocean when there was an urgent message to be heard. Jewel perked up an ear. She heard his voice. Her love was speaking to her.

"Aléshai, my cousin and new friend has taken me into her hands. Her father Belwin is full of malice wishes. Jesu has once again spoken to me. If you got my message, leave. Assist the Golden Kingdom in its troubles. The Riders will not be there. You may meet them on the way there, but you and your father, whose curse is now lifted, will be able to destroy at least two of them. Beware of their strength! Since they now ride all together, their power increases. Aléshai and I will meet you there in time and then will we make our attack on Apocalypse. As you head on your way to the kingdom, gather as many troops as you can from the other cities of the south that you encounter. As Aléshai and myself pass through the north, we shall gather troops. Look to the west gate towards the graveyards. Under Tahiti's gravestone there dwells the Horn of the South. As you leave the city, take it with you, for it will rally all of the southern troops and their citizens to you. Be safe, my love. Remember, love shall not go untested. I love you."

The wind brushed softly through her hair as she looked out upon Orés. All of her belongings had been packed. Or at least what had been left of them after Triaphor's fit. As she looked behind her to see the nations of Orés and Iristaniq prepare for departure, Ric and Salzahirz came up to her.

"Be strong my daughter," Ric said, "For a better leader have you been of this kingdom than I."

"My father," Jewel replied, "You and I together have made many faults over my 22 years of life. But one of all things I have learned, it is that we both rule the kingdom jointly. We both go together now to keep this kingdom and its people alive."

"And I by your side," Salzahirz spoke, "For even I have done evil unto you my brother, but love cannot go untested."

Jewel sighed with relief. Someone who knew what she felt. As the royal carriage appeared carrying the kings' things, Jewel hopped upon her horse and went for a ride. The rest of the two kingdoms made their way through the gate, following their fearless leaders. As she passed the graveyards, Jewel stopped only to pick up the horn and continued her steady pace.

Once again, the winds blew.

"Jesu is always with you."

***************************   ***************************

Reaching the Library of Rémitron, Aléshai helped Triaphor to the front door. There, they were stopped by guards.

"State your name and kingdom."

"Aléshai, daughter of Belwin the Merchant, residing in the city of Maesōrn."

"Triaphor, son of Biora, Prophet of Jesu, Lalrola of Prophecy, residing in the city of Orés. I am currently visiting in the home of my Uncle Belwin and his daughter Aléshai."

"You shall proceed. Aléshai, this shall go on your father's monthly. Have a nice visit."

The guards moved from the doorway and allowed the two to continue on their way.

"Monthly?" asked Triaphor.

"We have to pay monthly to stay in Maesõrn, which is why it's a city filled with merchants and politicians. Only they can afford to stay here. Like all northern cities, we don't have a king. We have a City Council, on which my father sits." Aléshai responded.

"Interesting."

Triaphor gazed upon the wonder of the Library of Rémitrôn. Ceilings made of stone in which were set crystals. The pillars that one passed while traveling through the library were built of pure marble. The shelves on which sat the scrolls were made of massive trees from the Golden Kingdom. The pearly golden floor had been fine crafted and burned by the fires of the Red Dragons of Ardenôs.

The wisdom of the entire world sat here. As one went to the shelves to search for a scroll in category, there sat massive thrones made of sapphire and it wasn't kings that sat upon these thrones. They were wise men. Men so esteemed as prophets, councilors, generals of war, builders, and inventors. Not one king sat there. These statues were made of ruby.

As Triaphor passed all of this in awe, they came across one statue. It stood at the end of all the shelves in a corner of its own. It was a monumental statue in the shape of Tahiti. On the bottom the inscription, made of gold from the Golden Kingdom, stated:

Tahiti, Prophet Of Jesu, who resided in the City of Orés, may honor and glory be bestowed unto. Blessings will come to whoever touches this statue.

Tears welled in Triaphor's eyes as he remembered Tahiti's greatness.

"Beautiful, isn't it?" Aléshai asked from behind.

Triaphor turned.

"Quite," he replied, "But… is it true?"

"What?"

"The inscription."

"The last line, you mean," Aléshai clarified, "No. This statue was set up by my father. It's a trick."

Triaphor looked at her in wonder.

"You see," Aléshai explained, "If someone were to simply come up to the statue and touch it, nothing happens. But say someone who was close to Tahiti sorta embraces the statue. It activates the magic set within the statue and that person catches a deadly virus, which is highly contagious. The city could be wiped out within a 10 day period."

"Clever."

"Yes… I found the scroll you were looking for."

"Oh… thanks."

The two sat down and went over the scroll. It was a part of the ever so popular Prophets of Orés series of books. These were the ones written by each prophet during their time until the vision of the Apocalypse was given to Trílautûs. This was the one speaking of the coming of the Lalrola. It was entitled Lalrola Rises. Triaphor thought that perhaps this would shed some light onto what his next move should be. As he casually scanned the scroll, he came across something speaking of Belwin and the Elders of Magic. Skipping that line, he found a line concerning the Four Riders.

"Here it says," Triaphor spoke, "that when the Riders are unleashed, they will set out to destroy all the kingdoms of the world before these kingdoms rally to destroy them. With them they bring their allies' troops. The armies of Ardenôs are assisting in this escapade. War, the White Rider, will take his troops to the four northern kingdoms.

Pestilence, the Red Rider, will assemble his troops and they will attack the southern kingdoms. Famine, the Black Rider and Hades, the Ashen Rider, will join forces to attack the eastern Empire of Orés. But that means that…"

"What?" asked Aléshai.

"How long did it take us to get here?" Triaphor questioned.

"About 4 hours, why?"

"Jewel left about 4 hours ago. She may just have an encounter with Famine and Hades…"

A look of panic crossed Triaphor's face.

"If she's as strong as you claim, she should be able to take on both single-handedly, let alone with two entire nations at her back." Aléshai confirmed.

***************************   ***************************

Hades and Famine led their skeletal armies across the eastern plain. As the evil Riders made their way through the eastern scope of Névorn, something did not seem right. Sentinels had been posted throughout the entire landscape of the eastern world, but they'd all been empty. None of this made any sense. The Prophecy did not speak of such things. Somehow, the Ashen Rider began to believe, they were being tricked.

But then, something shone in the sun so bright that it would've blinded any normal-sighted person. To the Riders, this light only meant one thing. Somebody from the royalty of Orés was happening upon them. Hades commanded the armies to halt. As the armies came to a freeze, the Ashen Rider disembarked his sickly colored horse, walked up a near hill and looked down upon the oncoming army. His black-clad cohort joined him at his side, robe flapping in the wind.

"Dost thou see what I see?" Hades beckoned.

"A pretty large challenge, don't you think?" Famine asked in return.

"No more fun than attacking a hunting party…" Hades grinned under the scowl of his hood.

"So this is how the Sultan of Iristaniq chooses to ally himself? With traitors of War's good name…" Famine hissed.

"He shall receive his payment…" Hades snickered.

This Famine knew. Hades had somehow managed to keep under control his seemingly massing amount of power. It was he who claimed he was most powerful, though War alone had proved him otherwise. Famine and Pestilence knew that Hades and War had a secret bet going on between the two of them. In their release from the gates of Apocalypse, Hades had exchanged looks with War for he knew that the Lalrola was somewhere, but where was just the thing that one of them was going to find out. Though Pestilence would have it easiest of all with the southern kingdoms, where all the Riders had ruled out that anyone of importance could possibly be but Salzahirz, War had wanted no one to accompany either Pestilence or himself. He knew that it would be a challenge for Hades to work with others, as his best work was done alone, but now Hades knew that by killing the essential to Orés' survival, he would create a bait and therefore rid the world of the Lalrola forever. Then he, in all his glory, would dethrone War and begin his reign over the world in its entirety.

"Do you desire slaves?" Famine requested.

"We are finished with Orés and Iristaniq is an experiment well worn out. Kill them. Kill them all."

********************************   *********************************

Jewel had felt them before she glimpsed the hoods of the morbid men of Apocalypse. She knew what she had to do. Unfortunately, this was one of those times when she didn't want to do it without Triaphor. Feeling now that she could fully trust Salzahirz with her people, she left all the citizens with him as she and her father went onward with the armies to battle the deadly foes.

"My father," Jewel spoke as they ascended a hill, "This moment shall be the hardest I've ever embarked upon, but I must encourage you to help me destroy these monsters."

"My daughter, it won't be easy," Ric responded, "But on my life I have your protection in my hands."

"Thank you my father."

As they reached the top of the hill, expecting to find a full-fledged army, they looked down in the plain and saw nothing. There was no one to be seen. It was as if they had all fled at a moment's notice. What confused Jewel the most was that she didn't think that their presence had been given away.

"Where did they go?" Jewel asked her father.

Ric could not respond as he looked on in disbelief. There was no way that the entire army could have possibly disappeared. Then he stared harder. The grain upon the fields was moving. At a steady pace, like children hoping not to get caught, they crawled, Ashen and Black Rider at the rear, waiting for the perfect moment with which to strike. But before he had the chance to even utter the faintest of all whispers, someone grabbed Jewel's ankle. She drew her knife and stabbed. Her eyes widened in horror.

"Orés!!! Iristaniq!!! Attack!!!"

As Ric and Jewel raced forward into the center of the debacle, bodies rose from the once silent plain and began to boom with the clash of over thousands of swords. Arrows whizzed from Jewel's armies as they attempted to kill as many of their foes as possible.

Famine and Hades advanced forward to where their last soldier had been and stood. They watched as the fight escalated to a raging war in front of their eyes. Hades smiled to himself as he spoke magic and he and Famine's horses reappeared.

"It is time…"

Jewel took the two knives of a very fancy curvy design and began to slice and dice her enemies to pieces. The little flesh that hung from their seemingly frail bodies flew in the wind as she tossed them like salad. The Living Dead is what they were known as, for they served the Riders as though they were alive but suffered as if they were dead.

One corpse came at her, swinging its massive arms in her direction. She jumped as its sword was aimed at her feet and flipped, landing a precision aimed kick into its chest. As she bounced up and over him, she threw down her knives into its body and looked into the distance. She heard footsteps fast approaching. With a closer glimpse, she saw that it was the Riders. Her father ran up by her side, slaying a soldier in his path.

"Here they come," he spoke.

"Ready for this?" she asked in reply.

He nodded and they charged, knowing that it would end up better for them if they did. Jewel could feel Triaphor in the air as he struggled to control the magic that Hades was so strongly trying to use. Jewel drew another knife, this one bearing the emblem of The Golden Kingdom. She threw it, directly striking Hades' horse in its Ashen chest. Ric took his sword and lifted just as Famine came riding upon him and connected it with the flesh on Famine's stomach. Striking him with the blunt of his blade, the Rider fell to the ground and was knocked unconscious, a move Ric did not expect.

Jewel ran up to Hades, bow poised and ready to shoot with precise skill.

"Drop your weapon. Your death is upon you."

Hades laughed to himself.

"Do you think that your fool of a prophet can keep you safe from afar? Do you not know that things have already been weighed in the balances and the scale is heavier on my side?"

He laughed once more and then stared at her. In her head, Jewel heard a voice whisper,

"I'm sorry…"

She knew what it meant. She dropped the bow upon the ground in seeming defeat. Ric looked on in confusion. Jewel eyed him with a look that only he would understand and Ric continued to hold his sword to the neck of Famine, who had by now arisen to view the scene.

"It seems that the king does not realize what you do, princess. Perhaps I shall inform him." Hades spoke.

As he turned to look at Ric, the king thrust his sword quickly into the Black Rider's stomach, withdrew it and threw the blade to Jewel. Jewel poised the sword at the neck of the Ashen Rider.

"You might as well use that magic to dig yourself a nice grave." Jewel looked him square in the eyes.

With his eyes flaring, the Rider said,

"Or perhaps your father would like one…"

He spoke magic that instantly darkened the sky with tornado clouds and the wind blew ferociously. Lightning struck the grain on the field at a certain angle so as to entrap Ric in a ring of fire. Jewel's sword melted from the tip of the blade until it reached the hilt. Jewel dropped the sword and did a rolling flip in the grain to reach her bow. The ferocious princess nocked an arrow as she landed on her knees and faced Hades.

Hades looked from Ric to her.

"The fire burns inward. Your father only has but so long to live."

The winds began to blow with such a furious rage that it was hard to balance one's own body. Jewel could feel Triaphor coming. She knew that he would not be long. But she also knew that her father did not have long to live either. All she could do was hope on Triaphor. Other than that, there was only one thing to do and she did not want to resort to that.

**************************   ***************************

Triaphor and Aléshai flew at a rapid speed, racing to get to the Field of Soltran before the devastation of Jewel and King Ric. The griffin on which they rode had belonged to Aléshai since she was but a little girl. He had been nourished from birth and trusted only people Aléshai trusted. The griffin, whose name was Bryan, would hopefully get them to the field safely and quickly enough to ensure the life of the King of Orés. But if Triaphor's vision was right, no such luck would come to him.

Then Triaphor sighted them. He saw Hades being held at bay by the princess and Ric standing with a circle of fire that grew ever inward, about to kill him. Triaphor knew exactly where to land Bryan. He whispered in his ear and the great bird made his descent.

Jewel could not wait any longer. She felt the winds getting stronger and knew that Triaphor would not arrive in the exact time she needed him to. This she also knew: she had to shoot her father. She aimed the arrow as best she could. Hades looked on in confusion as he began to speak.

"What are you going to do Princess of Orés? You can't kill me and you won't kill him and your precious Lalrola is so far away that his control here cannot even stand a chance. I alone have the advantage of power. So what is your final decision?"

An arrow whizzed straight past his face and connected in the perfect spot on the king. Ric howled as the arrow struck him square on his shoulder, knocking him to the ground.

Just as Ric hit the ground, the fire was out by the biggest gush of wind.

Hades looked and upon a massive griffin sat the Lalrola and a dark-complexioned girl that he noticed. Aléshai, daughter of Belwin the Prophet of Evil. Hades was alone now and knew that he could do almost anything. This was an advantage to him, he believed.

"Ah," Hades grinned, "Nice of you to drop on by."

"Don't waste my time with your pleasantries, oh Ashen one." Triaphor snapped.

Aléshai disembarked from the griffin, sword out and poised for attack.

"Don't… you… move…" she said, eyeing the pale rider down.

Hades knew not what to do. Two powerful humans with a warrior princess at his back and a griffin in front of him, there was nowhere for him to run. His army by now had long been disbanded and now it was time to take into consideration the magic he had been so long in holding back.

Hades spoke and acid rain began to fall upon the ground. Barely escaping the grasp of the black clouds, the acid rain was instantly destroyed as Triaphor spoke to Bryan and he flapped his giant wings. The ground shook and disrupted the balance in the sky and the rain dried up.

"Any more tricks?" Triaphor mocked.

Hades scowled at him and drew his sword.

"It appears to me that you want to continue this battle at a later date…" Hades struck the ground and it opened for he and his fellow fatally wounded Rider. They sunk into what seemed to be a black hole, but Triaphor knew better. He let them go.

*********************   *************************

"WHAT!!!!" Belwin was outraged.

The messenger had come back only to find Belwin in the house, bellowing around, looking for Aléshai and Triaphor. When he was convinced that the two were long gone from Maesõrn, he was quite ticked. Since the messenger had witnessed such an outrage, he decided it was best to tell his master of the message that Jewel had instructed him to give to Triaphor.

War stood in the courthouse of Belwin's master house and overheard the messenger speak. As he was inspecting Belwin's lifestyle, he stopped and turned to the door. Peering through it at the messenger, he asked,

"The Golden Kingdom, you said?"

"Yes, your Greatness," the messenger replied.

War accelerated his pace as he stormed out of the house. Belwin was in hot pursuit as the White Rider embarked his horse.

"What must I do, your Grace?" Belwin inquired.

"Go to Apocalypse," War responded, "Await for us to return, for it shall be soon. I, King Asta and the Lords of Ardenôs have things to do."

"Yes, my Lord…" Belwin left.

War rode off as Asta and the Lords of the Sky lifted off to follow the White Lord and his armies. It had taken them a long time, but from the message, War couldn't have salvaged better directions from a map. The Golden Kingdom would suffer great pain for their repeated offenses against Apocalypse.

***********************   ************************

Triaphor and Aléshai had departed a long time ago now and Jewel, along with her father and Salzahirz of Iristaniq, had almost brought the two nations to the very central location of the Southern world. Here was a tiny town that consisted of only a few villagers, most of them owning shops that would lightly replenish all of the resources that had been used thus far. Here is also where Jewel would use the horn to call upon the forces of the South to aid them in the attack against Apocalypse.

But as they arrived, they noticed that the town, known as Partrécious, was no longer there. Standing there in its place…

"Stop!" Jewel commanded everyone.

"What is it?" King Ric asked.

Jewel hoped that she was completely wrong in viewing what she had seen, but her sight was near perfect. Unfortunate for her, bright red shined so flawlessly in the light against the desert floor.

"Father," Jewel whispered, "Do you not see that the Riders intend on killing us and making us their slaves under every circumstance possible? We must kill this one right now…"

As Jewel was talking, Ric reached for his sword. By this time, the Red Rider, Pestilence was his name, had realized that this was Princess Jewel and her father from the Empire Of Orés. He charged his scarlet-clad soldiers to stop their steady pace and await his instructions.

Jewel, King Ric and Orés' finest archery division stepped to the head of their kingdom. Looking Pestilence square in his face, Jewel knew that if she had held two at bay, that this Rider would be quite effortless in a fight against her.

"Give up, oh Evil One!!!" Jewel shouted.

The Red Rider stepped forward.

"What shall be done to me if I choose to do otherwise?"

"Your death will be slow and painful…" Jewel gritted her teeth.

Pestilence could see that she meant business. Without his brothers by his side, it would be difficult to defeat her. Still, if reports went back to War that he had simply forsaken his duty to battle her, disgrace would be poured upon his head for centuries to come. It would be said in the future, that one of the Riders, the rulers of the world, had stepped down to one of his slaves. This could not be.

The sands around them began to stir and Jewel began to lose her balance. Her feet started to slide into the desert floor as did her father's and the archers'. She drew a knife from her shoulder and threw it at the Red Rider. His concentration had been so strongly focused upon the death of the princess that the knife struck him directly in the chest. The dust blew off their feet and Jewel watched as the Rider's cohorts gathered round their leader. As they did, a dust storm blew up in their faces and when it had cleared, the only red that could be seen was where Pestilence's blood had spilt.

"He got away!!!" Jewel shouted angrily.

"Let it be," Ric advised, "for it is obvious that his rampage of the Southern lands is complete. We no longer have allies here but the Iristaniqans that have joined us. We must march onward to the Golden Kingdom. There's a portal not too far north of here that we can take. If the message that they sent you is as urgent as we think, then we must go quickly."

Jewel knew that her father was right. She had still wanted to find some sort of victory over at least one Rider so that when they reached Apocalypse, the fight would be that much easier. But Jesu's will was not such.

The Empire Of Orés alongside the Kingdom of Iristaniq continued on their journey to the portal that would lead them to the Golden Kingdom. As they marched onward, Jewel began to worry for Sésad, hoping that he and his realm were in no need of assistance, but inwardly she knew that this wasn't the case.

*********************   ************************

Triaphor guided Aléshai's griffin towards the landing area outside of Belwin Manor, her father's house. As they landed, Aléshai noticed that there were no servants walking around, performing the daily duties that had been assigned them by Belwin. She moved uncomfortably behind Triaphor as he landed the griffin. As they disembarked, Triaphor asked,

"Is something wrong?"

"Triaphor," Aléshai said lightly, "Father never gives the servants a day off and even if he did, the very first thing they would do when someone returned from a journey, like ours to the library, is greet us with a drink. The house seems empty."

Triaphor quickly glanced around and felt a strange disturbance. He ran inside through the halls that led to the room in which he had been cared for. As he rushed, he observed that no one was residing within the household at this moment, but as he reached his room, he realized that no kind of damage had been done to the house either.

"No one attacked the house," Triaphor stated, "But someone of an overwhelming sinister character has been in this house. I felt it more around the landing area."

Triaphor slowly sat upon the floor and crossed his legs over themselves. As Aléshai examined his actions, she asked,

"What *are* you doing?"

"Prophesying..." Triaphor answered.

"You can't prophesy unless the event is going to happen!" Aléshai got heated.

Prophesying, the art of viewing current and/or future events by focusing on a certain person who is to be involved in this event, was a well-known craft that prophets from every kingdom used to keep trouble from erupting before it started. Many times, prophesying on one's own didn't work very well.

"There was a prophet of Orés," Triaphor began to explain, "who figured out how to prophesy past events by simply sitting on the floor, crossing his legs, closing his eyes and thinking upon the last time he saw a certain person in the situation. This I must do by thinking of your father and from there I'll get a full picture of what he did from the time he left my room to now."

"Wow..." Aléshai was shocked.

She watched as the prophet, who was her cousin, closed his eyes and let Jesu overtake him.

As Triaphor closed his eyes, he remembered his Uncle Belwin's suspicious mood and smile as he exited the room. From that moment on, what he saw would've frightened anyone with less power than what Triaphor contained.

Belwin left Triaphor's room and Triaphor saw a room filled with guests. These guests were not strange to Triaphor, for he'd seen them before. Beginning at the door that had brought his malevolent uncle into the room, there was a couch that stretched around the back wall of the room and reached the counter that connected to the kitchen. Upon this counter were many delicious treats that any man would dream of comprising.

Beside the couch, closest to the door, was Aléshai, who appeared to be enjoying herself. This worried Triaphor because she was in the midst of such iniquitous revelry. Upon the cushion nearest the door sat what appeared to be Asta, king of the Lords of the Sky. Beside him was a councilor of Maesörn who was known as Councilor Ranglicius. Ranglicius' notoriety was as one of Maesörn's toughest warriors and a former counselor to the Riders back when Tahiti was a young prophet. Triaphor had read of Ranglicius' ferocity when reviewing history as an infantile boy. Many had stated that he would've been the fifth Rider if he had learned to contain their power.

Next to Ranglicius sat who appeared to be the new chief advisor to the Riders, whose name was Lord Tantricus. Tantricus' tyrannical character had almost qualified *him* to be a Rider, but once more, there was a lack of power, yet being War's closest consultant put him in a position that scared most people. Most wouldn't dare to even look upon his face. Tantricus was known for encouraging the Riders to execute thousands of slaves in a torturous manor that would teach the nations to fear them. Sweat rocketed from Triaphor's body as he witnessed such a room filled with people.

Next to Tantricus was, of course, his master, the Riders' fearless leader, War. The White Rider sat upon his seat, looking dignified, feeling that he already had control over much of the world. The only thing that seemed to worry him was the fact that he felt the presence of the Lalrola beaming from the adjacent room. Not even the group next to the Rider could've filled him with more terror than knowing that the Lalrola, the most powerful being in Névorn at this moment, was this close to him.

The final people that Triaphor noticed were probably the most fearful looking and the dread that eluded from their presence sent more sweat pouring from Triaphor's body. Aléshai watched Triaphor in horror, hoping that he wasn't seeing what she thought he was.

The Elders of Magic presiding next to War and Belwin seemed to grin the widest as he greeted them last. Their grim nature caused them to barely even raise a hand to return the prophet's seemingly kind demeanor. The Elders of Magic resided under the earth, in dim dark dungeon-style cages that only released them if too much magic was used in any part of the world of Névorn. *This* explained Belwin's trip down south. The Elders were commonly referred to as the *judges* of magic. Whoever caused them to be *awaken*, as the saying went, would suffer a great amount of pain, usually under the spell that they had performed. This had caused many giant massacres of the inhabitants of Névorn by magic to cease.

Belwin, after acknowledging the presence of each man in the room, stood to speak.

"Men of Névorn," Belwin shouted, "In the room adjoined to this one lies the Lalrola of Prophecy and here amongst us we have very distinguished guests who we're all enjoying the presence of at this moment."

War looked upon Belwin with almost disgust. His facial features could barely be seen under the cowl of his deep white hood.

"My friends," Belwin continued, "The men we know as The Elders of Magic have joined us in this escapade of conquest that the Riders have so graciously shared with us. One day we'll all rule under War's splendid kingdom of paradise."

Rounds of applauding praise resounded for the White Rider. His calm demeanor almost seemed ungrateful, but everyone knew that War was an exceedingly mellow character. Having ruled the Land of Apocalypse for centuries, he was used to speeches flattering his work.

"The Elders of Magic will assure us safe passage to Apocalypse as we take the Lalrola back and when we reach the gruesome city, they will begin the process of extracting his power from him and dividing it amongst Apocalypse's soon-to-be top leaders." Belwin finished.

Clapping continued as Triaphor noticed that Aléshai, who'd been listening quietly by the door, slipped out of the room, not even catching her father's eye. His pride would be his undoing through his own daughter. This calmed Triaphor as the scene skipped ahead to Triaphor's now empty room. As Belwin shouted, there returned the messenger that he'd sent to Orés.

"Pray to Jesu. May He speedily come to thee with a message. To the Golden City will He send you. There you must go. Love shall not go untested," the messenger said.

Next Triaphor saw War, the White Rider, reading the mind of the messenger and through this, saw a complete recollection of exactly where the Golden Kingdom could be reached. Triaphor's eyes quickly opened as the realization crossed his face.

"Let's go!!" he shouted.

"What! Why?!" Aléshai shouted back.

"To the Golden Kingdom we must go before it's too late…" Triaphor rushed to Bryan. He jumped upon his back and flew into the sky, speaking words of magic as he took off. Aléshai was behind him as she saw the heavens burst open into a portal that would send them into the Golden Kingdom. The griffin flew straight into the portal and what they beheld was a terrorizing sight.

Triaphor and Aléshai had been flying for what seemed to be days upon Bryan. It would take them longer to get to The Golden Kingdom now because of the trap that had been set by the minions that were to see to its destruction.

Throughout the trip down the portal, the two had encountered all sorts of would-be tragedies. Giant piranhas, almost the size of Bryan's paw, came at them as they passed through the water stage of the portal. When going through the sky sequence, dragons seemed to continually chase them until Triaphor felt safe enough to speak magic and destroy them in a swift stroke.

Now it was drawing upon the 48th hour of their elongated journey and Triaphor didn't seem to be slowing down a bit. Aléshai used magic to fight herself from falling asleep. It was rumored in legend once that a princess fell into a deep sleep while traveling through a portal and in the portal's second stage, which had been the land phase of her trip, she was devoured by a massive cannibal. Never had such a story been repeated in any of the history scrolls or legends.

"Triaphor," Aléshai inquired, to take her mind off of her well-needed slumber, "Just out of curiosity, what did you see during your prophesying session?"

"Quite a lot…" Triaphor responded vaguely.

Aléshai could sense his feelings. She knew that he was ticked off at her because she did not mention this to him at all. As they had been voyaging the portal, Triaphor said not one word to her save for in their attacks. Feeling that it was her fault if The Golden Kingdom was in any way harmed, his demeanor had been one quite less than pleasing to deal with.

"I could not tell you…" Aléshai started.

"…and why not?!" Triaphor interrupted abruptly.

"Because knowing your life's history was more important to what was internationally known at the time," she finished.

"THIS!" Triaphor explained, waving his arms spastically, "could have huge repercussions simply because your priorities were completely backward!"

"Now wait a minute," her tone began to harden, "Don't talk to me as one would speak to a fool! I may not be as wise as thee, but I definitely know where to place my priorities, else I would have told you nothing save my name."

This took Triaphor by surprise. Such shrewdness he'd not experienced since his last argument with Jewel. The majority of women in the world of Névorn were quite submissive to the men that they knew. But women of authority, such as Jewel and Aléshai, saw no need for anyone to openly surrender their will simply because of gender or race.

"I have wronged thee," Triaphor apologetically began, "and for that *I'm* all to blame. But my friend and cousin, I must tell you that because of unfortunate circumstances, we may be in for more than we bargained for with this war. Dost thou know what I saw?"

"If I had known," Aléshai sardonically replied, "I wouldn't have asked thee, *'What is it that thou hast seen?'*"

Realizing that this was true, Triaphor adjusted a bit on Bryan the griffin and began to explain. As soon as he finished, Aléshai asked,

"I'm not quite sure what to think of this."

"I have my suspicions, but I'm hoping that they're wrong." Triaphor said.

Dead wrong! is what he was thinking.

"What suspicions?" Aléshai couldn't help but ask.

"I feel…" Triaphor hesitated, "…as if, through my clout, they're trying to create a whole government of people possessing unspeakable power and thus rule the world with torture as their ally."

"They're trying to create a regime of Riders?"

"Precisely."

Aléshai's eyes widened in horror at the thought. How much power did the fool in front of her encompass? But as she began to think, she began to dream and as the dreams unfolded within her mind, her eyelids initiated her sleep syndrome. Her mind fought against it.

"Relax," Triaphor said calmly.

By this, she knew that they were safe for the remainder of the trip and she could rest soundly.

**************************   ******************************

Jewel, bloodstained and battered, walked down a flight of stairs. She looked up and she saw women and children streaming from the palace. Horror filled their eyes. As they looked upon her a tiny bit of hope flashed in their faces, but it was only a miniscule anticipation.

Ric, king of Orés, met her in the midst of the courtyard.

"The king…" Ric spoke, "…is dead."

"Just as I had figured." Jewel said.

The two walked side by side between two broken pillars. The entrance to the palace that had once been so grand was now tainted with blood. Jewel looked upon the situation with fleeting hope.

"What is it my daughter that you fear?"

"Death…" Jewel said, "death of a friend and ally."

"Triaphor?" Ric asked, concerned.

"No, though I wish he too was here."

She always wished for his presence. His confidence always uplifted their situation and made men stronger. Triaphor knew the meaning of courage. By his own courage, he knew how to instill it in others as well. His power was usually an added bonus.

The king and his daughter walked slowly down the golden hallways of the dead king of The Golden Kingdom. Servants lay everywhere with stone crushing some and blades embedded in others. Some servants had fought for the lives of others and lost theirs in return.

They finally reached the double doors that signified the throne room. Jewel began to push them open, but they would not budge. She pushed again and ended up crashing to the floor.

"Father, these doors are heavy. Do something."

The king pushed against the doors himself.

"Surely the pure gold cannot weigh this much." Ric said to his daughter.

"The only thing that's ever held doors heavier than these is..."

Jewel stopped mid-sentence. The Riders!!!

She leaned her ear close to the door. Ric looked upon his daughter in confusion. As Jewel listened, she heard voices that sounded familiar. Ric watched his daughter's actions, but suddenly heard footsteps. He quickly drew his sword and turned.

"Cover me." Jewel instructed as she continued to listen.

A light shown at the end of the hallway they were in. This frightened Ric. He held his sword in an attack position. Suddenly, the light disappeared yet the footsteps continued.

Jewel was touched on the shoulder by a gentle hand.

"What is it father?" she asked.

"I don't know. I can't see the light any longer."

"What?" Jewel was confused.

She continued to listen as what felt like someone's lips brushed her ear.

"Father, what do you want?" she was agitated.

"I said nothing."

Jewel commenced with her listening and her shoulder was graced again. This time she stood and turned.

"If you don't..."

There stood Triaphor, beaming with white light, Aléshai beside him. Ric put his hand over his eyes as he turned to see him as well. The light dimmed down.

"You scared me to death," Jewel stated.

"We believe the Riders..." Ric started.

"...I know." Triaphor said, "I can get us in there."

"Wait..." Aléshai spoke, "What's in there that is valuable?"

"An old friend and ally," Triaphor responded.

Jewel knew that he spoke of Sésad. She watched as Triaphor closed his eyes.

"Hold this." He handed his staff to the princess.

He pressed his hands against the door.

"Morélis, moréli...

 Morélis, morélu

 Morân, morð, moré, morísan."

A gust of wind rushed through the hallway.

"Stand back!" Triaphor instructed.

The wind beat against the golden doors ferociously. Triaphor and the rest looked on as the wind formed what looked like hands and pushed. The golden doors broke from off their hinges and crashed into the throne room.

Four Riders turned to see Triaphor, Princess Jewel, King Ric and Aléshai, daughter of Belwin, standing there.

Sésad, strapped to the floor by The White Rider's magic, looked up in relief to see his three friends and a strange dark-complexioned woman standing in the entryway. His foot, one of the only body parts that could freely move, supplanted itself into the right calve muscle of Hades. The Ashen Rider fell to the floor, giving Ric the chance to rush to the aid of Sésad.

"Rise up, my friend." Ric said, handing him a sword.

Sésad stood, grasping hold of the weapon. Strapping the belt to his waist, he drew the sword.

"Your time is over, you filthy skinks!!" Sésad eyed Hades.

Triaphor looked War, the White Rider, square in the eyes. Aléshai flanked him on his left, poised to attack Famine. Jewel, flanking her husband on his right, glared at Pestilence.

"You can't escape this time!" Jewel said to the Red Rider.

"If you fools think," War spoke, "that we're afraid of your petty threats..."

The Four Riders of Apocalypse drew their swords simultaneously.

"Its time for the death of Névorn's top leaders. When we're finished with you all, who will defend this planet? Even this supposed God of yours cannot stop us!"

The three facing Triaphor, Aléshai and Jewel lunged across the throne room. Sésad and Ric attacked Hades with ferocity.

The small battle escalated within the walls of the Golden Palace. Triaphor's strokes on the defensive were powerful but the White Rider pushed him against the wall. Triaphor jumped over his head and struck towards the Rider's head. War ducked and the force of Triaphor's sword desecrated the entire left wall of the throne room. The others in the room turned to see the catastrophe.

Upon viewing such power, Sésad and Ric doubled their attack on the Ashen Rider. Hades' defense, however, was effortless and fearless, even after witnessing the power Triaphor held. He knew that if he'd killed the prophet before, he could do it again. But first he must lose these two fools. Hades began to attack instead of defend and Sésad along with the king began to lose ground. Hades struck a parry to Ric's left leg and swept him straight off of his feet.

Sésad, though, would not lose once more to these fiends. Using a low defense to ward off the persistent strike of the Ashen Rider, Sésad's skill used as little energy as possible. He knew that if he could ware out the Ashen Rider, he could prevail against his minion.

Aléshai pushed Famine back out of the opening that Triaphor had created. The two fought over the ruins of the once beautiful city of gold. Over dead bodies and destructed weapons the two battled endlessly. Famine, the Black Rider, found it hard to fight against the daughter of the evil prophet. She was a powerful warrior that knew sword techniques unique to a slain race of feminine warriors. They were known as the MorningStar Talsûrõn. The Riders had diminished them so long ago that Famine had almost forgotten their style.

Jewel, holding her two golden knives that Sésad had given her, pushed Pestilence against the right wall. She gritted her teeth with rage as she held the knives to his neck.

"I couldn't kill you the last time we met, but this time..." Jewel spoke.

She took her right knife and pierced the Red Rider in his jugular. The Rider didn't shriek or stir at all. She removed the knife and watched as the Rider fell to the floor of the throne room. Just as Jewel turned, she saw her father lying on the ground, wounded, as Sésad held Hades at bay. She ran to him.

"Father," she shouted over the clash of swords, "are you alright?"

"Just fine." The king said.

Jewel helped her father to his feet and watched as Hades took Sésad by surprise and stabbed him in his shoulder. Jewel readied her bow and shot an arrow. It struck the Ashen Rider dead in the eyes. A shriek roared from the Rider and he ran out of the throne room past War, his master, and Famine, the Black Rider.

Triaphor was shocked at how many magic beings filled this room and yet no one had used their power as an advantage. When he had struck the wall, he had forgotten that his power was extremely difficult to control. Fortunately, this had opened up a lot of room for the swelling battle.

He could feel that the White Rider was ready to pull a trick. Before the Rider could think to release his power, Triaphor began to control the air with his power. He knew that the Elders of Magic were all the way in Apocalypse, so they had no affect in the Golden Kingdom. Not to mention that they were in a completely different dimension. Triaphor could virtually do anything he wanted.

War began to speak a spell and just as he did, Triaphor's sword got too heavy to swing. Triaphor availed against the Rider nonetheless, but began to tire. As exhaustion began to take over his body, his control over the air withered. Triaphor pushed the Rider back into…

…the arrowhead of Jewel's arrow. Triaphor stopped his pursuit and dropped his sword to the ground. He spoke words of magic and from the White Rider's hands jumped the sword War had been using into Triaphor's hands.

"Trapped, are we?" Jewel taunted.

Aléshai struck the Black Rider in his arm and his sword dropped to the ground. She backed him up and he tripped over a stone, falling to the ground. The dark-complexioned warrior held the point of her blade to the Rider's neck.

"Don't you move… punk." Aléshai glowered at him.

War glanced around at his surroundings. The Red Rider lay against the right wall in the throne room. Hades, his Ashen comrade, had fled the scene entirely and the Black Rider lay with Aléshai's sword at his neck. What is it that he could do? He could easily escape and retrieve his power in Apocalypse, but he didn't want to do that. He would, once again, look like a coward in front of his enemies and that he refused to repeat.

"What will you do now, my White fiend?" Triaphor tested.

That was a good question. He didn't know what he was going to do.

"I'll make you a deal," Triaphor said.

This was a treat for War.

"If you depart these lands and never come back for eternity, I'll let you and your comrades go freely. But know this, Apocalypse *will* be ours when we come to stop your torture of this world. You will not control this world Jesu has given us." Triaphor commanded.

"You're right, great Prophet," War growled, "For you and I both know that this world is coming to a swift end. You also know that your time runs out. If you do not defeat us, then Jesu will hand the world to us and there will be nothing you can do about it."

Jewel lowered her bow and looked past War at her husband. This could not be true. She would not believe that Jesu had this pact sealed with such base creatures. But when she looked into his eyes, she knew that there was nothing truer.

"Is this true?" Aléshai asked, looking at Triaphor as well. The Black Rider arose from the ground.

Triaphor could not speak for his shame. Sésad, knowing many of the secret and ancient prophecies kept from the common folks, spoke for him.

"Yes, but it also says that in order for this to be fulfilled, the creatures must destroy us at the gates of Daréngir, the Dark City."

Before the conversation could commence, the Four Riders disappeared in a cloud of black smoke. Aléshai and Jewel walked to Triaphor. Bryan flew over the palace from the courtyard to join them.

"So what's next, babe?" Jewel asked.

"Well," Triaphor mustered all his strength to speak, "Now that we know Sésad is safe, we have our people here and the only thing that we can do for right now is what loyal allies should do in such a situation. Rebuild the Golden City."

All knew that Triaphor was right. It would not only be that much easier with two whole nations to help, but it would also take their minds off of their impending doom, should they fail. Their next move would have to be extremely careful. Whatever their next move would be.

Chapter 11 - The Golden River

Hooded and robed in white, Triaphor looked out upon the Golden City. Much had been restored since the time that the Riders had brought their attack to its gates. Sésad had taken over as ruler and lord of all the affairs of the Golden Kingdom. Triaphor's happiness had been restored to him as he and Jewel had spent much time together.

Months had gone by. Triaphor had not intended on it taking this long. Comfort had set in among the people. It would be hard to get them willing to move at the rapid pace they had been moving before. But Jesu continually prompted him. Nights of dream after dream after nightmarish dream had kept Triaphor awake. His prayers only received the same answer every time. MOVE!

He felt her presence before she spoke.

"What is it that you think of?" Aléshai inquired.

"The people of Orés…"

Aléshai could understand what he was feeling. It was hard for any leader to feel responsible over such a mass amount of people, especially when most of them didn't really know what war was like. Such warfare that they were forced to remain under until the end, was difficult and no man wished it upon anyone, especially not the entire nation.

"Triaphor, we've got to move." Aléshai advised.

He knew that what she spoke was true.

"Sound the alarm. Prepare the people. Send word to Sésad, King of the Golden Kingdom, that I seek an audience with him."

"My cousin," Aléshai responded, "It shall be done."

*   *

This is not how she wanted to leave!!! Why now? The timing seemed unfair. Just as she was completely finished decorating their house, it was time to depart. She was filled with anger. These were *her* people and he would not demand them to do anything without her consent.

"Triaphor, Son of Biora!!!"

Triaphor turned in the doorway to see a livid Jewel storming in his direction.

"My dear?"

"How dare you?!" Jewel bellowed, "How dare you give such instructions without first consulting me?!!! Now I understand that Aléshai is your cousin, but to have her giving orders under the circumstances that we stand in, I will not have it!!! I *will* throw her out Triaphor, watch me!!!"

Triaphor didn't know how to respond to her. He'd only seen her like this once and it was a council meeting. Justice was served at the right time in the right way. This, he could not understand.

"Are you even listening to me?" Jewel asked.

"Jewel," Triaphor finally spoke, "You must trust me. When I give orders, if you and your father do not agree with me, inform me, yes, but follow me please. I don't randomly command ridiculous things to be done unless it comes from Jesu first. Its time to move. Its past time to move. We don't have very much time left and you know it. Just trust."

Jewel peered through him like an arrow. She knew that he was telling the truth, but it seemed unfair.

"Where are all the other nations?!?!?!" Jewel roared, "Why can't they take this responsibility into *their* hands? Why must it always be Orés that suffers...?"

"...Orés is not the only suffering nation!!!!!" Triaphor shouted, "Jesu has chosen us because we're the only ones in Dimensia[1] left!!!"

This struck Jewel like a hammer to her heart. She could not believe that the Riders had succeeded in their decadent plans. Finally, the end had come. Time after time had she heard of this happening, but never did she suspect it to truly happen. Not in her time.

"Will you come with me to Sésad's palace?" Triaphor gently asked, reaching for her hand.

Jewel took hold and embraced her husband. Tears streamed down her face, as she felt desecrated. Simple had been the task before her, so she thought. Her love of her own nation and the comforts of life had been the downfall of all the other nations of Névorn's Dimensia[1]. Jewel cried in Triaphor's arms for what seemed an eternity.

Triaphor began to walk out of the door, holding hands with his princess. These two had ruled Orés since the death of Tahiti and long had the years seemed. It was time for them to secure Orés' safety, for it was just they and Iristaniq. The Golden Kingdom, belonging to another dimension than they, would render their services. So they hoped.

Triaphor stood at the egress to the cave with King Sésad and watched as the barges, one by one, exited the Golden Kingdom. Bryan and Aléshai stood closest to Triaphor, awaiting his embarking.

"Thank you for your help, Great Prophet," Sésad bowed, "It was much needed and we are in great debt to you and your kingdom."

"Your debt shall be repaid," Triaphor said, "For you will be with us at Apocalypse. But await my arrival, for I shall return. Alone."

"Yes, Great Prophet." Sésad returned to his kingdom through the cave.

Triaphor hopped on Bryan and they along with Aléshai rode off into the sky as the last barge came from the cavern. Jewel, upon the Royal Barge, looked up behind her and waved. Triaphor waved back, identifying that he was watching them from the sky, as she should command from the river.

The Golden River was a very long tributary that would lead them out of this dimension into theirs and to a nearby city that had been deserted. The City of Ivõrus was a secret hideout where no one would be able to find them. This would also provide the people with proper housing until they were ready to move on once more. But this time, they would only spend less than a week at Ivõrus, for they must continue moving.

"What do you think will happen to us?" Aléshai asked.

"I'm not sure. It all depends on our people."

This was true. If the people didn't want to cooperate, there was nothing that could be done. They would all perish in the destruction of the world if the Riders were not destroyed in the proper time.

He felt them!! Triaphor knew they were around here somewhere, but he could not place his fingers on them.

"Look!!!" Aléshai shouted.

Triaphor looked up and there they were. Famine, Pestilence and Hades, riding upon the Red Dragons of Ardenôs. Panic welled inside his people as, one by one, each barge realized they were in danger.

"What are we gonna do?" Aléshai asked.

"I've got an idea," Triaphor responded, "But you'll have to be a good driver."

"Trust me, Bryan knows what he's doing."

"Then," Triaphor grinned, "Draw your swords. Its time for battle."

Aléshai's swords left their sheathes as she prepared for what was to come.

The Riders began their tirade upon the barges. Triaphor knew that they could not lose one of those barges. He sent a message to Jewel.

"Get your archers ready!"

Jewel felt the breeze blow from the river. It was time to fight and she knew exactly what to do.

"Archers!!! Fire at will!!!"

The archers on each barge set themselves at a steady position. After securing themselves, they shot at the three beasts of burden.

All missed.

The Riders now focused their attention to the griffin that headed their way.

"Here they come!" Aléshai shouted.

Triaphor looked up and readied himself for the jump. He lunged towards the river and Bryan caught him with his massive claws. As Triaphor hung upside down, he felt Bryan speed up swiftly. It wasn't long before they were going to reach the Three Riders.

The prophet swung upward and struck off the head of Pestilence's dragon. Aléshai's two sword strokes cut off the right wing of Hades' monster along with the left wing of Famine's brute. The effort of the two cousins sent the Three plummeting towards the Golden River. Before the Riders' fall was complete, arrows whizzed by them from the barges.

"Nice work hottie!" Jewel shouted from her mind.

A large puff of smoke sent the three evil creatures back to Apocalypse. Triaphor regained his composure from being upside down for so long and jumped to the land next to the river.

"What's he doing?" Jewel asked Aléshai in the wind.

"I don't know…"

"The White Rider is here!" Triaphor cried.

Triaphor sheathed his sword and sprinted through the forest. He knew that he had to take out War for now or else they couldn't make their way to Ivõrus unseen. Without his cohorts, the White Rider would be easier to fight.

He saw him ahead in a clearing. Atop his pearly horse, the King of Vice looked dignified. Triaphor so wished that now was the time to bring this fool to his death, but he must wait a little longer. He drew his knives.

"I thought I told you never to return to these parts!" Triaphor demanded.

The White Rider only looked at him. Triaphor knew that he was ready to perform magic. He sensed them. The Elders of Magic were hiding in the trees. If Triaphor used any magic, it would have to be minimal or they were ready and willing to kill him.

Though angry, Triaphor had been taught by Tahiti how to be tactful with his power. The White Rider, on the other hand, was full of impious tricks that were unlimited in use.

Triaphor rolled on the forest floor and struck the legs of War's horse. The horse crashed to the ground and the White Rider leapt from his companion. Now the two were face to face as Triaphor rose from the ground.

Peering into the eyes of his enemy, the White Rider raised his hands. The wind blew with all its might. In order to stop the wind from blowing, Triaphor would have to use some sort of magic. No matter what kind of magic he used in this situation, it would be too much and the Elders would kill him instantly.

Triaphor could barely hold his position against War. He just stood his ground as best he could and waited for the White Rider to make one false move. War stepped towards Triaphor slowly. This was a bad move on his part. Triaphor threw his knives to the ground and drew his sword.

Still glaring at the Master of Ruse, Triaphor swung. The White Rider ducked, taking his focus off of his spell. Triaphor jumped over the Rider's head and stabbed him square in the back. Shrieks from the Rider were heard echoing throughout the forest.

"Return to thy Black Gates until your time comes you worthless mongrel!" Triaphor whispered viciously in War's ear.

In red smoke the foul sorcerer disappeared. Triaphor put away his sword and headed for the riverbank. There he saw that Jewel and Aléshai had led the people of Orés to the furthest point the river would bare them.

"Are you alright?" Aléshai asked.

"Just fine." Triaphor spoke.

By that tone, Jewel knew that he was tired and not really ready to move forward, but they had to continue.

"I've prepared a carriage for thee, Great Prophet. Lie and rest as we lead the people to Ivõrus." Jewel said.

"Ivõrus?" Autôw, leader of the War Council and General of His Majesty's forces asked, "Is there such a place? Rumor has it that this city is only of legend."

"Then I suppose we shall find out, won't we?" Aléshai sneered.

This, Autôw didn't take to kindly.

"If I want the opinion of a sorceress of the enemy, then I shall request it. Otherwise, your words can rot in the pits of hell as far as I'm concerned." Autôw spit back.

Triaphor grabbed the stubborn dupe by his neck and hoisted him against a nearby tree.

"Aléshai is a loyal ally and companion! You will treat her with higher respect than that you would give me!! She is not only my cousin, but she is your commander! In all things, when she speaks she is to be respected or you will rot in the pits of hell along with your opinion of her words!!!" Triaphor snapped sadistically.

All who witnessed this suddenly grew either afraid or esteemed of Triaphor and Aléshai. To Aléshai for not harshly responding and to Triaphor for doing so. There were many people in the kingdom who wished they had done the same thing. Even though Autôw had many supporters—most of them War Councilors—most people also knew that Autôw was a bit of a power seeking mongrel.

Jewel walked up to her husband and patted his shoulder.

"Get some rest, my friend."

Jewel led the people through the Wilderness of Westcott even though she grew tired and anxious. Determination drove her as well as the fact that she knew that if she didn't do it, no one else would have the strength.

Aléshai walked beside her. They had not spoken to each other the entire journey. They knew of each other's existence and that each one of them meant something different to Triaphor, but they didn't really *know* each other. Jewel, in her own mind, was a bit frightened of Triaphor's cousin. She, aside from Tahiti she discovered, was the only family member of Triaphor's that she had the privilege of knowing. It was a shame that they really hadn't had time to get to know one another.

"So," Aléshai spoke first, "What was it like living without Triaphor for so long?"

Jewel couldn't believe it. If she had been a rude person, she would've gone with her instant inclination to not respond. But her disposition only came from shock.

"Unbearable really," Jewel let the words part her lips, "I couldn't understand why Jesu was allowing such a time to happen. But ya know, after awhile I realized something."

"What's that?"

"Sometimes," Jewel loved every moment of this, "its good that people should separate from each other. It isn't healthy for someone to constantly be in your face. This is why I fear for this nation. We've only spent time *together* for almost a year and this can only damage the relationships that I know many of us have worked hard to garner."

"This is very true," Aléshai talked back, "Although another great truth is the fact that in togetherness we often achieve greatness at its best and even though it grows tough to be around the same old people doing the same old thing, in the end, we've become an unstoppable force if only we've learned to live, love and work together. There will be those times that we fight and argue, struggling endlessly within ourselves because it is with the closest people that we often battle, but if we overcome them, we turn out the better for it. Gold is polished in fire."

Aléshai was a brilliant person. Jewel was almost taken by surprise at how much she had learned in such a short lifetime. Jewel knew that Aléshai was about 3 years younger than she, but for a nineteen-year-old girl, she exceeded in knowledge and wisdom. She just supposed it ran in the family.

"Jewel," Aléshai beckoned, "I've been wondering, how many kids do you and Triaphor wish to possess?"

Jewel had thought out this question so many times. She wasn't really sure how many Triaphor wanted to have, but she loved children and it never really occurred to her before this time that it didn't matter how many she had, she would love them endlessly.

"I'm not really sure," Jewel responded, "It seems to me that children in today's complex society are getting harder and harder to rear. Though I'm sure I wouldn't really have that tough of a time, knowing Triaphor."

"I was thinking more along the lines of you. I don't think you could stand a misbehaving child!"

"Its true," Jewel said.

The two continued their talk throughout the Wilderness of Westcott. It meant not a thing that either one of them knew not exactly where they were going. Triaphor was right. It was only safe to trust in Jesu. Just trust. Jewel would never forget those words as long as she lived.

They came upon a clearing that appeared to be a field. Jewel stopped the people. She and Aléshai looked upon the field and it stretched as far as the eye could see. Triaphor walked up behind the two.

"The Field of Rulers…"

Jewel felt his arms wrap around her waist. The three stood, tranquil as birds, staring out upon the field, gazing at its wonder. Secretly in their hearts they all wished to be home. That final day that they could make that trip back would be the best day of their lives.

"Cousin," Aléshai looked at Triaphor, "Where exactly *is* this City of Ivõrus?"

"Borisón, bísõrjiýon!"

Before their very eyes appeared the grandiose City of Ivõrus.

"They will never find us here," Jewel said.

"My dear," Triaphor responded, "Never doubt the strength of evil men on the pursuit. When there is wickedness to be done, they shall not sleep until it is either completed or they're destroyed."

Triaphor, filled with relief, viewed Ivõrus with joy and excitement. He knew that here his people could regroup and live life as if they were back in Orés because this particular city was once inhabited by past citizens of Orés.

"The legends say," Aléshai spoke, "that this city was once a complex society of men and mysterious creatures called Elves. But then, after a time of confusing warfare and endless quarrel with Orés it was reconstructed as a refuge for those servants of Jesu that traveled through the Wilderness of Westcott."

"Fortunate for us," Jewel said, excited to see the progress being made.

"But why," War Council Leader Autôw began his usual inquiry, "is the city impossible to view unless magic is spoken?"

"It was not always this way," Triaphor informed him.

As Autôw almost opened his mouth to ask another sarcastic question, Triaphor put a finger to his lips to signal that no noise should be made.

"Cousin," Aléshai whispered, "What is it that you see?"

"Look," Triaphor quietly responded.

The three leaders along with the War Councilor turned their heads to the right and the sight that they observed was quite immaculate. A magnificent cerulean horse pulled an impressive carriage and behind the cart walked what appeared to be millions of elegant creatures.

"The Elves of Ivõrus," Triaphor muttered in wonder.

Clad in silver hooded robes lined in jade from head to toe, they were led to the city gates of magnificent Ivõrus. Triaphor, Aléshai, Jewel and Autôw watched in awe as these graceful beings made their way.

"We must follow," Triaphor instructed, "Come, quickly, gather the people. Sound the charge."

The leaders of Orés took the initiative of the roles they were meant to play. Triaphor, Jewel and King Ric on their horses, led the people of Orés and Iristaniq behind the Elves of Ivõrus and their mysterious leader. Aléshai could only help but wonder how these elves had come to know that Orés and Iristaniq planned on arriving at this time. The elves seemed to slow their pace as they realized, without turning a back or a head to look upon their followers, that Orés and Iristaniq sought an obvious dwelling within the city.

The gate of Ivõrus, known historically as The Gate of Rulers, was grand in appearance. Sculpted into the stone were the faces of kings, princes, prophets and Aléshai noticed that one of the MorningStar Talsûrõn's leaders was even amongst these great warriors of history. Jewel was astounded, as was Ric, to see her father's face carved directly across from the face of Tahiti, now revealed as Triaphor's father.

"We've taken on the role of our fathers, my love," Jewel whispered to Triaphor.

"And what role is that?" Triaphor inquired.

"We're the last leaders of our people," Jewel responded, "You as a prophet and I as royalty. This was meant for us. It was our destiny. Our call in life by Jesu was to follow in the footsteps of our fathers."

"Then let us make the best of what Jesu has ordained."

As they reached the marketplace and center of the city, they stopped. Disembarking the carriage was its apparent rider, dressed in a blue robe that was quite similar in style to Triaphor's. Triaphor, knowing innately who this was, allowed the hooded rider to reveal himself first.

"My friends," Tahiti spoke as he removed his hood, "It has been a long time since I've had the privilege of leading you forth. Unfortunately, my current task is over.

These," pointing to his hoary-robed friends, "are the Elves of Ivõrus. They have come to your aid and assistance."

"But how, great master," Aléshai asked, "for have they not been dead for centuries?"

"My dear niece," Tahiti addressed, "in the kingdom of Jesu, He who dwells within the holiness of the White Temple, they have been well preserved. He has sent these, His loyal servants, to militarily give you an advantage over the Riders. Trust in Him, my friends, for He, not Lalrola, is the only one who can save you from the chaos the Riders have caused."

Tahiti embarked his carriage once more. The horse, so pure in its cobalt color, sprouted wings and flew the old prophet back to the serene White Temple. Oh, how Triaphor wished he could've returned with him. His task, he wished could be easier to bear.

"Triaphor," Jewel snapped him out of his thoughts, "we must house the people quickly so that they may receive their rest."

"Of course," Triaphor said, "I want you and Aléshai to be in charge of making sure that everyone has a place to stay. There must be five elves to each family, do you understand?"

"Are there that many of them, my love?"

"There are even more," he replied, "enough for the palace to have ample security as well."

"Where," Aléshai asked, "are the War Councilors to be housed?"

"The palace," Triaphor answered, "for Council meetings will have to be held immediately."

The two, princess and warrior, went about their business and followed Triaphor's instructions flawlessly. Not assured of his position within the kingdom, Triaphor went for a walk throughout the palace gardens. As evening rapidly approached, he looked up into the sky.

There, painted across the evening horizon, stood his Lord. Jesu, appearing in less light and more body than before, stood, still blinding Triaphor with His luminance. Triaphor, astonished and ashamed, bowed the knee to the Master of his life.

"Speak," Triaphor garbled, "I listen."

"Yet you still doubt," Jesu spoke poignantly, "How, after all the things that have happened to you thus far, can you still have doubts about who you are and the task set before you?"

"My Lord," Triaphor said, "I try my best not to lose my patience. It is so difficult sometimes to move on. I just wish sometimes that my life's work was finished, so that..."

His words ceased to come from his throat. He began to feel choked. The harder he tried to speak, the more difficult it became to breathe. Triaphor gasped for air, hoping for relief. None came. His ears perked up and he began to listen to his Master's instructions.

"From this point forward," Jesu gently commanded, "You will rise up, Lalrola of Prophecy, as a Prophet of Jesu whose confidence and trust resides solely in Me. You will not doubt your abilities, for your abilities come from Me. What you have become and the task that you've been given is a reflection of My plans for Névorn. Respect yourself and honor will be yours. Embrace the charge that I've set aside for you. May My blessings be upon you, Son of Biora. Son of Tahiti."

At the mention of his old master's name, Triaphor's breathlessness was relieved from him. Tears strolled down his face as he felt two gentle hands clutch his shoulders. One, as pale as the city stone and the other, as dark as cherry tree bark, both embracing the man who would lead them to triumph.

Choosing not to speak, the three enfolded within each other, all taking on the task that lie before them. The leaders of Orés and Iristaniq and now the ancient soldiers of Ivõrus. As they clang to each other, the arms of Jesu wrapped around them, providing them with confidence and strength with which to follow through with His will.

*   *   *

Triaphor awoke. He glanced at his wife in all her beauty and saw that she was still happily at rest. Serenity had been granted them this gorgeous morning. The sun rose energetically and ready to start a fresh day. A new age had dawned upon them. More and more did the sun rejoice in appearing.

The prophet walked over to the crib. He picked up the 7-month-old baby boy and held him in his arms. Embracing his child, Jõniathor was his name, had pleased him for a long 7 months. Triaphor, every day since his son's birth, had never stopped smiling. With trouble in this world behind them, he could finally relax and spend time with his family.

A knock came at the door. A servant looked at his master. Triaphor nodded and the door was answered. Aléshai, long black hair flowing just below her shoulder blades, entered the room, grinning widely.

"Nothing is more precious," she said, "than watching you hold that child."

"Do you wish...?" Triaphor asked.

"No," she replied, "I enjoy watching you feed your son."

A bottle had been planted in Jõniathor's mouth. As the baby sucked upon the bottle's plastic nipple, Triaphor led Aléshai to the massive window that overlooked Orés' grand spectrum. Blood, sweat and tears had been duly shed for this vast landscape.

"Being king," Triaphor said, "I swear sometimes is more difficult than all that we went through for this city."

"Yes, well..." Aléshai began, when a knock at the door interrupted her statement. The servant opened the door... one... last... time.

The servant's head rolled upon the floor towards Aléshai, whose swords were already drawn. Jewel, still sleep in this turmoil, gently opened her eyes. Mouth agape, she rolled off her bed so that she could be hidden between the wall and the bed.

Aléshai fought off the warriors as best she could, but there was nothing that she could do to save herself or, for that matter, her cousins from danger. The soldier, clad in White, flung the Talsûrõn warrior, across the room against the hard wall, knocking her unconscious.

The Four Soldiers, one wearing Black, another in Red, the White one and the final soldier in Ashen, a color of sickliness, drew their swords. Triaphor glanced around him, searching for them. He knew that they were here. He could feel their presence breathing down his throat.

The Elders of Magic appeared behind him, near the window, as a familiar hand grabbed his shoulder.

"Nice to make acquaintance with you once more, my friend," Belwin, his malicious uncle said.

Jõniathor, screaming at the top of his lungs, was snatched out of a helpless Triaphor's hands. Shirtless and defenseless, Triaphor was knocked to the floor by the flat of the White Soldier's sword. Landing hard on his knees, Jewel broke the rest of his fall.

In her arms he fell and looking into her eyes deeply, he whispered,

"Retrieve my son,"

      *   *   *

Triaphor sat up in bed, sweat exuding from his body.

He looked over at Jewel, who was peacefully at rest. Glancing around the room quickly, he tried to spot a cradle. Not able to find one, he went to the massive window that overlooked the bright city of Ivõrus. Some of the city's lights were still glowing. Homes seemed so tranquil as the night wind gracefully blew through his shoulder-length hair, a trait that most dark-complexioned men were not fortunate to have. Salzahirz, a man of caramel color, did not even possess such a rarity.

Triaphor's mind was greatly disturbed. Though he and Jewel had spent many months of calm in The Golden Kingdom, utilizing the pleasures of marriage, he highly doubted that a child was on its way. Jewel seemed to be working faster than ever these days and harder, at that.

A knock came at the door. Jewel stayed fast asleep as she gently turned herself over.

Triaphor, having stationed a servant at the door, only turned his head. Expecting her, he sent the servant from the room as he spoke freely.

"Aléshai, I'm scared."

His gracious cousin walked up to the window behind him. Planting herself beside him, she gazed into his eyes. Fear welled up inside of him. She could not understand why he was feeling this way. Jesu had just blessed them all, yet he was afraid once more.

"They're drawing near here," Triaphor said.

"Who?" Aléshai solicited.

"The Elders of Magic."

The MorningStar Talsûrõn warrior knew now why he felt this way. Belwin, his uncle (her father), had drawn in the Elders to aid the Riders. Triaphor knew, as well as his enemies, that this could create chaos.

"Listen," Aléshai spoke, "If ever you feel that you need assistance, fear not to call upon me. I know some magic that's good enough to defeat the Riders in a battle, but not powerful enough to draw the Elders nearer to us."

"Aléshai," Triaphor responded, knowing now what he had to do, "Call a meeting of the War Council. Make sure that they are all in attendance. Call upon the king, Sultan Salzahirz and the elven Prince Kyliõn. Jewel and I will be there shortly."

"But the hour is late…"

"…I know," Triaphor interrupted, "but this is a dire emergency. They must be equipped and prepared."

Aléshai, sensing the urgency of the situation, rushed from the room. With speed, she made her way around the palace, arousing the councilors and the other royalty that were to appear.

Triaphor, still haunted by his dream, kissed Jewel lightly upon her forehead. Her eyelids opened. She sat up in her bed and walked to the window. Seeing that the sun had not yet peeked through the clouds, she looked back at Triaphor. He was sitting at the edge of the bed, head buried in his hands.

She sat with him, holding him and brushing her fingers through his hair.

The War Councilors sat on either side of the lavish pool that lay in the center of the courtroom. The royalty—Ric, Salzahirz, Jewel, Triaphor and Prince Kyliõn of the Elves of Ivõrus—sat up front, facing the pool. Autôw, angry to have been awoken for such a session, glared at Triaphor as he took his seat.

"War Councilors of Orés, Iristaniq and Ivõrus," King Ric announced, "Triaphor, Son of Biora, Prophet of Orés and Lalrola of Prophecy, has words to speak to you."

"Friends," Triaphor began, "The Riders of Apocalypse, our eternal enemy, are at this moment marching upon us. Unfortunately, the city can no longer be shielded through magic."

The room went up in an uproar. Triaphor had expected such. Prince Kyliõn, garbed in a royal green, his maroon hair laced in silver from his headdress, glanced around the room in agitation. Jewel traded looks with Aléshai, who sat directly across from Autôw. Feeling their presence draw nearer, Kyliõn lifted his pointy ears.

He could hear drums. Big drums. Massive footsteps were made in the Field of Rulers. They were progressing quickly. There was no time to waste. Knowing that he would draw attention, he bolted from his throne, the farthest to the right and closest to the courtroom window. He peered outside, over the wall and looked to the field. His eyes widened in horror.

The War Councilors, having stopped their fussing, all waited for his response.

"They've recruited help." Kyliõn said.

"We've got to go." Triaphor rushed from the room.

*********************   *************************

Triaphor, flying upon Bryan, viewed the scope of the armies that had been brought by the Riders. It was an extensive amount of people. The Red Dragons of Ardenôs, being ridden by their competent masters, growled at Bryan. In a shriek, the griffin snared back. The sun had come out, bright and fair, on a morning where Triaphor knew much blood would be shed.

Landing Bryan on the Gate of Ivõrus, Triaphor disembarked, meeting Kyliõn and Aléshai in the center.

"How many?" Kyliõn asked.

"About 1,000,000 of the Lords of the Sky alone," Triaphor said, "Not counting the armies of The Dark City."

"We need archers," Aléshai advised.

"Just as I had feared," Kyliõn said, knowing that his people were the best archers in the world.

"Don't worry, prince," Triaphor comforted, "I have a plan that may work. Gather the archers of Orés and Iristaniq on the city floor. Jewel shall take command of them. You, Aléshai, shall stay here with me and give order to the archers of Ivõrus. Kyliõn, you, my friend, shall take the combined armies of Orés, Iristaniq and Ivõrus, those who are not archers, and meet the Dark Alliance in battle."

Kyliõn was shocked at Triaphor's plan.

"How many shall I take?" he asked.

"A thousand men."

Aléshai gave an astonished look. Kyliõn and she traded eyes. Trustingly, the two followed orders. Aléshai directed the archers from Ivõrus to where they should stand upon the wall. Jewel, who'd already decided to lead the archers of Orés and Iristaniq into battle, rushed to the Gate of Ivõrus.

"What's going on?" she asked.

"Triaphor's come up with a plan," Aléshai told her, "You are to lead the archers of our forces in the city square."

Jewel, knowing now to just confide in her husband, did as she was instructed.

"On your word, my prince," Aléshai told Triaphor as she awaited his command.

"Open the gate!!!" he shouted.

Kyliõn, armored in silver, emerald cape flapping in the wind, led the soldiers of Orés, Iristaniq and Ivõrus onto the Field of Rulers. Piercing through the eyes of his enemies, Kyliõn's strength and courage uplifted the spirits of the soldiers he led.

"I hope this works," Aléshai muttered.

************************   *******************************

War, sitting upon his horse, viewed the situation before him. Learning, in all his experience, never to underestimate the enemy, he spoke not a word. His Three comrades, though not as calm as he, watched in silence as well. The Elders of Magic, those who never felt fear in any manor, sat upon chairs resembling skulls in appearance, observing what seemed to be mass confusion amongst the enemies.

It was Belwin, the Prophet of Evil, who worked himself into a tizzy. Looking upon the Gate of Ivõrus and seeing Aléshai, his daughter, and Triaphor, his nephew, seemingly organize themselves, frustrated him to no end. But when glancing around and noticing that not even Asta, King of Ardenôs, sitting in his filth, worried over the outcome, he chose his words carefully.

"What are the fools doing?" Belwin barked, "Dare they think that they can take us on with a thousand men? And who is this cocky red-haired lad who leads them?"

"Kyliõn, Prince of the ancient Elves of Ivõrus," one of the Elders of Magic answered. His eerie tone made all but the Riders shiver.

Belwin was ready to take his men into battle, but the Riders held back on this.

"We must let *them* rush *us*…" War commanded.

The Elders of Magic seemed amused at the whole ordeal. This war, without their presence, could've been settled between Triaphor, Aléshai and now Kyliðn and the Riders alongside Belwin, if they had not been there. Knowing, though, that Triaphor possessed more power than them all combined, Belwin thought it wise to recruit the Elders. He'd paid a heavy price for their assistance.

*************************   ********************************

Commander of the Troops and Leader of the War Council, Autôw had spent a lot of his time in battle. He, not really being his normal self, actually appreciated Kyliðn's presence.

"My prince," he tapped him on the shoulder, "Perhaps we should rush them."

"That is exactly what they want us to do," Kyliðn had picked up on their plan.

Seeing, though, that he might not have a choice, he turned to Autôw.

"My friend," Kyliðn said, "Sound the charge."

"With pleasure."

Aléshai, atop the Gate of Ivðrus, standing beside her cousin, looked upon the faces of the enemy.

"They seem unfazed," she told Triaphor.

"That will soon change."

The charge was sounded and Kyliðn, along with Autôw, led the men into battle. Peering at them, War grinned.

"Prepare to march."

Belwin looked upon his master in shock. Asta blew upon his horn and shouted the command. The drums began to beat. And in the Field of Rulers, the Riders, Belwin, Asta and the Lords of the Sky made their descent upon the foolish one thousand.

Triaphor, watching the spectacle unfold, listened intently to Jesu. He was instructing him as to what should be done, step by miniscule step.

"Jewel!" he shouted, "Fire!!!"

Jewel and her archers, about twenty thousand in number, drew their arrows upon their bows. The arrows whizzed past them and Triaphor raised a hand. The arrows stopped in midair. Jewel was shocked and her mouth dropped.

"Aléshai," a concentrated Triaphor spoke, "Command your archers."

"Fire!!" Aléshai bellowed.

Sixteen thousand archers from Ivðrus, having laced their longbows with five arrows apiece, released.

Those arrows froze as soon as they were let loose from their bows. Triaphor's hands were both in the air now. His eyes closed, he used all his might to hold those arrows wafting in the sky.

Belwin, lit with anger, took his horse back to the Elders of Magic, who'd remained seated.

"Do you not see this?" he yelled, "Is this not illegal?"

"Any man of power could perform such a trick," another ghostly response came forth.

The Riders, amazed at the sight, fell back to the Elders as Belwin had done. However, Asta, Ruler of the Lords of the Sky, lifted off into the air upon his dragon. His soldiers, over 1,000,000 in number, followed their fearless leader. The foot soldiers and horsemen of the Riders, The Living Dead, from Apocalypse continued their charge without their masters.

"Draw them back Aléshai." Triaphor commanded.

Aléshai embarked upon Bryan immediately. With speed she flew to Kyliõn's aid. Asta, wishing to shed blood, sped up and drew his sword. Aléshai, knowing the operations of the sky better than he, took Bryan down, closer to the battle at hand. She drew her swords.

"Kyliõn!!!" Aléshai shouted, "Get the men out of there!!!"

Not even raising his sword to strike one man, Kyliõn sounded the charge and the one thousand troops fell back. Autõw, in confusion, still obeyed merely because Kyliõn was in command. Upon his unicorn, whose name was Spéliskir, Kyliõn raced for the walls of Ivõrus, his soldiers in a close line behind him.

"Asta you fool!" Hades said in anger.

Aléshai swooped up and cleaved his head from his shoulders. Bryan dug his massive claws into the head of Asta's dragon. The two went plummeting to the ground. The Lords of the Sky, his faithful countrymen, came upon the battle with more speed now. Aléshai and Bryan booked it back to the Gate of Ivõrus.

The Gate of Ivõrus opened for the retreating soldiers, but Kyliõn turned to see what Triaphor was about to perform.

Eyes still pressed shut, Triaphor spun his hands as quickly as they would move. Spinning the arrows in motion, a gust of wind of seismic proportions gathered to him. Stopping his hands from their busy work, he let them drop to his side, sending the arrows forth with ten times more power than they'd been shot.

The arrows connected firmly into 100,000 of the soldiers of Ardenôs. Kyliõn's mouth stood agape just as Aléshai and Bryan landed inside the gate.

"Get inside now!!" Aléshai urged Kyliõn.

Snapping back to attention, Kyliõn led his men back into Ivõrus. War, astonished at such a display of power, looked back at the Elders of Magic. They sat comfortably, not moving even one finger. This angered him, but he knew that if such a great feat had been deemed a small trick, then he could not win this war without the Elders. Triaphor's power seemed to excel beyond anyone's possible imagination.

"Bring back my forces!" War commanded, "And sound the retreat!! Back to the Dark City!! Back to Apocalypse!!!!"

The drums boomed once more. This time, the soldiers marched to the beat of a different tune. One that did not welcome them.

Kyliõn, allowing his troops to all enter before he would dare pass through the gate, almost got plowed through by a dragon that looked as if it would crash into the gate. Aléshai screamed and Bryan flew over the Gate of Ivõrus rapidly. Aléshai stretched out her hand and picked Kyliõn right off the ground. Realizing almost too late that he was still riding Spéliskir, she spoke a small spell of magic that gave her strength to fly them back into Ivõrus. The dragon ended its fall right in front of the gate, just where Kyliõn had been standing.

Triaphor sighed. Relief flushed over him. Jewel, who'd joined him after Aléshai had made her flight, smiled at him. Her people had been saved once again. The two drew near to each other.

"I love you," she said.
Together they kissed on the Gate of Ivõrus.

*************************   *************************

It had been two days since the dream. Two days since that climactic battle that sent the Dark Alliance running. He'd developed fear into the eyes of his enemies and it wouldn't be long until they reached Apocalypse to regroup and plan another strategy.

Triaphor looked out upon the city. Elves, cream-colored men of Orés and men of the South, their dark-complexioned skin matching his, scrambled about, preparing for their departure. The War Council had argued relentlessly that the people needed rest for much longer. Somehow, the royalty had all agreed and convinced the council to side with them. Even Autôw, he who was usually a terrible force to reckon with, was cordial.

Jewel joined him at the window.

"Love," she said, getting his attention, "We're ready."

At the Gate of Ivõrus, Triaphor and Jewel met up with Aléshai and Kyliõn. In the Royal carriage sat King Ric and Sultan Salzahirz. More and more people filed behind the leaders of Orés. The War Councilors had crafted two carriages for themselves. Autôw had commanded this to be done.

"'It should speed up the process', he said to us," Aléshai told Triaphor.

The Prophet of Orés rolled his eyes. Only Autôw would wish to rush into the hands of the Riders so quickly. Though Triaphor had wanted to continue their voyage, he didn't want to fight those beasts any sooner than he should have to. For once it seemed that Autôw had finally gained some courage.

"The midwives, are they ready?" Triaphor asked.

"Their carriage shall be pulled between the Royal one and the two for the War Councilors." Jewel had monitored the situation to make sure that all the nursing mothers had a safe place along the rough road.

"What of the physicians?" Triaphor inquired.

"They are in the process of packing their things upon their designated horses." Aléshai reported.

"Why do they not have a carriage like the other groups?" Kyliõn wished to know.

"Because," Jewel answered, "if anyone is in need, it is easier for one physician on one horse to attend to that person than to have to stop a whole carriage, find the person and then attend to their needs."

"I see."

Triaphor wanted to quickly remove himself from this place. Time was growing short. The other thing that pressed upon his mind was the fact that he wished to take Jewel to The White Temple. If indeed she was pregnant or going to be in the near future, he wanted to be done with his task so that, like his dream, he worried not over the safety of his family.

"Jewel, Aléshai," he called the two girls to him, "Check the caravan and see who's ready and who's not. If they're not, get them ready. We must depart soon."

The girls nodded and went about their business. Kyliõn could sense Triaphor's impatience, but also his worries.

"You're worried about your child," he spoke.

Triaphor did not respond. Kyliðn had been of a great aid in the Battle of the Rulers' Field, but he felt he did not owe his pointy-eared ally an explanation. But the elf pressed on.

"You know," Kyliðn continued, "This task cannot be completed any sooner than is time for it to be finished. All things that hang in the balance do so because of Jesu. Do not think to rush His assignment, for…"

"… I know what is to be done!!!! I know that time in which it shall be done!! I know the worries that I possess and I know that my family needs safety!!!!"

Triaphor, filled with anguish, crashed to the floor of the city. Kyliðn, gently and kindly, held the prophet as he wept upon his shoulder. The Prince of Ivðrus cared about Triaphor because the man had saved his city from peril. His hope was that the two could become more than just allies, but friends. Triaphor had no male friends that he could speak to of things that were just too difficult to talk to a woman about, for they would not understand.

Jewel and Aléshai returned from their inspection. Kyliðn had helped Triaphor into the Royal carriage.

"He was in need of rest," he told the girls.

Ric and Salzahirz had come out and were on their horses, ready to go. Jewel, having not been to Apocalypse, let her father lead the way. Aléshai took Bryan into the sky. His shrill call led the people from the gates of Ivðrus. Taking a sharp left, Ric led the people of Orés, Iristaniq and Ivðrus away from the Field of Rulers, the Wilderness of Westcott and the City of Ivðrus.

Chapter 13 - In the Woods of Wyrdrías
_____

The Fortress of Daréngir, tower of pain and death, and home to the Riders of Apocalypse. Murky shadows of mist and deception crowded this torturous territory that belonged to the debauched sorcerers of Névorn. The Four Riders had called it their habitat for centuries, falling far from the place that they were created.

War, the eldest of his Four Brothers, had always suppressed the other three. Ever since birth, he'd taken command of their every daily task. Never had he let them do anything without him first knowing about it. Hades, the next in line, had always resented War's prying attitude. He'd felt that *he* was to one day rule the kingdom that their father had possessed for so many years.

Hades, ashen looking from his first day, had never been a favorite in the palace. His father's servants would always tease him. The mistresses that his mother owned would generally walk by in a state of pity, saying,

"Look at the poor child. His parents aught to be ashamed of themselves, allowing such a stank creature to live."

The days of his youth were tormenting. To this very hour, the words of those mistresses haunted him. He always knew that if ever he got the chance, he would obliterate them in such a way that history would never forget.

Pestilence and Famine, the twins of the family, were born in a time of war. Their eldest brother had just turned 13 and was ready to swear an oath that would make him legal as an adult. War felt that he was mature enough to even go to battle, but his father, King Tântrígõr, held him back. The White Rider snuck into an envoy of soldiers and went against his father's orders.

Hades, 12 at the time, was stuck raising Pestilence and Famine, when the battle was lost. His mother, the queen and his father, the king had both been lost in the debacle. War could not be found, for they'd taken him prisoner.

For over 10 years, the search for War continued. Hades had hassled around with his twin brothers for this amount of time, teaching them everything he possibly could about conducting themselves as Princes of Ivõrus. Though 25 was the proper age that a new king was coronated, the people of Ivõrus, his councilors and the nobility had seen the work of Hades and wished to make him Lord of Ivõrus.

Just as the time had come for the coronation service, War rode through the city's gates, carrying a cloth that seemed to cover something round. This angered Hades that his brother would return just in time to claim the crown and take the throne from him.

They'd argued extensively for months over what was to be done. The ten-year-old twins watched as their elder brothers struggled for power. To please Hades and the nobility that had taken his side, though War could've defeated them if the affair had become civil, he crowned Hades Crown Prince of Ivõrus.

"Now about this treasure," Hades had questioned his brother for months over what he'd brought into the city upon his return. War refused to answer. Instead, he locked it into the Palace Treasury and never spoke of it again. Hades continued to ponder over it.

For 10 years, there was peace in the land of Ivõrus. The eastern kingdom of Orés, their allies, had kept the Southern kingdoms in check while Ivõrus did so with the North. But Maesõrn would not be silenced. They rose up against Ivõrus once again.

War commanded Hades to stay behind and watch over the twins. Even though the twins had remarkable skills as archers, War refused to lose his brothers like he'd lost his parents. As a result, War led a great victory against Maesõrn and discovered a portal that would lead them to Dimensia³. Dimensia³ would lead them to such kingdoms as the newly famed Golden Kingdom and a dark mountain known as Eléctrasûmõn. This interested War greatly. He wished to be ruler of two dimensions of the world of Névorn.

But, on the home front, Hades, 32 years of age, had come down with a deadly disease. Pestilence and Famine loved their brother dearly and did not wish for him to die. There was no cure and no physician that could make him feel any better. Upon the passing of Hades, War finally came home from his rampage of the North. The twins grew angry and ordered that War be removed from the throne.

Fearing that this would cause a breakout of civil rivalry, War respected his twin brothers and released the debated treasure from the Palace Treasury. The cloth still upon it, the twins took it up in their hands and entered Hades' chamber. War, afraid of its power, commanded his brothers to set it upon the table nearest Hades' bed.

Pestilence, Famine and War took the cloth from the treasure. Underneath it lay an orb. The orb rolled off of the table onto the concrete floor of Hades' chamber and shattered. Blasting the three living brothers clear across to the other side of the room, War was the first to notice movement from his brother's bed. Hades, by the power of the orb, had been awakened from death.

Throughout time, the Four brothers relished in the new power that they had discovered. But one day, Trílautûs, Prophet of Jesu from Orés came to Ivõrus upon command from Jesu. He spoke to the brothers of the new powers that they possessed.

"War," the prophet said, "You cannot hold on to such power. It will corrupt your mind and you will become more evil than anyone could possibly imagine. Do not do this to yourselves."

War, already power-hungry and not willing to turn back now, killed Trílautûs by drowning him in the pool that was in the courtroom at Ivõrus. Killing the prophet was not a thing that he should've done, therefore Jesu was angered with him and sent Orés, once their allies, against them to destroy them.

Pleading for help from his brothers, War promised them the highest positions. For Hades, he would make him Ruler of Orés. The twins would rule jointly at Maesõrn if they swore allegiance to their eldest brother. Not willing that War should die because of his sin, Hades convinced his twin brothers to forgive War for continuing his slaughter of the North and not returning to assure life for him. Pestilence and Famine agreed to this proposition and they took up four horses and rode out to battle together.

Ivõrus was not easily conquered, for War was a powerful warrior. He used his new powers to wipe out thousands. A new prophet of Orés, Sõnércus, knowing how to utilize his powers more than War, went to the front of the battle line. Using his staff, he struck down the crazed King of Ivõrus.

Hades was angry, but knew that there was no way he could possibly fight such strength. He waited until the battle was over. He and his twin brothers took the wounded War, bandaged him and called a search for a strong magician. Deep within the Woods of Wyrdrías they found a man. He was known as the Warlock of Wyrdrías.

The Warlock came to Ivõrus and healed War. What the Warlock did not know was that War had garnered half of his power. The Warlock's power, added on to the strength that the orb had given all four of the brothers, caused War to excel rapidly. If anyone didn't want to listen to War's instructions, he would simply hold up his hand and whatever came to his mind transfused through his fingers. Hades and the twins marveled at this power. But the people of Ivõrus, who had been angry about their broken alliance with Orés, didn't find War's power remarkable, but despicable.

With the help of Sõnércus, the Prophet of Jesu, Ivõrus banished the Four brothers from their midst. Filled with resentment, the Four, upon their horses, went deep into the Woods of Wyrdrías and found the Warlock. They questioned him about the orb that had exploded and initiated their power.

"The Orb of Uthir Pañé," the Warlock informed, "has three brothers. You see, these orbs are meant to work together. But you have broken one, so I'm not sure how you will be able to salvage their intended power."

"All we wish to know," War was intent on gaining more power, "is where the other three are laid."

"You must look on the Mount of Eléctrasûmõn," the Warlock said.

All Four wanted to make the trip, but War insisted that his three brothers stay behind. Hades, knowing how this would end out, refuted his brother's word more gamely than did the twins. They ended up staying with the Warlock, who began to train them in the ways of Black Magic and spell speaking. Witchcraft was a daily practice for the three men.

Hades excelled in the lessons at a pace irregular.

"You, my son, were born for power," the Warlock told him.

His twin brothers did not resent him, for Hades didn't lord it over them. He'd grown tired of War doing that to them. When War returned, he would show him what powers he possessed and then dare his older brother to take it from him.

War, once King of Ivõrus, trekked up the Mount of Eléctrasûmõn. There he discovered a sorcerer.

"My name," the sorcerer told War, "is Eléctrasûmõn. For a century, I've waited for this moment. Where is the Orb of Uthir Pañé?"

War described the situation to Sorcerer Eléctrasûmõn. The sorcerer, though irate with rage, took War to the side and showed him the other three orbs.

"These," he informed the former king, "will bring to you unspeakable power. But you cannot possess them without the other. It just does not work in that fashion. But if you bring the shards of the Orb of Uthir Pañé to me, I know of someone who can restore it to its full capacity."

War, eldest of his Four brothers, rode back to Wyrdrías. The Warlock heard of what the former ruler had to perform. He gave him a robe by which he could shield himself. He would not be seen if he wore it.

"It is pure white," the Warlock said, "made from the skin of the Unicorns of Skyrõs. I have three more for thy brothers. One is red, the other is black and the other…"

He pulled them from a wardrobe as he spoke. As he paused, he yanked a pale colored robe of the same design as the others from the closet.

"This," the Warlock eyed Hades, "is for you, my son. You were destined to don this from the day of your birth."

The Four brothers took the robes, thankfully, from the Warlock. Not informing their companion of their plans, they stole away from Wyrdrías in the middle of the night. The Warlock never saw his boys again. Elderly in his days, he had taken them under as sons. The twins found it hardest to depart from their master, but War and Hades were hasty. They didn't want anyone, except the Sorcerer Eléctrasûmõn, to know about their plans to rebuild the Orb of Uthir Pañé and then wipe Ivõrus and Orés from the face of the earth.

The Four departed quickly from Wyrdrías and entered into Ivõrus under the shadow of night. The orb's shards had been placed in a jar and deported to Orés. Upon discovering this, War grew livid.

He took his brothers to meet Eléctrasûmõn upon the mountain. The sorcerer was well pleased in them, especially Hades. He provided them with troops and a naval fleet so massive in size, that it could've enveloped the whole of Orés. The Four brothers made war with Orés from the ocean.

Sneaking upon them in darkness, they did not expect Sõnércus, the Prophet of Jesu, to know of their intrusion. The soldiers of Orés had been prepared to do battle upon the arrival of the Four. Sõnércus' two protégés, Belwin, the elder of the two, and Tahiti had been entrusted with the charge of the military. Bulldozing past the two weaker prophet trainees, War and his brothers left the skirmish and entered Orés, unable to be seen because of the robes they'd been given by the Warlock.

Sõnércus met them in front of the Temple of Jesu. He battled the Four brothers in a dispute of power. Just as Belwin and Tahiti came to assist their master, they found him dead on the steps of the temple. Hades, using all the Warlock had taught him, had taken a knife and stabbed the prophet in the pancreas. Belwin and Tahiti entered the temple to find the fools responsible for this murder.

Upon finding the shards of the Orb of Uthir Pañé, the Four heard a voice. Removing their hoods, for their disguises did not work any longer, they searched eagerly for from whence the voice came. In front of them, next to the table with the shards, stood a being of such a luminescent presence that it nearly blinded them. They could not look upon Him.

"Four fools!" said Jesu, the God of Névorn, "This day have you infuriated the wrath of Jesu. Forever will you wallow in blood, anguish and shame. War, for all eternity you shall possess the talent of leadership. This talent will win you many battles, yes, but because of it, one close to your heart will be the cause of your death. Hades, your looks have always been of a sickly manor. Now you shall become the most handsome young man anyone will ever see for all of forever. But because you died and were raised with the power of the Orb of Uthir Pañé, the orb shall be yours. From it, your power shall come. You will always possess less power than your elder brother War. And since you have led your twin brothers into your debauchery, you will lose them within the first hour of the battle that will take your life. Twins of Tântrígõr, King of Ivõrus, as you have followed your brothers into open sin, so shall the nations follow you. So shall people fear because of your names. Your power shall take on the meanings of your names and for this reason, nations will fear you the most. But, Twins of Tântrígõr, you shall also inherit that which you will have the power to give. Pestilence, you will be sick with a new disease every day, rising in the morning, not knowing which disease it shall be for that day. As for you Famine, you will starve for the rest of your life. Never will your appetite be satisfied. Your brothers will struggle to feed you until the day of your death. Many warriors will stab you in your stomach, causing it to rupture and rupture continually. Never will you heal."

The brothers, kneeling in fear, still unable to look upon Jesu, began to tremble. Sweat rocketed from their bodies as He spoke. Belwin and Tahiti, who'd entered the room unable to see, listened intently as Jesu finished His sentence.

"Young fools, you will reek havoc upon the inhabitants of Névorn until the end of time. But know this, when your Day of Reckoning comes, it shall be swift and cold. Those who serve you your death sentence shall not think twice upon your death. Pity shall not be yours for the rest of your life. Go!! Go!!! Rise up!!!! Thou Riders Of The Apocalypse!!!!!!"

The temple shuddered as the Four brothers looked upon themselves. The changes had already begun.

"I feel sick," Pestilence gasped. War's eyes widened in horror. His younger brother heaved up what looked like what he had eaten for the last 22 years of his life. Hades, so used to supporting his twin brothers, grabbed him.

"It will be okay," Hades comforted, "I'll find a physician, I promise. Perhaps, even the Warlock will be able to help."

"You heard the Man," War reminded Hades, "Never will he be well again. It's too late. We've crossed the bridge and burnt it. We've passed the point of no return!!!"

"I will not let you talk me into anything else, War!" Hades shouted.

"But you know what was spoken is truth!!!!" War retorted, "Don't try to deny…"

"…I'm hungry, guys," Famine interrupted his brothers.

War and Hades looked at each other, then their other twin brother.

"What did you say?" War asked, tensing up.

Famine, unable to walk without holding his stomach, fell to the ground in the attempt.

"Get him!!!" Hades yelled.

War, possessing the jar containing the shards, picked up his brother and Hades, holding Pestilence tightly, led them through the temple, out of Orés and back to the ships. Tahiti and Belwin, having watched this entire engagement between their God and these men, ordered their soldiers to stand down.

The Four returned the fleet of ships to Sorcerer Eléctrasûmōn. The Orb of Uthir Pañé was refurbished and given to Hades, as Jesu had prophesied. Pestilence, having thrown up the whole trip back, was provided with the Orb of Uthir Cíliōn, the orb that would ease his pain, making it bearable the majority of the time. Though Hades was relieved slightly, he still watched out for his brother carefully.

"Everyday, for the rest of our days," Hades told Pestilence through tears, "I pledge to keep you safe. I love you brother."

Pestilence, lying upon a bed, held out his hand for Hades to hold. Hades clutched his brother's hand firmly. The elder brother wept on the younger for hours into the night. Famine, stuffing himself with food and still finding no satisfaction, was given the Orb of Uthir Mínýōn. It wouldn't sedate his need for food, but it would make him crave it less. His stomach would tell him that he was full, even if it really, nutritionally, desired more.

War, feeling terrible for leading his family into this turmoil, weeping for his brothers' plight, accepted the Orb of Uthir Áthéris. This orb would provide him with the power he would need to rid the world of Ivōrus. The authority given to him through this orb would allow him to create their future home.

After accepting these treasures from the Sorcerer Eléctrasûmōn, the Four got upon their horses and rode down the mountain, back to the dimension they'd lived in all their lives. Upon arrival at the Fortress of Daréngir, their horses turned the colors of their robes.

Around the Fortress of Daréngir, War constructed, using the orb, a wall and planted a dark, empty forest full of death, mystery and all forms of evil imaginable. He then called his kingdom Apocalypse. His brother Hades, though resenting his older sibling, crowned War king of Apocalypse.

"We need soldiers that will do battle for us," War suggested.

"We can take them from Ivõrus, my brother." Hades bantered.

This pleased War. He took charge of the arrangements for battle. The Four Riders of Apocalypse rode forth that very hour and demolished the inhabitants of Ivõrus, save for the Elves that dwelled there led by King Éisõräl, father of Kyliõn. Hades, using the Orb of Uthir Pañé, transformed the citizens of the city into the Living Dead. The Living Dead has served them from this day forth.

Each brother took their share of the Living Dead, War taking the largest of them. They cloaked them in robes from the Unicorns of Skyrõs, whom they slaughtered, and in colors that represented each of them. The mistresses that had spoken so ill of Hades as a child, were kept alive. He laid with each and every one of them as a husband lays with his wife (most of them willingly because of his changed appearance). Then he blasted them from the face of Névorn.

**************************   ********************************

Triaphor awoke in a cold sweat. The dream had come again. He was growing to fear this dream. He didn't like the fact that with every night he fell asleep, this dream would bring the doom of his child closer. He looked around and noticed that he was in a tent.

Separating the flaps of the tent, the prophet exited the pavilion. As he took a look around the camp, he saw smiles upon the faces of the people. This pleased him, for he had been very worried about the journey ahead. There was dangerous territory that they were embarking upon, Apocalypse the scariest of them all.

He took a step and felt the ground vibrating with the hooves of horses. Kyliõn, his newfound elvish friend, stood next to him.

"Horses," he prophesied, "Two of them. From the enemy."

"You're sure of this?" Triaphor asked.

The elf nodded. Clad in an olive robe, Kyliõn glared at the trespassers. Archers, attentive, on duty and given the command by Jewel, nocked arrows on their bows.

"Hold!" Triaphor demanded.

The two horses continued forward until they felt they'd traveled far enough. Two men jumped off of their creatures of burden. Triaphor knew who they were, once they got close enough for him to see. One was garbed in a red robe, a cape attached to the robe. The other, older in appearance and more experienced in their field, wore a black robe of the same design.

Tantricus and Ranglicius, advisors to the Riders. Ranglicius had been the old chief counselor to the Riders and Tantricus was the young man who'd filled his position. Ranglicius donned red robes because of the amount of blood that he'd shed in his lifetime, leading the Living Dead into war against the peoples of Névorn. Tantricus, on the other hand, wore black because it represented the quality of his heart. At an early age, the Riders had reared him to fear no man and he'd become just as malicious as they had. The only trait that he lacked to becoming a Rider was whatever fed their power.

According to the legends, the Riders had each been given orbs. The Orb of Uthir Áthéris, War's object of power, had been made into a crown, so that his power would always be with him. The Orb of Uthir Pañé, Hades had turned into circlet. This circlet, although not a crown, symbolized Hades' forever hunger for the power and authority that War possessed. Hades would never forget the day his brother returned and stole Ivõrus from him. Pestilence and Famine, eternally bound by the day of their birth, decided to turn their orbs, The Orb of Uthir Mínýõn and The Orb of Uthir Cíliõn, into chain mail shirts. These, they wore under their robes so that it would protect them both from the pain they would suffer had they not worn them. Especially since Famine had acquired a stomach problem under the curse.

Triaphor, Kyliõn, Aléshai and Jewel stood together as the two from the enemy stepped forward. Pride filled them from head to toe. Knowledge of their sins bothered them not. They cared not that they were working for who had become the most wicked men to walk the face of Névorn.

"What is it that the Sons of Sin wish to speak to us about?" Triaphor inquired.

"I'm surprised, Prophet of Orés," Ranglicius taunted, "that you do not know the errand of our masters."

"I don't commonly think upon my enemies' intentions during my sleep, Lord Ranglicius. It's not healthy." Triaphor retorted.

Ranglicius was astounded at the response.

"Well," Tantricus took over, "Great Prince Triaphor of Orés, our masters have come to wonder what a man such as yourself is doing, dwelling in such a dangerous place?"

"There is no danger here," Aléshai said sternly.

Triaphor looked around him. A breeze blew up his robe and his heart fell stone cold.

"There is a power here at work that I knew not of when we entered this place," Triaphor shivered.

Tantricus grinned, knowing that his work was completed. Ranglicius knew that his partner wished to depart. The two evil men turned to board their horses. As they embarked their creatures of burden, Triaphor spoke to them.

"Wait!" he shouted, "Listen, how do I repel this creature that lies within these Woods of Wyrdrías?"

The two eyed each other.

"How can we tell Lalrola to do what Lalrola alone can do?" Ranglicius was the first to ride away. Tantricus, following his wiser elder, laughed as he rode off.

"Kyliõn," Triaphor called to the prince, "Hand me my staff."

Triaphor, Son of Biora, took the staff in his hand. He knew now that his power, though not unlimited, could be used to fight whatever evil lay within these woods, for the Elders of Magic were far from here. Walking slowly, Triaphor kept his senses up and his eyes attentive to everything around him.

"Legend has it," spoke Aléshai as she and the others followed Triaphor through the forest, "that in this woodland there lives a powerful man. He is known as the Warlock of Wyrdrías. It is rumored that long ago, it was he who helped the Riders utilize their power."

"That is no rumor," Triaphor muttered in fear.

Triaphor and his companions happened upon a cottage. This cottage rested upon a hill and was infinitesimal in size. Upon the door rested a symbol. Four orbs laced together in a panoramic universe. These four orb replicas changed colors. From red to black to an ashen color and then forming into white. In a continuous cycle did these orbs change their colors.

Trembling, Triaphor knocked upon the door. Wearing his wine-colored cloak from the White Temple, he was afraid that he might have to use the silver undergarment on this Warlock. He didn't really know what kind of power that garment held, but hopefully it wouldn't destroy his comrades.

No one answered, but upon a second rap on the entry, a voice boomed in the air.

"His power!" Kyliõn was frightened, "It comes from demons!!"

The voice spoke with a tone exuding wickedness.

"Who dares to disturb the Woods of Wyrdrías!" the voice hollered, "Who are you to think that you can live and prosper under the roof of the Warlock of Wyrdrías?"

"Come out, servant of Evil!" Triaphor yelled back, "We have questions to ask of you. Do not think to hide, for I, Triaphor, Son of Tahiti, Prophet of Jesu and Lalrola of Prophecy have the power to bring you forth. Come out!!"

Lightning flashed and standing there in their presence was a man of considerable height. Wearing a traditional wizard's hat and a long brown robe that matched, it was the staff that Triaphor noticed. Atop the summit of the Warlock's stick were Four hooded heads.

"What was your relation to these Riders?" the prophet asked.

"I," the Warlock replied, "was their master and teacher. Since the death of their parents, I'd kept a watch on the boys and the City of Ivõrus, knowing that they would one day cross my path. After the explosion of the Orb of Uthir Pañé, they had to come to me. But, of course, they decided to wait until *they* could best benefit from me."

"After the war with Sõnércus." Aléshai stated.

"Precisely."

Wondering to herself why they were conversing with one of the most iniquitous men Névorn had ever birthed, Jewel gazed into Triaphor's eyes. He knew what had to be done to the Warlock, but he wanted to garner valuable information first.

"Master Warlock," Triaphor addressed him, "Why? Why did you help spawn these demons?"

"Was it my choice?" the Warlock posed.

"Whose choice would it have been? You're the only fool who lives in these woods!" Jewel infuriated.

"People who serve The Dark Spirits have no choice," the Warlock informed, "The Dark Spirits take away all knowledge of choosing one's destiny. Ever since I began delving into their world, *they* took control and *they* decide what I must do…"

"…and *they* provide the power to do it." Aléshai finished.

"Then why," Triaphor couldn't believe it, "would you put someone else through those tortures? Especially those Four young and innocent men?"

The Warlock didn't respond.

"Answer me!"

Triaphor's anger was aroused. How could someone who'd lived in this situation for so long willingly subject anyone to their torture? He faced the Warlock and glared into his eyes.

"Why?" Triaphor asked through developing tears.

Jewel didn't know what to think. She couldn't quite grasp the concept of the Warlock's intentions either, but it was enough to make her kill him, not begin feeling compassion for the Riders.

"Those boys craved more power." the Warlock said, "They would've gotten it from someone else had it not been me. I wasn't going to let some *other* magician take the claim for them. These were to be the biggest terrorists of Névorn. If anyone was going to be known for helping them along the way, it was going to be me."

Triaphor's tears dried up. Anger boiled in his face.

"Thou fool," he spoke, "You wanted acclaim. You wanted to share in their power. You didn't worry about whether they were going to come for you or not if you had denied them. No! Instead of stopping these men from becoming the monsters they are, you've *turned* them into these morose creatures.

For this treachery against our world, you will suffer a death most unimaginable. Your powers shall be taken from you and thou shalt be reduced to a man of normalcy. Then, you will travel with us to the Land of Apocalypse. There, you will be suffered to watch the death of your Four precious boys. Upon seeing this, your heart will fail you and you shall die. And it will be known amongst the generations that the Warlock of Wyrdrías, the fool who thought it best to help the Riders, perished on their Day of Reckoning."

The Warlock, thinking that he might be able to escape even now, eyed his four enemies. Kyliðn, knowing the Warlock's craftiness, drew his sword and struck the Warlock's staff. The Warlock paralyzed Kyliðn by knocking his sword to the ground and striking his leg with his staff. Aléshai, upon seeing this, drew her swords and advanced toward the magician slowly. As she went to lop his head from his shoulders, the Warlock raised his staff to the sky. Bees of enormous size distracted Aléshai and as they held her up, Jewel shot a series of arrows. The Warlock then disappeared.

"Pôrl man míntas de príagrõmâs!" Triaphor shouted. This healed Kyliðn, destroyed the vicious bees and made the Warlock appear in his sight alone.

"Now where will you run?"

Triaphor pinned him against a tree. Shoving the Warlock a considerable distance, the other three heard the resounding thud. Glaring ever so intently into the eyes of the dark magician, Triaphor concentrated greatly.

"Through this power," Triaphor began, "and through the power of Jesu, the One and Only God of Névorn, I revoke from thee the Dark Spirits that feed thee thy power. May they perish!!! May they cease!!! May they desist from ever being able to give you any more commands or powers with which to carry out those commands!!! I RELEASE YOU, THOU WARLOCK OF WYRDRÍAS!!!!!"

Shrieks of terror filled the forest. The ground underneath them shook as the Warlock appeared in front of Aléshai, Kyliðn and Jewel. In pain, the Warlock was released from the Dark Spirits' hold upon him. As they came out, the Warlock roared out in agonizing horror.

The Dark Spirits, not intending on letting the Warlock loose, attacked Triaphor aggressively. The Lalrola, full of fury, struck the Spirits with his staff. Speaking magic, the trees above them separated so that the sky could be seen. Getting down on one knee, Triaphor closed his eyes and beat the ground with the staff. The Dark Spirits were instantly sent soaring through the clouds, their fate in the hands of Jesu.

After this dissipated, Triaphor fell prostrate to the ground. A throbbing and an aching pain enveloped his head. Jewel rushed to him as Kyliõn and Aléshai arrested the Warlock.

"Oh my god, are you alright?" Triaphor's wife asked.

He was unconscious.

The Royal Pavilion was usually a very quiet place. The royalty saw it as not only living quarters, but also as a place of judgment, much like the palace at Ivõrus and the castle of Orés. Tonight, though was very different. It was not very tranquil at all. For someone who had developed a terrible headache, this was not good.

Triaphor awoke from his unwilling slumber. He removed his blankets from him and placed his sandals on his feet. Wearing a long scarlet half-robe, resembling a towel with strings and extending from his lower hips to his feet, the topless Prophet of Jesu walked casually into the main area of the pavilion. Before he stumbled upon the room, he saw a table containing a flask of wine. The prophet poured himself some wine in a silver cup.

Hearing the shouts as he drew closer and closer to the area, he figured that there was a council meeting in session. Triaphor stood by the entrance to the room, waiting for someone to notice him. Aléshai, constantly feeling his presence, turned her head in his direction. As she was about to open her mouth, he motioned for her to continue listening to the meeting and not to say a word.

She did as instructed.

"I just don't understand," Autôw was speaking, "what we're doing suffering this dangerous man in our presence. His powers are inconceivable!"

"His powers," Jewel interrupted, "are unavailable to him! He cannot do anything that he was once able to perform. I was there. I watched it happen."

"But how do we know that the Warlock spoke the truth about these *Dark Spirits* controlling him? His power could come from somewhere different and we not know it. Just because you saw Dark Spirits ascend to heaven from his body, doesn't mean that *that* is what fed his power."

A reasonable point, but not enough to draw Triaphor from his spot. He wanted to see exactly what response would come from this. He took a sip of wine.

"My friend," Kyliõn, Prince of Ivõrus said, "You cannot speak on things you do not know. The powers of this world are given to us by various sources, but those who do not obtain any kind of power do not understand how power works. The Dark Spirits were in possession of his body and they *are* what fed his power. Now that they are gone, there is nothing he can do to harm us."

"Nonetheless," King Ric spoke, "the Riders of Apocalypse will no doubt hear of this, for they too are controlled by the Dark Spirits. Will they not descend upon this place if they do hear of what Triaphor has done?"

The court went into an uproar. Once again, many people were taking sides over what should be done with Triaphor. Autôw and a number of the War Councilors continued to believe that he should return to The White Temple and send for a new prophet who could do better. Aléshai, Jewel, Prince Kylĩõn, Ric and Salzahirz of course disagreed. Only obtaining two or three of Orés' War Councilors on their side, it seemed that if it came to a vote, Autôw's War Councilors would win this debate.

Triaphor, sick of watching the dispute, finished his wine and threw the cup against the side of the tent. This caught everyone's attention immediately. They turned in his direction to see from whence the noise had come. A smirk arose on Triaphor's face. Mutterings from Autôw could be heard as Councilors tried to shush him.

"Kings, princes and councilors," Triaphor began, "for too long have I denied my rightful position over this land. Everyone in this room knows that I am the husband of Jewel, Princess of Orés and in turn, that means that I am Prince Triaphor of Orés. I have long declined this honor because I am merely a servant of Jesu, sent to guide you and do His bidding. Never would I have taken the liberty to command you had it not come to this."

Autôw snickered.

"I cannot tell you," the prophet continued, "how much it hurts me every time this discussion comes up in War Council meetings. My friends, it is no longer important what I feel. Work has to be done. It is no longer important what *you* feel. We've got to get moving. What many of you cannot seem to understand is that we are engaged in, not just a war, but the most significant war of all time. This war has been prophesied about since the beginning of time. *I* have been prophesied about since the time of Trílautûs. All of us were meant to be here, all of us were meant to fight and all of us were meant to take this world of Névorn into our hands. After this, Orés, Iristaniq and Ivõrus, for it shall be restored, will be given the authority over this earth. Dominion has been appointed for us all. But there is little time. Do not think that we have until the end of the world to destroy these Riders. For everything, there is an appointed time."

Intent on every word slipping from his lips, the Elves of Ivõrus, royalty of Orés and their War Councilors and even Salzahirz, listened carefully. Their eyes watched as his every step brought him closer and around the room he would walk. Taking a cluster of grapes in his hand, Triaphor continued his speech.

"My friends, examine the grapevine. There are only so many grapes on this one stem. It is only a matter of time when they shall all be gone and I have to grab another handful. So it is with the Riders. The Dark Spirits do not control them. No. They control the Dark Spirits. That is the extent of their power. These Riders of Apocalypse have craved power since their reign over Ivõrus began. These beasts do not wish to stop. As time increases, they will not hide in their fortress forever. Ric is right. They will hear about what I have done to their precious Warlock of Wyrdrías. That is why we must move now. We've got to get to that city and finish them off, once and for all."

"What," Autôw, sarcasm filling his voice, asked, "do you propose we do?

"Train the people to take a stand," Triaphor answered, "By doing this, all will be fighting for Névorn's safety. You will not defeat them with the number of soldiers that we have from each kingdom. Yes, the number is roughly 600,000, but we need more, for the Riders will draw all evil to them. They'll recruit much help from many places."

"How can any man take on such a task?" Autôw countered, "To train a whole nation of men and *women* and children to fight when most of them have never picked up a blade in their life?"

"I have a plan that will work," Triaphor said, "but you have to be patient and mature. Autôw, I'm putting you in charge of this. Aléshai, listen and remember all that I will say to you. The women of Névorn, those that are not nursing, taking care of children under thirteen or midwives, will learn under Aléshai. Bryan will call all of his griffin comrades to come so that the women can learn to ride them. Cousin, you must teach them everything you know. We will rebuild the MorningStar Talsûrõn.

All men over the age of twelve and under the age of seventy must prepare for combat. Autôw, chief of the War Councilors, you will divide them into groups. Each War Councilor is to take responsibility for one group of trainees. Deal gently with the young ones yet teach them ferocity. The Elves of Ivõrus, of course, will be guided by their captain and prince, Kyliõn."

"Forgive me for asking, but," Autôw pried, "what will you be doing during this time?"

"Jewel," Triaphor put out his hand towards her, "and myself will depart tomorrow at dawn."

"What?" Ric shouted.

"We have to recruit more people," Triaphor told them, "We need reinforcements. The other dimensions of Névorn must be held responsible for the upkeep of this world just as much as we are. This dimension was thoroughly wiped out by the Riders. If we lose this war, the others will be as well. We cannot expect them to survive where we could not. I will call upon them to fulfill their duty."

"But why must the princess go?" Autôw inquired.

"For reasons that she and I alone will keep."

Triaphor momentarily seemed disturbed. As he passed into deep thought, his eyes misted. It would take much strength to bare through what they were about to experience. But this is what had to be accomplished. This was the will of Jesu.

"Battle plans, my lord," Kyliõn caught Triaphor's attention, "We need battle plans."

"There are 6 governors of the Empire of Orés. All of them are War Councilors and capable of leading people into battle. There will be three governors to the West gate and the Eastern gate of Apocalypse. Each man shall be divided according to where they live. If they are governed by a certain viceroy, then that is to whom he will depart and that determines which gate he shall stand by.

The Southern gate will be stormed by the king, the Sultan, Prince Kyliõn, Aléshai and her warrior females and the soldiers from the Capital. There will be many tricks along the way, so everyone should be on their guard. Kyliõn will divide his elves into regiments and place them at every gate. Comprise a strategy among you that will secure your passage through the Land of Apocalypse. All of you will meet up after The Wastelands of Åbérdeen. There, I shall meet you. In front of you will stand The River of Hades. Do not, under any circumstances, cross that river until I give the command. Don't even draw near to it. Set your camp far away from it. Let sentries be placed to keep watch through the night.

The Riders will do all they can to stop the people from reaching The Wastelands of Åbérdeen and beyond. But once you view The Fortress of Daréngir, there is nothing that they can do to stop you until the battle begins. Be courageous."

"And what," Kyliðn added, "of the North gate?"

"It shall be used for another purpose." Triaphor responded.

Triaphor left the room. The War Councilors, the royalty and other leaders of Orés stared. Mighty had the young prophet become. They could not deny that he had been sent by Jesu to take charge and fulfill an important task.

"At dawn," Ric announced, "we will begin our work."

Triaphor turned over in his sleep. Expecting to find Jewel there, he awoke when he did not feel her hip. As his eyes fluttered open, his ears heard a faint sound. Smithies, hammers, clashes of swords and whizzes of arrows. He arose out of bed. A robe had been left on the other side of the bed. He smiled as he knew that Jewel had already prepared for this day. He donned the sky blue robe and walked outside.

Jewel was packing the last thing upon their horse that would fit. Luckily, she had packed lightly, for she knew that one day she would return to Orés. Triaphor only possessed robes from the days of his youth and the one that had been provided him at The White Temple.

Sipping upon his wine, Triaphor stepped towards his wife. Throwing his cup aside, he took a hold of her. Tears were streaming down her cheeks as Triaphor held her face.

"You've been crying, love," Triaphor noticed.

"Its just the cold," Jewel lied.

The prophet looked intently into the eyes of his wife. He knew that she knew of his dreams. Aléshai must've informed her. But he knew as well that she didn't know why they were leaving. He kissed her softly and lovingly held her in his arms. Afterward, he wiped her tears from her face.

"Listen," he spoke tenderly, "I will protect you no matter what happens. There are a lot of things you do not understand, but they all will become clear."

By these words, Jewel knew that she didn't have to inform Triaphor that she was pregnant. He had already known. They heard footsteps approaching and turned to see who was coming.

"My son," Ric said, holding something shiny, "This trinket is something that your mother wanted you to have. I withheld it from you until I felt the time was appropriate. Not knowing whether I would see you again, today I thought was perfect."

Triaphor took hold of a tiny necklace. The emblem of the necklace was an intricate "T" emblazoned in fire.

"She had it made when you were firstborn. She knew that one day you would come to power and save him." Ric explained.

"Who?" Triaphor asked in surprise.

"It is not right for me to say," Ric held back, "but do not worry. Time will reveal all that you need to know. Goodbye, my son."

Ric turned in tears. Wiping them quickly from his face as he walked away, he turned back and said,

"Triaphor, hold my grandson for me. Tell him that I love him."

As the tears began to well inside him once more, Ric departed into the pavilion. Jewel had already embarked their horse and was ready to leave. Prince Kyliðn and Aléshai, walking hand in hand, strolled up to them.

"Be careful my friend," Kyliðn said to Triaphor, "Come back to us in one piece."

Triaphor nodded, for he was too shaken by Ric to speak.

"Jewel," Aléshai addressed the princess, "Do not fear, for Triaphor will take good care of you. Thank you for the advice. Kyliðn and I are going to be happy."

The princess smiled. Kyliðn had fallen for Aléshai from the moment he saw her. Aléshai had only responded likewise when she saw his valor at the Battle of the Rulers' Field. Triaphor had been pleased for his cousin.

Aléshai embraced him. Triaphor began to cry.

"Be at peace," Aléshai comforted, "This was meant to be. Jesu will be with you. Take good care of Jewel and all will be well."

"I know." Triaphor said through tears.

He jumped upon their horse. The time had come for them to bid farewell, temporarily, to their beloved people.

"I will meet you at your camp on the banks of The River of Hades. Hopefully we will not lose many in The Wastelands of Åbérdeen. We love you."

Triaphor led the horse out of the Woods of Wyrdrías through The Field Of Rulers, passing onward into the Wilderness of Westcott. As they passed out of Wyrdrías, various people bowed in confusion. Continuing the work that Autôw had put them to, most of them asked no questions. Jewel and Triaphor traveled until they reached the banks of The Golden River.

"What now?" Jewel asked.

"We watch and wait."

The young couple sat upon their horse as they saw an amazing sight. From the Golden River there arose Sésad, King of The Golden Kingdom. He bid them to ride on until they reached the cave they'd exited so many weeks before. Triaphor took them to that cave and on the other side lay a fully restored Golden Kingdom. Jewel eyed the house they'd stayed in previously. She wondered if it was still fully decorated as she'd left it.

"Now what becomes of us?" Jewel speculated.

Triaphor silently rode on.

Chapter 14 – The Wastelands of Åbérdeen

The White Rider stood in the balcony of his dark throne room. His golden crown, the only light that shone in the gloom that was the Fortress of Daréngir, could be seen for miles. As he glared out into the dankness of Apocalypse, War observed the marching of The Living Dead. He knew that war would strike them soon. The news they'd just received was enough to send him from his gates, but there was nothing he could do until the day of the battle.

"My brother," Hades called, "We must do something."

"And what," War turned to his brother, "does Hades, Lord of Death, suggest?"

The Ashen Rider knew his brother's intentions. To make him look like a fool.

"Anything besides stagnation, my lord."

Oh, how Hades loathed bowing to his older brother. He knew that he could possibly kill him and take his position from him. Unfortunately, Jesu had cursed him so that this would never be.

"My feeble friend," War began, "The *great* God Jesu has decided that it is best for us to remain stagnated until the battle."

"But why?" Belwin piped in, "Why can't we advance on them? Women, children, young men, old men. We could very easily take them and defeat them. How many warriors doth Orés possess that we cannot kill? What are the powers of the Lalrola if we have the Elders with us?"

War sat upon his shadowy throne, listening intently to Belwin's case. If only Belwin really knew the balance of things, he wouldn't even begin to discuss the alternatives.

"Who can stop us now?" War questioned him, "If they do come upon these walls, it is they who will lose, not us. Why should we ride out and waste our energy? For when their warriors have been wasted away and all that is left of Orés and their allies *are* their women, children, their young men and the elderly…"

War, under the cowl of his murky hood, looked at his brother.

"…Hades can do his greatest work."

They all knew what he spoke of. Forcing the inhabitants of the world to serve them forever as The Living Dead. Miserable they would become, living yet appearing and suffering as though they were dead. Belwin was still unsatisfied.

"Do we not have allies besides The Lords of Ardenôs?"

"And *you* would be the one to call upon such creatures?" one of the Elders of Magic shrilly returned.

"And why not? Have I not released you from your cages? Can I not do the same with our other… friends?"

"Belwin, you fool!" Hades scolded, "You think too highly of yourself. Do you not know the strength of the forces that you speak of? They are not to be merely *awoken* in the darkness! There is more to these *friends* of yours than you know."

Belwin, Prophet of Evil, knew many of the secrets that lie in the deep shadows of Névorn, but he did not know them all. Hades, having been the one who studied the most incisive incantations while in the presence of the Warlock of Wyrdrías, knew that the inkiest unscrupulous characters possessed unspeakable power. This power had kept them hidden for centuries and only upon their time would they succumb to the tortures of the world around them.

"Could we not call upon such as the Harlot of Apôstasy?" Belwin begged, "Or perhaps The Grim Reaper of Grômrithoél, he who holds the Sickle of Sodom? The Merchants of Wormwood could even lend a hand. Does no one hear my pleading?"

"These creatures do not answer to any calling but their own," Hades continued the debate, "They will not come simply because we, The Riders of Apocalypse, call for aid. There are even more powers at work here in this world than you know. Hast thou not heard of the Four Beasts of Divulgence? Or perhaps your ears do not know of the Stars of The White Temple? You think that just because they bare the name of Jesu that they are holy? No! On the contrary, they are dark angels who are holding back the Four Winds of Strife and when they are *permitted*, not begged, they will release these Winds and a wickedness, unlike any ever known to mankind, shall plague Névorn..."

"...He is right," War interrupted, weary of the debate, "They will not come to our aid. They wait for the Time of the Apocalypse."

"How do you know such things?" Belwin questioned.

"We have seen it," Hades responded, "The Orbs of the Uthir have shown us everything that shall take place according to the destruction of this world. What many men do not know is the fact that *we* have a place in these Apocalyptic dealings. This Triaphor that rides with Orés cannot kill us. We *will* wipe them out. Trust me."

There, the argument ended. Even though Hades was more correct of the two involved, War knew that there was more to the Apocalypse of Névorn than even he'd been told. Every powerful being knew the extent of the Apocalyptic affairs, but none really possessed the full knowledge of Jesu's plans for Névorn.

***********************   *****************************

Triaphor sat in the courtroom of Sésad, King of The Golden Kingdom. On his throne, Sésad had listened to an incredible report of Triaphor's plans. He was left in shock when the prophet divulged upon the information of the training of his people. Nothing like this had ever been attempted in the history of Névorn.

"How big is this war?" he asked.

"This war," Triaphor explained, "will determine whether the Riders rule Névorn until the Apocalypse or not. If we do not stand up and fight now, the Time of the Apocalypse will be that much harder."

Sésad, aware of some of the climactic events that would soon befall them, looked upon Triaphor in horror.

"*All* nations must fight to protect us from this calamity."

Triaphor nodded in agreement.

Sésad arose from his throne.

"My troops will be there," he promised.

"You must," Triaphor instructed, "take the road through The Golden Woods. That is the quickest route from here to The Fortress of Daréngir. It should bring you directly to us on the battlefield. There's a portal there."

"Truly?" Sésad asked.

Triaphor affirmed it.

"Excellent," Sésad praised, "Now before you go, I have a guest that wishes direly to speak with you."

Triaphor gave the king a questioning stare. From the antechamber behind the throne of the Golden Ruler came a familiar sight. Tahiti, once Prophet of Orés, strolled into the throne room, clad in a white robe lined in gold. A golden fastening in the shape of a lion held Tahiti's cape in place.

"My friend," Tahiti grasped his son, "I have brought gifts from on High. There are weapons here that will do you well in the battle against the enemy."

From his cloak, Tahiti pulled out a sword. Handing it to Triaphor, the boy pulled the sword from its sheath. Emblazoned into it were intricate designs of lions, lambs and 10 crowns representing the Ten Elven Rulers of Ivõrus.

"This," Tahiti explained, "is the Sword of Tântrígõr. Jesu had it crafted years ago. It was originally an heirloom for the Four Sons of Tântrígõr. But as we all know, his Four sons never grew responsible enough to bare such a powerful weapon."

Lastly, Tahiti took from his robe a long staff, much like the one that Triaphor bore. But this staff was no mere wooden stick. Designed deep into its many edifices were symbols of Orés. Swords, elephants, arrows and horses were all things that Orés was known for using in battles.

"The Staff of Sõnércus," Tahiti said, "Many battles have been won from this staff. We've refurbished it. The Riders will not have forgotten Sõnércus from the Battle of Ivõrus. Trust in these weapons and you will win a great victory."

As soon as Triaphor finished basking in the glow of his new weapons, a servant brought a message to the king. Triaphor could feel it instantly. He knew the words that were about to come forth out of Sésad's mouth.

"Your wife needs you."

"Push!" shouted the midwife.

Triaphor, on his knees, grasped Jewel's hand firmly in his. Screaming at the top of her lungs, Jewel did as the midwife instructed. For 9 hours she'd been trying her best to deliver this child. So far it had been one hour for every week that she'd actually bore the child. Most women were pregnant for 9 months with their children, but ever so often a special child would come along. Only 9 weeks had been set aside for the woman bearing the child, for that child had been given a special purpose from Jesu.

"Hold out a little longer, my love." Triaphor comforted.

"Push!" the midwife yelled once more.

With one more effort, this one the strongest of them all, the child burst forth from the womb. Jewel relaxed quickly. In fact, it happened so fast that the midwives thought that she had died. Triaphor, restless over having a new child but also losing his wife, shook Jewel to see if the thing were true.

Her eyes fluttered open. She could barely move. The midwife who'd delivered the child handed it to Triaphor.

"You have a beautiful baby boy," she smiled.

Triaphor gazed into the eyes of his son. The day had finally come. With a smirk, the young prophet held him close. Jewel relished at the sight.

"What," Tahiti, who'd been standing at a distance, "shall you name my grandson?"
"The Spirit says," Triaphor responded, "that we shall name the child Jõniathor."
Jõniathor was the boy's name. The midwives took a recording of the name and like all babies that were born in the Golden Kingdom, they gave him a pair of gold sandals. Presenting the gift to Jõniathor's proud parents was Sésad.
"They adjust to his feet as he grows in stature," the king informed.
Triaphor put the tiny sandals on his son's feet. Sitting on the bed next to Jewel, he began to play with the child's fingers.
"Their so small."
Jewel smiled upon Triaphor's astonishing discovery. Oh how she'd lived for this moment. But she knew that it would not be long before they'd have to live in the real world once more. Perhaps, though, the baby's birth would prolong their time.
At least, Jewel hoped.

*************************   *************************

Aléshai, Kyliõn, the king, the Sultan, Autôw and the army behind them reached the Southern gate of Apocalypse. Dark clouds shrouded the entire land of the Four Riders.
"I never thought I'd behold this sight," Aléshai said.
Ric had already been here years ago. This time, the plans were different. This time, they were more prepared.
"What do you think lies in the Wastelands of Åbérdeen?" Autôw asked.
"Only Jesu knows," Salzahirz responded.
The five leaders awaited the signal. Aléshai had sent one of the MorningStar Talsûrõn around the kingdom to see what progress the others had made. When the time came, the warrior was to return with news. Depending on this news, Kyliõn was supposed to blow the horn that Jewel had taken from the Grove of Prophets outside of Orés upon her departure, The Horn of the South as it was called.
"Here she comes," Aléshai pointed.
"My lords," the female warrior bowed, blond hair blowing in the wind, "It is time."
Aléshai looked at Kyliõn. The five leaders bowed their heads in prayer. After prayer, Kyliõn took the horn in his hand. The signal had been given. They advanced quickly upon the gate as to destroy it. Aléshai embarked upon Bryan and led the MorningStar Talsûrõn into the strongest part of the gate. The archers upon the wall, those known as The Living Dead, fired at the MorningStar Talsûrõn.
"Kill those archers!" Aléshai demanded.
At her command, two of the Talsûrõn, the messenger with blond hair and another who sported wavy brown hair, took arrows and began to destroy the archers of Apocalypse.
Kyliõn, upon Spéliskir, took the Elves of Ivõrus and plowed right into the gate. Speaking what little magic he knew, the swords of the elves doubled in their strength. Even still, the gate would not surrender to their powerful strokes.
Ric and Autôw brought the newly trained soldiers of Orés into the debacle. The

archers upon the wall continued their rapid firing, making it difficult. Autôw looked at Ric in horror, knowing in his heart that it was going to be impossible to make it into the gate.

"This gate is too heavily guarded!" the general shouted.

"There is a way that we can succeed," Ric encouraged, "but we must give the Elves of Ivõrus more time, else we shall all perish here. Follow me!"

Autôw quickly pursued the king of Orés. Ric pulled from his armor rope that had been stored there prior to the engagement. He attached the rope to an arrow that could latch itself onto something. It was a special arrow of legend that had only been written of. Autôw's eyes opened wide.

"The Leeching Arrow!" he gazed in astonishment, "Impossible! But how...?"

Ric put a finger to his lips to silence him.

"Hold on to me!"

The king shot the arrow into a miniscule hole in the wall. Then, with all his strength, he climbed the high wall of the Kingdom of Apocalypse. Looking down at Autôw to secure that he was safe, he noticed that Kyliõn and the elves were struggling. He climbed faster and ever so faster. Upon reaching the top of the wall, he drew his sword.

"Let's finish it!" Ric shouted at Autôw.

Autôw, General of His Majesty's forces and Ric, King of Orés plunged into every archer they discovered on the wall. Much to Kyliõn's pleasure, the gate began to slip under their power. Salzahirz brought his Iristaniquan warriors alongside Kyliõn's elven troops.

With that help, Kyliõn's soldiers doubled their efforts. Efforts doubled, spirits high and Autôw, Ric, Aléshai and the MorningStar Talsûrõn taking charge of the gate's defenses, the Gate of Apocalypse slipped right under their hands. Crashing down upon them, Kyliõn cried,

"Fall back!!"

On the other side of that gate was a slew of archers waiting to attack. They took down a considerable amount of Kyliõn's finest warriors. This mattered not. Aléshai brought her MorningStar Talsûrõn in to swarm upon the archers. Swords drawn, the MorningStar Talsûrõn swooped down and took out the archers.

"Into the kingdom!" Ric shouted from the wall, "Quickly!!"

The Allies of Jesu moved into the Kingdom of Apocalypse in confidence. The soldiers of Orés that had once been citizens had been trained to fight valiantly and without fear. As Aléshai led the MorningStar Talsûrõn in the sky, it was Kyliõn who took charge of Ivõrus and Orés alongside Iristaniq on the ground.

"Trolls!" Aléshai screamed from above.

"Draw swords!!!" Kyliõn commanded.

Ric and Autôw joined Kyliõn on either side of him. Upon Spéliskir, Kyliõn drew the sword of his father, King Éisõräl. Green hilt gleaming in the darkness of Apocalypse, he lifted it in the air.

"Forward!!"

Upon that command, the army ran full force into the troupe of trolls that came their way. Kyliõn went head on with a troll of quite a clever conduct. As the elf leader swung his light sword at the troll, the creature dodged with all his might. Kyliõn would not be outsmarted by such a stank individual.

Thrusting with all his might, the elf, clad in silver armor and an emerald cape, much like his armor at the Battle of The Rulers' Field, plunged his sword into the gut of the troll. Withdrawing his sword from the morose being, he took on another troll.

Aléshai, riding Bryan, swooped down upon a massive troll that had raised his mace to clobber an entire force of elves. With her swords in her hands, the daughter of Belwin, the Prophet of Evil, went down and with a swift motion, she cleaved the head straight off the troll.

Ric and Autôw were triumphant over five trolls apiece. This feat was remarkable, considering the size of these monsters. Salzahirz, using his curved Arabesque-styled sword, struck the feet of the nearest troll off of his legs. When the troll came crashing to the earth, the Sultan of Iristaniq stuck his sword into its head. All of the Sultan's followers, the soldiers of Iristaniq, did as they had watched their lord achieve.

Victory over the trolls was only the beginning of their turmoil in The Wastelands of Âbérdeen. Aléshai continued to lead the MorningStar Talsûrõn in the aerial offense as Kyliõn took charge of his soldiers on land.

"Form the line!!!" the command rang out.

The troops of Orés, Ivõrus and Iristaniq continued their trip into the terror of The Wastelands of Âbérdeen. Aléshai only wished now that Triaphor had given instructions as to what should be done when in the Wastelands. Âbérdeen was known for consuming armies of this size before. She could only but trust in Jesu and her comrades for this next phase of the journey.

**********************   ******************

Triaphor and Jewel, riding upon the same horse that had taken them from the Woods of Wyrdrías into the Golden Kingdom, were staring upon a grand wonder. The city was massive in size and its beauty was unlike any the two had ever seen before. A river ran down the center of the city and an irrigation system had been built out of it.

When the couple reached the palace, their shock was rekindled. The colossal spectrum of its halls stretched far beyond the imagination. Upon the pillars that held up this structure were engraved figures of history. Each column was dedicated to a particular warrior. Some of them Triaphor knew and others he did not. Jewel seemed to know all of them. She had always been better at the history of Orés than he.

But it was the last pillar that shocked them the most.

"That's us!" Jewel gazed in wonder.

Triaphor stared at both pillars, one on either side of them. On one of them was carved, sure enough, the Lalrola of Prophecy and on the other, was the Princess of Orés. Arriving at the massive double doors to the throne room, a being of majestic authority begged them to remove themselves from their horse. They did so.

"How shall I announce thee?" the being asked.

"I am Triaphor and this is Jewel. We are the Prince and Princess of Orés," Triaphor enlightened.

The being, obviously the lackey for the king, opened the doors. The courtroom was just as grand as the hallway preceding it. Sitting upon a giant throne was the ruler of this kingdom. Triaphor was astonished because the king himself was… enormous in size.

"Entering," announced the lackey, "Triaphor, Son of Biora, Prophet and Prince of Orés, Lalrola of Prophecy with his wife, Jewel, Daughter of Ric, Princess of Orés to see his majesty, King Gângror of the Giant Kingdom of Álgrériðn."

"Enter, royalty of Orés!" Gângror commanded, "Long have we, the Giants of Álgrériðn, welcomed this day!"

Triaphor and Jewel stepped forward and bowed before the King of Álgrériðn. Peering into his eyes, Triaphor saw a hesitance there. He drew Jewel near unto him.

"Be careful what you utter," he whispered, "This king may not wish to serve us in the battle. If that is so, we must be prepared to accept whatever answer he is willing to give."

Jewel nodded.

As Gângror finished drinking his wine, he called upon Triaphor to speak of why he had come.

"My lord Gângror, King of Álgrériðn," Triaphor started, "The time has come for all the nations of Névorn to put an end to the suffering of our people..."

"Suffering?" the king interrupted, "What suffering has befallen us? If there is such suffering, it has not reached the halls of Gângror of Álgrériðn! Perhaps you have come to bring it."

"No, my lord," Triaphor politely continued, "You see, Dimensia[1] of Névorn has all been destroyed save for the three kingdoms of Orés, Iristaniq and Ivðrus, the elves that were restored to us from Jesu, the One and Only. It is up to us, my wife and I, to call upon aid from the other inhabitants of Névorn. That is, Dimensia[2] and Dimensia[3]."

The prophet gulped at the end of his sentence. For some strange reason, fear had crept into his soul. He did not know what the response of the King of Álgrériðn would be, but whatever it was, he didn't feel it would be positive.

Gângror laughed. His hearty chuckle turned quickly to fiendish cackles as his entire courtroom joined in with the king. Triaphor and Jewel glanced at each other and held one another tighter.

"I see what you would do," King Gângror stood, "You would have Dimensia[3] join in on your senseless war against these Riders of Apocalypse, only that we may be slaughtered alongside you in battle. And what honor is there in this? None! None, I tell you! For what honor can be gained in battle when one is allied to another? When the war is said and done, they will say that it was Orés and their allies that defeated the Riders of Apocalypse. Only will our names be mentioned by master storytellers if they decide to divulge information about who the other allies were, which in most cases, they don't. You would bring down the Great House of Álgrériðn with your spells and wizardry and force us to serve you like dogs, dare we refuse!!!!! THIS! I will not have!! Guards!!!"

Jewel looked sharply at Triaphor. His eyes approved. She grasped her sword hilt. The guards came into the room and with every step, the ground gyrated.

"Take these fools to the dungeon!!" Gângror commanded.

With an approving glance, Triaphor and Jewel drew their swords. The king laughed, as did his servants. The giant guards surrounded the young couple. Jewel, poised and ready for action, jumped upon the knee of the giant to her right. His hand tried its best to grab hold of her, but she would not have it. She stabbed his knee violently and he fell to the ground.

Triaphor, using the Sword of Tântrígðr, called upon his power. The sword lit and blinded the giants to the left and right of him. The Prophet of Orés jumped upon the head of the giant to his left. Triaphor, not wishing to slay the giant, stuck the Sword of Tântrígðr, lighted with power, into the right shoulder of his gargantuan attacker.

As his feet landed on the ground alongside the head and shoulders of his opponent, the other guards backed off. Triaphor and Jewel stood together and gazed into the eyes of King Gângror. Triaphor, using the Staff of Sõnércus, held him in his position on the throne.

"We," Triaphor spoke, "wish no harm done to you, Giants of Álgrériðn. But know this, Jesu has demanded that every nation must defend themselves in the fight against the Riders. If this is not done, when the Day of Judgment comes, you shall not know the pleasures which the One and Only has bestowed for us all. Will you stand and fight with us?"

Gângror, filled with remorse and fear for Orés, looked into the eyes of the prophet.

"What better honor," he said, "can there be than to fight aside our brethren, these faithful men of Orés."

Standing, for now he was able to move, the King of Álgrériðn took his sword into his hand.

"Assemble the army!!!!" he shouted.

Triaphor smiled in relief.

He'd been standing here for a long time, trying to convince this ruler of the consequences about to befall them. This nation, the Land of Réstôngrír, had stood alone for centuries, apart from all other kingdoms in Dimensia^2. This was the last kingdom of the four nations of Dimensia^2 that Triaphor had to persuade. The Dwarves of Gírgéthôr, the Eagle Riders of Énrísôr and the Secret Sisters of Séröndín had come forth willingly. Of Dimensia^3, Triaphor had salvaged their always and forever allies The Golden Kingdom and their new allies, the Giants of Álgrériðn.

The Fire Masters of Réstôngrír, on the other hand, adamantly refused to join Triaphor. For three days and two nights, Triaphor had tirelessly pleaded with their ruler, Lord Laúres, to help with the war effort. Nothing would persuade him. He was stubborn and would not dare plunge his people into a pointless war.

"Many centuries ago," Laúres was telling Triaphor, "My people counted on the dark Sorcerer Eléctrasûmõn from Dimensia^3 to give them a pleasant life, without war and without strife. But, much to their dismay, the Sorcerer tricked them and forced them into war against these Riders of Apocalypse. He felt that they had conned him out of his precious Orbs of the Uthir."

Triaphor had remembered this story from history. According to legend, the great Sorcerer Eléctrasûmõn had been the only one able to discover three out of four of the Orbs of the Uthir. These mystical orbs were only to be used together and in times of dire emergency. Long had the prophets of Orés wished to possess these orbs so that no one, like Eléctrasûmõn, could use them for their own malice intentions. Unfortunately, the

Sorcerer had found them first. He turned the nation of the Mount of Eléctrasûmõn into a wasteland much like that of Ábérdeen and took on the name of the mountain. The other orb had disappeared mysteriously.

The Great Trílautûs, Prophet of Jesu, residing in Orés at the time, knew that the Four Sons of Tântrígõr had the fourth and missing piece of the puzzle, the Orb of Uthir Pañé, the most powerful of them all. Jesu had commanded him to retrieve the orb from the brothers. Upon the prophet's arrival, Trílautûs discovered that the Princes of Ivõrus had broken the orb and obtained its power. He warned them against using it for evil. War, King of Ivõrus, would not listen and drowned the 2,007-year-old prophet.

When the four Orbs of the Uthir were finally reunited, Eléctrasûmõn grew greedy and held back on the promise he'd made concerning the Sons of Tântrígõr. With their combined strength, War and his brother Hades pinned the Sorcerer to the wall, stole the Orbs of the Uthir, absorbed their power and left that place. After establishing the Kingdom of Apocalypse, containing The Wastelands of Ábérdeen and The Fortress of Daréngir, the Riders were involved in their first war as the powerful beings they now were.

"Eléctrasûmõn," Laúres continued, "wanted his orbs back. Unfortunately, he used our people to do his dirty work. This happened right after Eléctrasûmõn had delivered a child to the Riders. It was a baby boy and around the child's neck was a necklace made out of the Orb of Dimensia^3. He wanted that back as well."

"Why," Triaphor asked, "didn't he take it when he had the child in his grasp?"

"I know not," Laúres glared into the prophet's eyes, "But… *we* betrayed him when he claimed that he wanted it back. It was we, the Fire Masters of Réstôngrír, who'd made the Orb of Dimensia^3 in our own fires. It was our volcanoes that forged the Necklace of Biora and we would not allow this insane Sorcerer to take this power from that child."

Triaphor recognized his mother's name.

"Necklace of Biora?"

"Yes," Laúres responded, "So, we killed Eléctrasûmõn at the Gate of Apocalypse, but unfortunately we lost many lives in the process. But, we travailed and ever since that time, I have been Lord Laúres, Ruler of the Fire Masters of Réstôngrír. I will not give up all that I have worked so hard to gain."

"But, my lord, this war…" Triaphor started.

"*This* war," Laúres interrupted, "is just like any other war. All wars are a struggle for power. Leaders call upon men to lay down their lives so that they can continue to live peaceably in their bravura palaces and their dazzling castles. No ruler really fights for the freedom of his people. It is impossible for there to be a war that does not have a struggle for power at its center."

Triaphor grew tired of debating with the Ruler of Réstôngrír. He always found some sort of excuse to dodge the real reason he would not battle the Riders. Laúres had mentioned a lot of things such as this Necklace of Biora and a mysterious child that Triaphor had never heard of in any of his studies of the Prophecy and that made him curious of Laúres' intentions.

"You're scared, aren't you?" Triaphor asked, looking into Laúres' heart.

The ruler shuttered.

"This," Triaphor read his heart, "is not about your people, as you would have me believe. You feel as if you cannot fight the Riders of Apocalypse and win. You fear the child who holds this Necklace of Biora…

    …no orb has more power than this power Jesu has given to Triaphor, his servant."
Relief flooded Laúres.

    "Fine," the Ruler of Réstôngrír said, "We will join thee, Triaphor of Orés, in this war. But I promise you this, you must understand that there is a power beyond reckoning in that necklace and it will not be easy to take the Riders."

    This, Triaphor knew.

*************************   *************************

    For three days, the Allies of Jesu had been wandering about The Wastelands of Åbérdeen. Kyliðn had not rested or stopped and neither did his followers. Aléshai and the MorningStar Talsûrðn kept a constant watch for enemies. Yet, for days their only enemy had been a barren land filled with unbelievable humidity, thick fog and detrimental health to many soldiers.

    The king wondered how well the other two forces were doing. His mind also thought of the safety of his daughter and their hero, Prince Triaphor, the Prophet of Orés. Just as Ric began to sink into a deep thought about them, Kyliðn stopped.

    "What is it, prince?" Ric asked.

    "I see creatures of an unspeakable number."

    Advancing towards the Allies of Jesu was a tremendous army of what appeared to be horned monsters. These creatures held axes and ran at them at a pace unimaginable. Kyliðn commanded his archers from Ivðrus to step forward.

    "Steady!"

    The archers held their bows at their cheeks. They, the Archers of Ivðrus, were well acquainted with the art of firing a successful shot. It was Kyliðn's hopes that the entire first and second line of the advancing army could be taken out.

    "Fire!!"

    The elves shot perfectly into the troupe of Minotaurs. The first, second and half of the third line of the Minotaur army dropped to the ground. Kyliðn held off his next order. Aléshai had a plan.

    "MorningStar Talsûrðn!" she shouted, "Swords ready!! Now!!!"

    The MorningStar Talsûrðn, upon their griffins, made a diving attack upon the Minotaurs. Heads and bodies went flying everywhere in front of them. The fourth and fifth line of the Minotaur army was taken out by another stream of arrows from Kyliðn's troops.

    "Allies!" Kyliðn bellowed the next command, "Swords!! Charge!!!"

    As they all drew their swords once more for another strong attack, there came a force of ghostly creatures from the midst of the Minotaurs. These ghosts were the legendary creatures that consumed all men who'd made it thus far in the journey.

    "The Phantoms of Åbérdeen." Kyliðn frightfully observed, "Forward!!!"

    Combining their powers, Kyliðn and Aléshai led all of their troops into battle against the Phantoms of Åbérdeen and the Minotaurs. Demolishing the remainder of the Minotaurs, it was the combination of Aléshai's powers and Kyliðn's small knowledge of magic that finished off the Phantoms of Åbérdeen.

    As Kyliðn struck down the last of the ghosts, he wiped his sword clean.

Disembarking Spéliskir, Kyliðn took a rest. The soldiers behind him stopped. Ric and Autôw came and stood alongside Kyliðn.

"My friends," Kyliðn said, "We've reached it. The end of The Wastelands of Åbérdeen. We dare not go any further."

Horns blew in the distance. Kyliðn and the rest knew that these were their friends from the other gates. Aléshai landed Bryan next to Kyliðn and the others.

"Kyliðn," the Talsûrðn leader said, "The River of Hades is 100 meters to the north. The others, they've made it."

The inhabitants of the kingdoms of Orés, Ivðrus and Iristaniq streamed into where they would end up setting up camp. Trees surrounded them. Looming across the River of Hades was the Fortress of Daréngir.

"The fortress," Aléshai shivered, "looks formidable. I'm not sure how Triaphor plans on taking it."

"Fear not," Ric said, "My son-in-law knows what he's doing."

"Has he not led us this far?" Autôw added.

Autôw's amazing amount of faith surprised even him. Kyliðn and Aléshai took charge of making sure that the camp was set up properly. Hoping for a place to put valiant sentries, the two looked to the trees.

"Those," Kyliðn pointed out, "will make brilliant hiding spots. Place our best archers there."

Though they knew that no harm could come to them while they were in this area, they thought it best to take Triaphor's advice on having sentries placed. Who knew what the Dark Lords of Apocalypse might try to pull. After all, they were in their land.

************************   ************************

Triaphor stood upon the steps to King Sésad's palace. He stared into the courtyard and viewed the organizing of his new allies. They were dividing themselves by dimension. All of the soldiers from Dimensia^2 were to his right and those from Dimensia^3 were to his left. Sésad stood next to him.

"So this is the war that wages before us," the king commented.

Triaphor said nothing. He held his son tightly to him. His dream still haunted him and Laúres, Ruler of Réstôngrír, had spoken of a child bearing a necklace. The prophet had given his son, on the day of his birth, the necklace that Ric had provided him with on the day he left his people. Triaphor was afraid to leave his baby in the Golden Kingdom.

"Worry not, my friend," Sésad comforted, "My people will take good care of your son."

So Triaphor hoped.

Jewel came striding beside him. She would take command of one of the dimensions while Sésad would take control of the other. She kissed her son on the forehead and then she kissed her husband.

"Good morning," she said.

"Good morning," Triaphor responded, "Listen. Sésad will take Dimensia^3—the Giants of Álgrériðn and his own soldiers, the Horse Riders of the Golden Kingdom— through the Golden Woods. You shall take Dimensia^2—the Dwarves of Gírgéthôr, the Secret Sisters of Séröndín and the Eagle Riders of Énrísðr—down the Golden River, through the Wilderness of Westcott, passing over the Field of Rulers and into the Woods of Wyrdrías. Through this route, you shall lead them to the North gate of Apocalypse. There are woods to the left of The Fortress of Daréngir. Hide there until the signal is given."

"What of the Fire Masters of Réstôngrír?" Jewel asked.

"I," Triaphor said, "shall be responsible for them."

Jewel embarked upon her horse, the one that had led them to the Golden Kingdom. She rode out to the soldiers of Dimensia^2. Sésad, upon his grandiose stallion, headed up the flanks of Dimensia^3.

"Ride now!" Triaphor shouted, "For this war is in our hands!! Jesu will not falter! Ride now to rid this world of pain!!!"

Dimensia^2 and Dimensia^3 were led in their separate directions from the Golden Kingdom. Triaphor looked on, as he knew that it was now time for him to take his flight. Handing his son to Tahiti, who had remained in the Golden Kingdom, he spoke.

"Take care of my son."

A tear stroked his cheek as he boarded Phôrastérõn. Phôrastérõn was a giant firebird known as a Phoenix. He had been given to Triaphor as a gift from Lord Laúres of Réstôngrír.

"If you are to lead us," Laúres had said, "you are to fly like one of us."

The Fire Masters of Réstôngrír all flew Phoenixes. The colossal firebirds of Réstôngrír were birthed in the volcanoes of Réstôngrír long before men had settled in the plain. It was the Phoenixes that taught them all the tricks to wielding fire. The Phoenixes, after a long war with men, decided to forever serve the inhabitants that settled in Réstôngrír only if they treated them fairly. The deal was settled.

Laúres and his troops also used swords enflamed in fire.

"These swords," Laúres informed, "are forged by the Messengers of The White Temple in our volcanoes. This way, we are able to keep our name as the Fire Masters."

Triaphor, upon Phôrastérõn the Phoenix, took flight. As the giant bird shrieked in the air, its brothers and sisters answered the call. A portal in the sky lit up as Triaphor flew the Fire Masters of Réstôngrír straight into it.

He did not know what lie in store for this world, but he knew what he must do in order to save them. It all lay on his shoulders and no matter how hard it may have sounded; he had to be the one to do it. This is what he was born in the world to do. This was what Jesu, Tahiti, Belwin, Sõnércus, Trílautûs and all the other 300,000,000 prophets had prophesied for centuries. This task was the final test.

Lalrola. That was not only his name, but also his purpose. He only hoped that he could live up to this purpose without worrying about his son.

Jõniathor, my son, he thought, *I love you. Jesu is with you. Be safe.*

Kyliõn, red hair glowing in the firelight, watched the motion of the flame that lay before him. As he glared into its magnificence, he began to realize that for many of the soldiers, sitting around various fires like this one, it would be their last night. Wives would lose husbands, fathers and brothers. Husbands would mourn the loss of their wives, daughters and sisters. The Battle of Daréngir, as it was later called, would claim many lives.

Sitting to the right of the elf was Autôw, General of His Majesty's army. The next day would be the defining moment of his career. He'd seen many battles and fought alongside King Ric for most of these, but none would compare to what he would face tomorrow. His love of Orés and its amassing Empire might cause the end of his life. But he did not care. He'd been through many trials and had learned numerous lessons. Gladly would he die beside such greats as Ric, his king, Aléshai, Sultan Salzahirz, Kyliõn the elf and yes… even Triaphor, the Lalrola whom he'd hated for so long.

On the left of Kyliõn sat King Ric. He worried over his daughter and the child he knew she was having. If this child was as significant as she thought he might be, Ric could only pray for safety. The Riders would discover the birth of this child as soon as it came from her womb. Jewel knew how to protect herself and others quite well, but could she keep her child from danger? Only Jesu would know.

Aléshai, proud of her new MorningStar Talsûrõn warriors, emerged from the tent. She'd been resting all afternoon. Only two days ago had they reached the end of The Wastelands of Ábérdeen and now wallowed in the shadows of The Daréngirian Vale. A messenger from The Golden Kingdom had come yesterday, informing them that Triaphor was on his way with a mass of reinforcements. Aléshai had heard of other kingdoms existing in the other dimensions of Névorn, but never did she really believe in them. Névorn's dimensions were never really close. It was as if they all lived in separate worlds of their own.

A sound came from behind the camp. Sentries had been set to watch the camp, so perhaps it was one of them, but just in case, Kyliõn, Autôw and Ric stood. Aléshai's hands rested on her swords. The four waited until the footsteps drew nearer.

"The news is urgent," Kyliõn said, eyes scoping what lay before him, "I can feel it."

As the footsteps began to halt, the person came into the light of the fire. It was indeed a messenger. In fact, it was one of the MorningStar Talsûrõn that Aléshai had trained. Her long wavy black hair flowed in the subtle wind of Daréngir. Her chest armor had an intricately designed "T" surrounded by a ring of stars. Each servant of the Talsûrõn Order was provided with a hooded red cape. Her silver boots were engraved with stars flowing down the side of each shoe. Knives sat comfortably at each side of the boots as well. The Talsûrõn warriors had sword sheathes on their backs that held their classic blades. These swords had stars in the same design as the boots.

"Sérínûs," Aléshai addressed the woman, "Speak."

"My Lady," Sérínûs answered and bowed, "My prince, Your Majesty and great general, there is someone approaching. We cannot see him but one of the Seers insists that he feels a presence. A powerful presence of a dangerous sort quickly comes this way."

Aléshai, followed by Kyliõn, jumped to attention and ran past Sérínûs. The warrior trailed them easily. As the three approached the trees where the sentries had been placed—towards the back of the camp—Kyliõn began to slow. His heart ached and pain welled up inside of him. He fell to the ground upon his knees and held his chest. Aléshai turned to face him.

"Are you alright?" she asked.

"The weight of their power is overwhelming my soul," the elf gasped.

Aléshai drew her swords. She would not lose this man now that she had finally found one. Even if she had to fight all Four of the Riders of Apocalypse single-handedly, she would have Kyliõn until a natural death took him. Sérínûs joined her trainer's side.

"Mistress," the woman called, "Who is it that draweth near?"

"I don't know." Aléshai quivered.

Apt for attack, the two MorningStar Talsûrõn warriors held their ground. The archers in the trees had their arrows at the ready. And then they noticed the being. His entire presence breathed that of power. Aléshai, for the first time in a long time, grew afraid. Sweat poured from her hands as she tried her best to hold her sword steady.

A man wearing a crimson robe of a wine complexion strode confidently towards the camp. Hood covering his eyes and hands in their robe sleeves, he walked with a sense of urgency yet courage. Aléshai tensed as Kyliõn began to cry out in pain. As this man drew closer and closer, the screams were louder and louder.

"Hush, my prince," the man spoke.

Aléshai lowered her sword. The archers lay their bows and arrows at their sides. The sentries climbed down quickly from their posts. All except Kyliõn and Aléshai bowed to the red-robed man.

"Triaphor?" Aléshai looked at him in shock.

He removed his hood.

"Cousin," he greeted. He put forth his hand to help Kyliõn from the ground.

"What has happened to you?" the elf asked.

Triaphor looked into his eyes. Never meaning to stare, Triaphor's gaze lingered as he thought of The White Temple. His mind dwelt upon the moment he'd first awoken and seen his master looming over him. He remembered the Invocation Of Power and what it felt like to be in the presence of his Lord.

"Triaphor?" Kyliõn snapped him to attention, "What's wrong, my lord?"

"Nothing," Triaphor said, "I was only reminiscing. My friends come. I have much to speak with you about."

Aléshai could not speak. Overwhelmed by the sense of power that Triaphor had compared to when he'd left them not more than a week ago, the girl was astonished. The archers followed the three leaders as they made their way through the camp. As they passed by, people who were guarding their tents bowed in obeisance to the Lalrola. A herald ran forth before him shouting,

"The Savior cometh! The Savior of Névorn is coming!"

Ric and Autôw looked up and saw the three walking towards them. Automatically, as if something had befallen them, they bowed as well. Triaphor seemed more than calm about such changes. It was Aléshai and Kyliõn who couldn't believe what they were seeing.

"What is it that has happened to my lord Triaphor?" the king asked in shock.

The prophet smiled.

"These robes," Triaphor said, "They come from The White Temple. Last night as I approached the camp, I prayed over them. Jesu heard my call. He sent to me two Messengers of The White Temple. As I still prayed, bowing upon my knees, the Messengers, with their enormous wings, covered me. A light filled the skies unlike any I've ever seen in my life. My companions, the Fire Masters of Réstôngrír, told me that this light means that I now have some special purpose in the Apocalypse. Ever since that time, my power has increased, my confidence is sure and now I know that, without a doubt, we shall succeed tomorrow in battle."

Ric, Aléshai, Autôw, Kyliõn and the archer-sentries listened in amazement. They could not believe that such a man of a powerful force sat in their presence. Jesu would preserve their nation once more. They knew that through Triaphor, their world would be saved only for a time. Hopefully, peace would be restored to them until the Time of the Apocalypse.

*****************************   *********************************

Hades stood in the throne room of his brother, King War of Daréngir. The Ashen Rider stared at the seat that his brother often ruled from. Anger filled his soul as he remembered how War had paraded into Ivõrus and stolen his one chance at ruling as a Lord of Ivõrus. For centuries, he'd lived with one talent. He had the ability to skillfully murder anyone he pleased. Unfortunately, the only person he could never destroy was his own conniving older brother.

His stride led him around the pool that lay in the center of the throne room—for Daréngir's palace was shaped much like that of Ivõrus—to the throne itself. His fingers graced the armrests. His heart stirred with an overwhelming sense of passion and for the first time in what felt like forever, tears streamed down his face. The High Prince of Daréngir fell to his knees and wept bitterly upon the throne.

His rarest gift—the craft of murder—and his finest treasure—the best looks one could ask for—did not save him from the sorrow he'd feel for the remainder of his life. For it was too late to turn back now. But Hades, the Ashen Rider of Death, knew that if he could, he would readily join Triaphor in his pursuit to stop the Riders from ruling Névorn.

Footsteps resounded in the darkness. Hades felt his presence. In fact, he was one of the only beings who could. The Ashen Rider's hatred was kindled against the King of Daréngir so much, that he could feel his every pulse within his own soul. He stood and turned to see his brother. For once, War's hood was not covering his eyes. Hades and the twins never wore their hoods at Daréngir.

"Like it?" War asked his brother.

Hades did not respond.

"You know," the White Rider began, "I used to crave power like our brother Famine desires food. I begged for it, I stole it and I even lied to attain all the power in the world. Without even realizing it, I have lost the most important power of all."

"And what," Hades wiped his cheeks, "would that be?"

"The Power of Love."

War, The White Rider of Authority and King of Daréngir, last elven Ruler of Ivõrus embraced his brother, Hades, High Prince of Daréngir, Lord of Death. The two wept upon each other's shoulders. War had finally noticed what was missing in his life. Though he would never turn from his ways now, he had finally learned what it meant to love first and let nothing stand in between that love.

The Twins of Tântrígõr, Pestilence and Famine, donned in their black and red robes, witnessed such a repentance. This sight was unbelievable. The two glanced at each other knowingly. One of them was lying, but neither of the twins knew which one. It could have very easily been both of them.

War needed an advantage in the upcoming battle. Hades was born to end lives. Not only did he have the ability, but the power with which to back it up. The White Rider would do leagues better if he had his Ashen brother at his side. Hades, on the other hand, could very easily pretend to make amends with his older brother, only so that it would make it more stunning when the Ashen Rider betrayed War in the battle.

"What do you think?" Pestilence asked his black-robed twin.

"Time," Famine responded smoothly, "will reveal all."

*****************************   ******************************

Jewel trudged onward through the Woods of Daréngir peacefully yet in much fear.

The Princess Of Orés knew only one thing as she led the troops forward. Triaphor had the battle plans complete in detail. This was unlike him. He usually showed up to the battle prepared to just use his power as best he could in the enveloping situation. But this time, Triaphor had done quite differently. His plans were extensive because he knew that in order for him to do his best work, the Elders of Magic must be terminated.

Jewel could feel the fear that dwelled within Triaphor as he mentioned the task to her. But if it was one thing that she'd learned about him thus far it was that he would never allow fear to assume control over the situation. She loved him very much and would stand beside him in great support in the upcoming battle. One of those Riders would die upon her sword. Which one, she did not know, but she knew that she'd kill one of the Four Sons of Tântrígõr.

She reached the edge of the forest. Jewel looked out and could see the Fortress of Daréngir looming in the distance.

Here goes nothing. The princess thought.

****************************   ******************************

Triaphor lifted back the flap to The Royal Pavilion. It had been a restful night but from the look of Kyliõn's eyes, it hadn't been so for him. The deep circles that had formed around his optics were as dark as the night that had just left them. The elf, yawning from his tired state, held a silver cup of red wine in his hand.

"Have you noticed something?" Kyliõn asked.

Triaphor gave a questioning glance.

"The sun rises," the elf pointed.

The Lalrola looked into the sky and saw the gigantic ball of light peeking from behind a pallid cloud. This was unusual for the opaque land of Apocalypse. From the moment they'd entered the terror of the Apocalyptic Land of the Riders, The Allies of

Jesu were unable to tell whether it was day or night. Traveling wasn't really difficult simply because they knew that if they didn't keep on the move, death would befall them through attack.

"It is His sign," Triaphor said, "He's telling us…"

"…He's watching," Kyliðn finished.

"Moreover," Triaphor corrected, "He's with us."

The elf smiled lightly. It was difficult for Triaphor to see him like this. Kyliðn, Prince of Ivõrus, was usually on point with everything that was going on around him. But today, the biggest day of all their lives, the prince seemed less alert. This worried Triaphor, for he knew that if victory was to be achieved, all the leaders of the nation must be keen in every sense.

"Are you alright?" the prophet questioned.

Kyliðn stared deeply into his eyes. Triaphor read every thought.

"I'm not sure."

Autôw had been up before the crack of dawn preparing the troops for battle. With Orés, there were 1,000,000 soldiers doing all kinds of different exercises that would strengthen them for the battle to come. Salzahirz, the Sultan yet Commander of his forces in Iristaniq, was drilling his 600,000 men. The elven soldiers of Ivõrus, 2,000,000 in number, were standing at attention, awaiting orders from their prince and ruler. Kyliðn walked beside Triaphor to his troops. The young Prophet of Jesu was inspecting the progress.

"Kyliðn," Triaphor said, "Where is my cousin? Where is Aléshai?"

"I don't know," the prince replied, "I haven't seen her all morning. I know that Sérínûs is drilling the MorningStar Talsûrðn. Where Aléshai is, I cannot say."

Triaphor wasn't worried. No matter where his cousin went, he could tell whether the MorningStar Talsûrðn Leader was in danger or not. The king, Ric of Orés, emerged from The Royal Pavilion as Triaphor made his way around the tent to the other side.

Standing in the plain behind the pavilion was Aléshai, Lady of the MorningStar Talsûrðn, breeze blowing through her hair. Something, Triaphor couldn't put a finger on it, was bothering his cousin. Usually she was more than ready to fight the Riders of Apocalypse, but today was different.

"My father," Aléshai spoke first, "is on the other side of that wall. He willingly leads their armies into war as do I with ours."

"Are you ready to do what we discussed?"

"Triaphor," Aléshai gazed with concern into his eyes, "My father was the sole supporter since the death of my mother, but he was never really my father. I've never had a father, Triaphor."

The Prophet of Orés embraced his cousin closely. Tears fell from her eyes. As she began to weep silently upon Triaphor's shoulders, the Lalrola felt her sense of emptiness. Their connection from her birth was something special that had been set by Jesu. What she felt so did he and vice-versa. Her spirit longed for a father figure and Triaphor's heart burned for her longing to come true. Tears filtered onto Triaphor's cheeks as well.

Kyliðn came around the corner. Though he knew there was something wrong with his love, he didn't want to interfere. Triaphor let go of his cousin and turned to the elf. He'd felt his presence.

"My lord," the elven prince said, "The soldiers are ready."

The three leaders glanced at each other in assurance.
"It is time." Triaphor stated.

*****************************   ******************************

Marching. Constant marching. The incessant noise of endless marching filled the ears of Belwin, Prophet of Evil. The Riders had given him sole authority over their forces. Everyone that had come to join The Dark Alliance in the war effort had already been placed. As the corrupt prophet looked out on the Plains of Daréngir, he saw what caused the sound of marching.

It was the Allies of Jesu. They'd finally made it. He'd felt a familiar presence. The Riders along with the Elders of Magic had assured him that the night before Triaphor, Son of Tahiti, had come. Belwin was afraid of no one.

The Riders rode out to meet him at the gate. They climbed the stairs and stood atop the gate alongside the Prophet of Evil. Glaring down at the Plains of Daréngir, War was shocked.

"How many?" Belwin asked.

"About 3,600,000." War prophesied.

Hades glanced quickly at his brother.

"But how?"

"My guess," Belwin answered, "is that they must've trained their entire nation to fight. At a time like this, desperate measures are assumed."

"But no one in the history on Névorn has attempted such a task!" the Ashen Rider exclaimed.

"These," War explained, "are no ordinary inhabitants. Something feeds their hunger for our defeat."

All agreed.

"Belwin," War called, "are we ready?"

"Yes, my lord."

Aléshai and the MorningStar Talsûrõn stood along one side as they watched the soldiers of the Allies of Jesu position themselves. It was wise how Triaphor had placed them. No soldier of Orés stood beside another. He or she would be standing beside an elf of Ivõrus who would be placed beside an officer of Iristaniq. By this, they would learn to fight together as one.

In front were the swordsmen. There were about 300,000 of them. Though every soldier was equipped with a sword, it was these soldiers who carried the most blades amongst everyone. Two swords on their backs, a sword at their hip and knives on one side of each boot.

Behind them stood the archers. All 600,000 were prepared for a long battle. Ever since Triaphor and Jewel had left the camp, each one of them were given the daily task of creating arrows for themselves. By the time Triaphor had arrived at the camp the night before, each quiver was expected to have a thousand arrows. One would expect the weight of such an amount to be heavy, but these arrows were made from the skin of the

Bakrôns of Bélgôrith, the cousins of the Red Dragons of Ardenôs. This caused the arrows to be lighter than feathers, but sharper than a two-edged sword.

The troupe of elephant riders came next. The number of elephants that had been brought from Orés had increased largely since their departure. Since the citizens of Orés used elephants for most big battles, they'd kept a goodly number of them in the kingdom. In fact, Ric had built an entire city to house these giant creatures and their keepers. Over 20,000 elephants were with them that day. These beasts were heavily laden with 30 archers and 5 swordsmen.

The next group of troops was the largest of them all. 2,000,000 horsemen made up the tale end of this massive army. The cavalry of the Allies of Jesu was most important to Triaphor. Though he knew that King Sésad would bring 200,000 horsemen of his own, the Prophet of Jesu thought it best to counter the Riders with a good two million *riders* of his own.

There was two of what Triaphor named Special Task Forces. These groups stood off to the side, not in alignment with the other troops. The MorningStar Talsûrôn, whose number was approximately 500,000, was responsible for aerial raids. The Fire Masters of Réstôngrír, ranging around 700,000, were placed wherever they were needed most.

The Lalrola had carefully placed commanders over each of these divisions. Aléshai was, of course, to direct the MorningStar Talsûrôn in their special task. Triaphor himself was to lead Laúres and the Fire Masters of Réstôngrír into battle. Autôw had been placed in charge of the swordsmen. Salzahirz would head up the archery division. King Ric wanted to be personally responsible for taking charge of what he considered to be his best asset, the elephants. Triaphor's prized cavalry would be lead into battle by Kyliðn, who would be riding Spéliskir, his unicorn friend.

Riding upon Phôrastérôn the Phoenix, his personal firebird, to view the scope of his armies, Triaphor smiled. The sun was shining, his troops were well trained and there were more on the way. He only hoped that Jewel remembered the signal by which to enter. Everything was timed perfectly and there could be no mistakes made.

Triaphor landed next to Bryan and Aléshai. The two cousins disembarked their beasts of burden and looked back upon the army.

"Fear," Aléshai stated, "It seems that they do not know it."

"Yes," Triaphor agreed, "They've seen too much of it before. I think they've become immune to it. Hopefully that will serve us instead of destroy."

Aléshai nodded in approval. Triaphor looked at her.

"Ready?"

"When you are," she responded.

The two walked towards the dreadful River of Hades. The river was on low tide currently and they could easily cross. It wasn't they who need fear crossing this river, but their soldiers. Hades, Lord of Death, knew how to use his powers well and would do so to make this battle easier for the Riders.

Triaphor, fearing no darkness, took the first step. He felt the evil exuding from the river. Aléshai, holding his hand tightly, took a step. As the two looked up, they noticed that Hades stood atop the Gate of Daréngir witnessing them. Triaphor spoke a silent prayer. This would easily prevent their fiend from killing them or others as they tread across the river.

After the cousins had crossed, they heard a sound. The gate was opening and

Triaphor saw people stirring. As he and Aléshai came to a halt in the middle of the Plains of Daréngir, they could clearly make out who their advancing foes were. Belwin, Prophet of Evil, rode upon a black horse and was flanked by what appeared to be ten men.

"The Elders of Magic," Triaphor said.

Suddenly, ten chairs of a similar style as the ones the Elders had used in the Battle of the Rulers' Field became visible. Off to the side these chairs rested. Belwin continued his stride towards the cousins as the Elders of Magic made their way to their seats. Degradation filled Belwin's eyes as he saw his daughter.

"I see you've decided to permanently ally yourself to these fools," Belwin spoke to Aléshai.

She said nothing.

"We," Triaphor raised his voice so that all could hear; "The Kingdoms of Orés, Iristaniq and the restored City of Ivõrus have come to make war with The Riders of Apocalypse, Rulers of Daréngir and The Dark Alliance that follows them. May the winner take home possession of Névorn until the Time of the Apocalypse."

Belwin laughed to himself. The Riders, his masters, watched in disgust from the gate of their fortress.

"Listen," the Prophet of Evil responded, "All my lords want is your loyalty. There is no need for this useless bloodshed. We all know with whom the victory lies. So all the Riders request is that your nations return to their abandoned cities and for the leaders of these kingdoms to come to them. We shall all sign a treaty that places you in charge of your people, but you will have to answer in authority to War and his brothers. Otherwise, we will defeat you here and kill the leaders of the Allies of Jesu and then make slaves out of its inhabitants. Forever."

Triaphor knew the game that they were trying to play. For this reason, Jesu and Tahiti had instructed him to not cave in or give into any agreement. He was to hold firm to all that he stood for.

"What say you?" Belwin asked.

"We shall," Triaphor started, "not comply with your masters' wishes. We've made up our mind and it is settled."

"Fine," Belwin replied, "but not with my daughter on your side. Aléshai, daughter of Belwin, come back to your father. I will make your life pleasant. Are you not as beautiful as thy mother? Come, marry me and you shall not fall into the same fate as your friends."

Triaphor eyed his cousin. Aléshai walked forward and embraced her father. She stroked through his hair gently. Belwin, who'd not been married since Aléshai's birth, held on to his daughter, as he would've grasped his wife.

"Kiss me, father."

Momentarily, Belwin paused. He looked into his daughter's eyes in surprise. This was unlike her. But, the Prophet of Evil could not refuse such an offer. War and his brothers looked on in hysteria.

"What is he doing?" Hades asked.

Belwin kissed Aléshai. The Leader of the MorningStar Talsuron held her knife closely to her abs. She took a hold of it and stabbed her father in his gut. Blood poured from his lips as she pulled hers away.

"A war is what you wanted," Aléshai stated, "A war is what you shall receive."

Belwin, Prophet of Evil, dropped dead instantly. Hades and War glanced shockingly at each other. The twins, Pestilence and Famine, did the same. Aléshai wiped her knife clean and placed it back in its sheath. Triaphor lifted up his voice once more.

"Come forth, Sons of Tântrígõr," he said, "and face the fulfillment of Jesu's prophecy spoken to you long ago in His temple at Orés."

They paused and for what seemed like an eternity, no one stirred. Then, like a whirlwind, the gate flew open and 100 trolls came at the cousins. Ric, wanting to advance the army, commanded,

"Steady! Steady, men!"

Triaphor had told them to stay in their places until the signal was given. He and Aléshai drew their swords. Like a rushing wind, the two stormed upon the troupe of trolls. Each of them felled numerous amounts of their foes. Both of them had been well trained in the art of fighting huge groups of people at one time. They also spoke tiny spells that killed off many trolls as well.

Hades, knowing what they were doing, glanced at the Elders. They shook their heads. By this, he knew that they were completely legal and the Elders of Magic could do nothing. Yet.

After the trolls were dispatched, Aléshai and Triaphor waited for more. The gate flung wide open again and this time, there came forth the Vampires of Irísylvânia. They were riding upon the Bakrôns of Bélgôrith. Aléshai eyed Triaphor and the Prophet of Jesu nodded his approval. She blew her horn.

Forth flew the MorningStar Talsûrõn across the River of Hades. Along with them came Laúres, leading the Fire Masters of Réstôngrír. Bryan and Phôrastérõn, as geese fly in sync, came to their masters, the two cousins. Swords drawn and poised for attack, the MorningStar Talsûrõn and the Fire Masters flew into battle with the Vampires of Irísylvânia.

The debacle grew fierce, but they handled it well. Suddenly, a horn blew from the fight. Ric and the others knew that it was the signal they'd all been waiting for. Upon that sound, Autôw led the swordsmen into battle. Following him were Salzahirz and the archers. Behind them came the king and the elephants. Kyliõn and the horsemen ensued closely behind Ric.

The Allies of Jesu plunged into the skirmish, fighting to the death. The swordsmen killed many of the Vampires, even though they were riding upon the gargantuan beasts of Bélgôrith. Autôw seemed to fight the hardest, as he'd long been enflamed with wrath against the Riders.

Salzahirz and the archers slowly made their way into the scene. It was difficult for archers to get a hold of enemies in such a mass of confusion. But nonetheless, Salzahirz took the archers into battle and they shot at whoever they could find. They had been commanded to stay in formation, just in case they were needed later.

Ric and the elephant riders traveled swift as eagles.

"Fire!" Ric shouted to the archers on each elephant.

The command was quickly followed. As the Bakrôns of Bélgôrith flew down upon the Elephants of Orés, they were destroyed. If the mass of arrows didn't kill the Bakrôn and its rider, then one of the five stationed swordsmen did. Ric even took out a couple of Vampires himself.

The Riders of Apocalypse watched as this mêlée unfolded in front of their eyes.

War had many other allies at his disposal, but he waited to see if the Allies of Jesu could sustain. If so, he knew exactly what his target would be. Though he was surprised at the ferocity with which these newly trained soldiers fought, War didn't expect the Allies of Jesu to last his next barrage of troops.

****************************   *******************************

Jewel had been awake since the dawning of the sun. It had actually surprised her that the glorious ball of light chose to shine on such a day. In Apocalypse, she'd not expected such. The Dwarves of Gírgéthôr hadn't rested all night and it had been hard for her to rest. For constantly, she heard the sounds of blacksmiths crafting their tools for the battle. She only hoped that these newly sharpened weapons would serve them victory on the Plains of Daréngir.

"Your Highness," spoke King Hûram of Gírgéthôr, "The troops are ready."

"I know," the princess replied, "But we must wait for the signal from Triaphor."

"But there's more lying behind that gate and you know it!" Hûram shouted.

The King of Gírgéthôr had argued with her, Eärísaél, Lord of Énrísôr and Síntrînãs, Princess of Sérõndín the entire trip there. Frankly, Jewel was tired of listening to his senseless babble. She turned her eyes from the battle and stared directly into Hûram's eyeballs.

"Listen," she said fiercely, "Just because I'm a woman doesn't mean I don't know how to lead. I've fought in many wars of my time. I even lead Orés to victory against the Spiders of Tortroc. But here's something you must understand. We stand together. We must listen intently to every word our commander, Triaphor of Orés, has spoken. He said that he would give us a signal. Therefore, if we must wait until the end of time, we shall not march until that signal has been given."

Eärísaél and Síntrînãs, who were standing close to Jewel, applauded her words. Hûram hung his head low in shame. He knew that he'd overcompensated and should've backed off a long time ago. Jewel looked upon him in understanding.

"Lift up your head," she told him, "Today is a day of victory. No one should feel let down or sad. We've all made our mistakes, but now is not the time to dwell on them. Now is the time to take back what is ours!"—at this she raised her voice to the soldiers— "This is our moment to live freely!! We will no longer be oppressed by the ensnarers of wickedness! Their reign has come to an end. Stand up and fight!!!"

******************************   *******************************

Triaphor had fought bravely against the Vampires of Irísylvânia. But as time wore on, he realized why they'd been sent. As he struck down a vampire from the air with the Sword of Tântrígôr, he looked to the gate. There, he saw the Riders giving orders. He knew another assault was quickly on the way.

The Prophet of Jesu was convinced that the Vampires of Irisylvania had been sent purely to tire out the Allies. He took flight with Phôrastérõn and soared over the battle. There weren't many vampires left. He needed to warn them. Fast.

With much speed, he and Phôrastérõn flew down to Kyliõn.

"Prince of Ivõrus!" he shouted, "Reform the line!"

At first, Kliðn, who was slaying a Bakrôn whose rider had died, did not understand. He looked at Triaphor in disbelief.

"Reform the line!!" Triaphor repeated.

The elf nodded. His emerald cape flapped in the wind as Spéliskir took him around the battlefield. Shouts erupted. All commanders were giving the same orders. Triaphor could hear even Aléshai demanding the Talsûrðn,

"Reform the line!!!"

Just as the last vampire was killed, the Allies of Jesu stood in alignment as they had prior to the battle. A noise came from the River of Hades. Triaphor, now on the ground with Phôrastérðn, turned his head towards the cursed stream. Aléshai landed Bryan beside her cousin.

"What is it that disturbs the water?" she asked.

"I'm not sure." Triaphor responded, horror filling his eyes.

From the mysterious river burst forth giant piranha plants. These plants towered over the elephants. One by one they formed a line behind the Army of Jesu. Everyone turned to face this new threat.

"What devilry is this?" Ric questioned.

The Piranha Plants of Hades marched forward into battle.

"How many?" Aléshai solicited Triaphor.

"I'd say 500,000," the prophet replied.

"Good."

Triaphor knew what she was thinking. With an order, Phôrastérðn took off. Upon seeing this, Laúres blew his horn and the Fire Masters of Réstôngrír followed their leader into the fight. Aléshai and the MorningStar Talsûrðn soared directly after Triaphor lifted off. Swords drawn and arrows nocked, the aerial Allies of Jesu flew upon the Piranha Plants of Hades.

Jewel, who'd been waiting patiently for a signal, finally heard Triaphor blow upon the horn. He wanted Eärísaél's eagles. The Princess of Orés eyed the Lord of the Eagle Riders.

"Farewell," he said.

His Eagle Riders lifted off into the air. The Riders of Apocalypse looked sharply towards the Woods of Daréngir. Bursting from there like rain from the clouds came,

"The Eagle Riders of Énrísðr!" Pestilence shouted.

Hades and War looked at each other, stunned. How had Triaphor managed to get them?

Énrísðr, Réstôngrír and Talsûrðn clashed directly into Hades' army of piranha plants. Aléshai took Bryan in between two plants and with her swords, severed their heads. Triaphor flew low upon Phôrastérðn and chopped one piranha at its foundation and quickly glided up to destroy another at the head.

Eärísaél had fought many foes, but never had he been forced to fly upon flowers. The Lord of Énrísðr could not totally grasp what kind of war they were fighting. What sort of powers caused even plants to sprout wills enough to fight? And how viciously these piranhas fought. At times, Eärísaél found it hard to strike them down.

Triaphor took the Sword of Tântrígôr and shoved it directly down the throat of an enemy. As he finished off his flowery fiend, he directed his attention towards the gate. It was opening once more. This time something more deadly was coming. Kyliðn, becoming more and more alert as the day drew long, ordered all the troops to turn around and the army was to reposition itself.

The Elders of Magic, they who usually showed no kind of emotion, sat up quickly in their seats. Turning their heads towards the gate as well, they saw a mammoth force of unimaginably formidable creatures. Their armor was the thickest any had ever seen. The Elders watched as the armies before them trembled.

The Living Dead came forward from the Gate of Daréngir. Triaphor had flown all the way to the front of the battle line. By this time, all divisions had switched places. The horsemen were in the front, behind them Salzahirz's archers, next in line came the swordsmen and in last place were the elephant riders with Ric. Kyliðn, upon Spéliskir, met Triaphor as he landed Phôrastérðn.

"We cannot face them," the elf shuddered, "There are too many."

"Keep faith," Triaphor said, "If we, the leaders of our people, do not hold fast, then who will remain standing?"

Kyliðn knew that this was true.

"What then," the elf asked, "shall we do?"

"I will lead Laúres and Réstôngrír in first," Triaphor explained, "and then you shall take your men to the left. Autôw will come forward, yes, even in front of the archers, and the swordsmen will flank us to the right. After we've attacked them, the archers will fire ten volleys and draw their swords. Next, the elephants will come forward. Those who lose their elephants must fight as though they were a swordsman or an archer. Do you understand?"

"My lord," Kyliðn responded, "It shall be done."

As the Army of Jesu fell back from the wall—for before they'd been too close—Kyliðn spread Triaphor's new plans across the allied forces. Autôw, Salzahirz and Ric, thinking that the prophet's plans were brilliant, quickly adjusted themselves and their troops. Laúres flew in beside Triaphor.

"What," the Lord of Réstôngrír spoke, "are we to do now?"

"You," Triaphor rejoined, "shall bring the Fire Masters of Réstôngrír to the front, behind me. When I command, we shall go into battle."

Laúres nodded and went to inform his soldiers of this new arrangement. The Living Dead, the most treacherous of all servants to the Riders, strode forth. Leading them, Triaphor noticed, was Tantricus and Ranglicius. Each of them was wearing special robes over their armor. The tunic was black while the cape the two wore was blood red. This outfit sported a pair of white gloves for each of them and their boots were of an ashen color. Behind them was The Warlock of Wyrdrías. He had escaped sometime during the night and crossed over the River of Hades to join the Riders. Triaphor had expected this to happen.

The ground pounded senselessly as The Living Dead marched onto the Plains of Daréngir. Triaphor could only hope that his plan would work. He looked over to the Woods of Daréngir. He knew Jewel was watching. Soon, he would have to bring her into this catastrophe. He could only wonder how long it would take Sésad to get here.

Laúres and the Fire Masters of Réstôngrír returned to his side.

"My lord Triaphor," Laúres bowed, "We're ready."

The Prophet of Jesu took one last look at the Riders of Apocalypse. They smirked. That's all that Triaphor needed to see.

"Draw swords!!"

All did as he instructed. Autôw sent the command through his division. Kyliðn shouted so that his horse riders could hear. The sound of sliding metal resounded throughout the battlefield. The marching of The Living Dead was suddenly silenced. Triaphor took a deep breath.

Phôrastérðn, with a tap from his master, shrieked as loud as possible. Giving the signal to his fellow phoenixes, he lifted off into the sky. The Fire Masters of Réstôngrír ascended into the air, ready for whatever befell them. Kyliðn watched as Triaphor bravely led them into war. He eyed Aléshai. She nodded in approval.

"I love you," he whispered.

She blew him a kiss.

The Prince of Ivðrus bid Spéliskir to begin his gallop. The horsemen of the Army of Jesu rode forward with amazing speed. The wind blew through his burgundy hair as Kyliðn felt relief sweep over him. Jesu was with them and would protect His people.

Autôw shouted. All of his men did the same.

"For the freedom of Névorn!!!!" he bellowed.

Thrusting his sword into the air, he ran into battle. Flanking Réstôngrír, Kyliðn and Autôw valiantly took their troops into the war of the century. Shouting all the while, Autôw and the swordsmen were the first to hit The Living Dead. With his first swing, he killed three of them instantly.

Salzahirz commanded each of his archers to nock three arrows. Every man, whether Iristaniquan, elven from Ivðrus or pale-skinned from Orés, had this many arrows on their bows. He held up his sword.

"Volley One!"

The archers fired. The entire first line of The Living Dead fell prey to arrows.

"Volley Two!!"

The next two rows of the Army of Apocalypse collapsed.

"Volley Three!!!"

Death came upon swift wings to the next line.

"Volley Four!!!!"

By this time, Hades had noticed Triaphor's plan. Before Réstôngrír or the horsemen had taken their first blow, six lines of their army perished. He would not stand idly by and watch this happen. These were his slaves and so far, his future slaves were winning. He turned to War, who knew his brother's thoughts.

"Patience," he said, "Tantricus knows what to do."

Indeed the Chief Advisor to the Riders had been well instructed on whom to kill. The person responsible for the most damage. Tantricus looked back. The closest soldier to him was someone in the spear division. The Chief Advisor took the weapon from him. With this, he rode forward past the Fire Masters of Réstôngrír. Triaphor, so intent on his advance, did not even notice him. Kyliðn was the one to bring it to the attention of the archers.

"Kill him!!" the elf shouted.

The archers in the front of their division fired a volley. Tantricus' eyes widened. Though he was afraid of so many arrows coming his way, it was the fact that they had been frozen in air that shocked him, not the fact that they were being shot at him. He looked back at the gate. War had spoken a pretty deep spell to hold them in the air. But even this spell could not hold the arrows. He initiated the help of his brothers.

Aléshai, who'd been watching all of this unfold, looked to the Elders of Magic. They had been unfair and they knew it. But the wicked judges of magic's use had been corrupted by her father. She flew upon Bryan at once.

Tantricus leaned back and threw the spear of his servant. Salzahirz did not realize what was happening until the spear was too close. His mouth dropped…

…Aléshai was too late. Into the Sultan's throat was thrown the spear. As Triaphor's men clashed into battle, Aléshai looked up and saw King Ric advancing forward with the elephants. She flew above them only to insure safety and from the gates of Daréngir came another force.

The Lords of Ardenôs rapidly burst over the walls of the Fortress of Daréngir. The MorningStar Talsûrõn, aboard their griffins, flew over the Elephants of Orés. Aléshai and her loyal Order of Talsûrõn Warriors struck down many Dragon Riders of Ardenôs. Aléshai cleaved heads off of two soldiers of Ardenôs. They were no match for the MorningStar Talsûrõn because of the fact that they were leaderless. The Talsûrõn Order had been restored through Aléshai and though they'd been newly trained, they knew what to do in almost any situation.

******************************   ********************************

Jewel looked upon the battle in horror. Bloodshed. Slaughter. So much death for the cause of one word. Freedom. Though she knew that this was necessary, she definitely couldn't wait until it was all over. Half the day had already been spent and the Riders hadn't even come from their fortress yet. Sésad hadn't come on the scene yet either. The Secret Sisters of Sérõndín were just as willing as she to join the scuffle and the Dwarves of Gírgéthôr were growing more impatient by the hour.

Finally, the moment came that they'd all been waiting for. The Horn of the South blew and Jewel knew that it was time to advance. The Dwarves of Gírgéthôr were the first to appear from the trees. Axes ready, the miniscule men rushed the left side of The Living Dead. Dragon Riders of Ardenôs flew down upon them. Jewel drew an arrow as her horse led her into battle. She shot it and killed a rider. The Sisters of Sérõndín followed Jewel's example.

This was definitely better than sitting on the sidelines.

******************************   ********************************

Triaphor swung his sword and chopped off the head of a soldier. He looked up to witness what was happening. Jewel was coming into the battle now. The Lords of the Sky had tried to stop the Dwarves of Gírgéthôr from advancing but between the MorningStar Talsûrõn and the Secret Sisters of Sérõndín, they failed.

The Prophet of Jesu was beginning to wonder about Sésad when he heard a noise coming from the far right end of the battlefield.

"The Golden Kingdom has arrived!!" someone shouted.

Indeed they had. Hope was rekindled among the soldiers as they saw not only the 200,000 horsemen of The Golden Kingdom but also Gângror and his Giants of Álgrériõn. Triaphor smiled and returned his mind to the battle at hand. Ranglicius had made his way skillfully to the Lalrola.

He's a brave one. Triaphor thought.

Ranglicius swung at Triaphor's head. The prophet ducked and chopped at the horse's legs. He hated the way that felt every time that it was necessary for him to do it. He rolled on the ground and stood to face the Old Advisor to the Riders. Ranglicius charged Triaphor.

The prophet parried continuously. Ducking and striking equally, the two began to play a sort of game. One would lead the other around for a little bit while blocking and ducking all at the same time. Then Triaphor pulled something Ranglicius didn't expect. He jumped over the advisor's head. Without having the reflexes to turn quick enough, the blade was shoved into Ranglicius' back. Peering through to his stomach, the Chief Advisor looked down at the blade piercing him.

"Goodbye, Ranglicius."

Triaphor released him.

The Riders of Apocalypse witnessed the entire brawl. So many forces had come together to do battle against them. Hades grew steadily impatient. He was waiting for the words to be spoken by his brother. If only he'd had the guts to go out there when Tantricus had killed Salzahirz. He knew that he could turn the tide of this war just by showing up on the battlefield.

"Servant!" War called.

One of the servants to the Riders strode forward, bowing as he came. Hades listened intently.

"Gather the horses." War commanded.

A smile crossed the shadowy face of The Ashen Rider.

"Brothers," War spoke, "Prepare for battle."

The Sons of Tântrígõr scurried to don their armor.

*****************************   *****************************

Aléshai, riding upon Bryan, was growing ever tired. She'd been up since the fifth hour of the day preparing for this moment. Her sword had been active since the moment the trolls descended from the gates. Still she was shedding blood. It was a relief to see Jewel. She flew Bryan over to her.

"I will disembark and fight with you, my sister!" she shouted.

"And I shall do the same," Jewel answered.

The Princess of Orés sent the horse back to the woods. It would hopefully find its way home to Orés. If not, Jesu would look out for its well-being. Aléshai and Jewel looked at each other.

"Are you ready?"

"Let's do this!!" Aléshai confirmed.

The two went forward with new zeal. Swords poised, they struck down soldier after soldier. The Living Dead flanks were falling rapidly by the power of their attack. Kyliõn looked up and saw them coming on with such confidence. It boosted he and his men and they continued to drive The Living Dead into the earth.

Triaphor, who'd been riding upon Phôrastérõn the whole time, glanced over at the Elders of Magic. They'd sat there, undisturbed by anyone. Too many people feared their presence. He knew that he had to be the one to do something about it. The prophet commanded Phôrastérŏn to fly him over there. The Phoenix of Réstôngrír, braver than ever, did just that.

The Elders, though very quiet, were no fools. They knew who he was and what he wanted. The ominous Elders of Magic stood. As they did, their seats disappeared. Each one of them drew their swords. Triaphor disembarked Phôrastérŏn.

"Go!" he shouted, "Go defend your fellow phoenix brothers!! Go!! Protect us all, Great Firebird of Réstôngrír! Go!!!"

The phoenix nodded, shrieked in approval and left. Triaphor faced his enemies. By this time, all ten of the Elders of Magic surrounded him. Their swords were all pointed in his direction, ready to soak up his blood.

Triaphor withdrew the Staff of Sŏnércus. Hades, who'd changed the fastest of his brothers, looked on with horror. He remembered how that same staff had struck War down with sickness. This wouldn't happen to the Elders of Magic, he was sure. They would bleed him like a stuck pig.

"Prepare to die, Lalrolian filth!" one of the Elders spewed.

Triaphor closed his eyes. Focusing on The White Temple and the Invocation of Power, he knew that this was the moment. This is what the Lalrola had been called forth upon Névorn to do. Finally, his task would be over. The Elders knew that he was about to speak magic, so they raised their swords.

"Bayasí, bayasŏ, bayasím,
Irígir, irígÿ, irígiðn nayâsúm."

As Triaphor spoke the words of magic, The Elders brought their swords higher and higher into the air. By this time, all Four of the Riders had gathered at the top of the gate. The Twins of Tântrígŏr watched in amazement at what Triaphor did. War and Hades were terrified. They didn't know what was going to happen next, but Hades had a feeling it was going to be disastrous.

"Rísiãlé, ríesûlŏr, rísiâléasŏ,
Triaphor irâ mantas pantha éstrías.
Lalrola ayäsím sín sitûway asa!"

At the last word, the swords of the Elders were brought down. Triaphor, before a blade touched him, removed the red cloak. Underneath it was a shiny silver robe. Shrieks came from the Elders as they were blinded by its light. Clouds filled the sky as though a storm was approaching. One by one, each Elder of Magic dropped their sword.

Using the Staff of Sonercus, Triaphor struck the first elder with the rod. When that Elder disappeared into thin air, the others saw it and ran. But Triaphor would not allow them to escape.

"O Messengers of Jesu, descend ayäsím siyístâÿañ tríâs!"

Calling upon higher power than even he possessed, suddenly the Messengers of The White Temple, their massive wings spread, appeared in a circle around the fleeing Elders. The Elders of Magic picked up their swords, deciding to defend themselves.

Four elders advanced forward to attack. Triaphor hit the first one as the other three filed in on top of him. Rising from the pile, the Prophet of Jesu consumed them as well. Four more Elders of Magic strode forward. Lalrola glared into their eyes.

"Enough," one of them spoke.

He nocked an arrow on a bow. As soon as he shot the arrow, Phôrastérŏn came and swept Triaphor right off of his feet. The Elders of Magic lifted off into the air and followed them. Surrounded by them, Triaphor swung wildly, trying to get at them. He caught one of them as Phôrastérõn took them close to the River of Hades.

"Right!" Triaphor shouted to the bird.

The phoenix took him hard right and Triaphor hit another Elder. Two down, two to go. Phôrastérõn led them through the many facets of the battle. Soldiers fell over each other, trying their best to steer clear of the Elders. Fear erupted their souls as the two passed through the crowd, trying hard to get at the Lalrola.

"Fly up! Up!!"

Phôrastérõn did as instructed and Triaphor held the staff with two hands. He quickly thrust it into one of the two—the one on his right. The last Elder left, stabbed Phôrastérõn in the side and sent Triaphor rocketing across the battlefield. Triaphor flew so far that Aléshai and Jewel, who were now fighting back to back, turned their heads. They ducked as the Elder of Magic came soaring past them.

Triaphor stood to face him.

"Give up my brothers, Lalrolian filth!" the Elder commanded.

"Or what?"

No reply came. The Elder breathed in and blew a gust of wind into Triaphor's face. As he did thus, the ground rumbled and began to split between the prophet's feet. Triaphor tapped the ground with the Staff of Sõnércus. The rumbling and splitting stopped immediately. This was not enough to convince the Elder. He threw his hands forward in front of him. From his fingers came lightning with the strength of a storm. As if Phôrastérõn hadn't had enough, the giant bird came once more and received all of the lightning into his body. Gyrating senselessly, the Phoenix of Réstôngrír shrilled out in pain.

"No!!!!" Triaphor yelled.

As tears burst forth from his eyes, the Prophet of Jesu leaped over his beloved friend and landed...

... the Staff of Sõnércus into the gut of the Elder of Magic. Triaphor rolled on the ground so that he could land properly. The prophet ended up with one knee on the ground and struck the ground with the staff. Suddenly, a great beam of light shot up into the clouds. Separating them and changing their color from black to red to ashen and then back to white, he sent the Elders of Magic soaring into the heavens.

It was such a powerful moment, that all fighting ceased. Everyone watched as they saw what seemed to be winged creatures robed in white receiving each of the Elders of Magic. They chained them up and the clouds closed up and disappeared. Triaphor was on the ground, yelping in pain. Tears fell down his face as the pain enveloped his entire body. Jesu was there, comforting him, he knew, but he was also aware that this was going to be a painful process.

As soon as the beam of light was gone, Triaphor slowly regained his strength. The Staff of Sõnércus disappeared and the Prophet of Jesu went over to Phôrastérõn. The great firebird was no longer enflamed. His fire had died along with him. Triaphor wept bitterly upon Phôrastérõn.

"Aisté pertisto. Peace be unto you, my friend."

Triaphor had little time to mourn, for through the gates of Daréngir, a sound resounded. Horse hoofs pounded in the Plains of Daréngir and all knew who was coming.

Triaphor stood and drew the Sword of Tântrígŏr. On his right stood Kyliŏn, Prince of Ivŏrus. To his left was his wife, Jewel, Princess of Orés who stood beside Aléshai.

"This is it." Jewel said.

The others drew their swords. The four lifted them into the air and joined them at the tips of their blades. Bringing them back down to the earth, they watched as the Riders came forward. Aléshai, Kyliŏn, Jewel and Triaphor, the Lalrola of Névorn, ran to meet their opponents in battle.

Swords clashed and they all took the Riders from their horses.

*****************************   *******************************

Aléshai took on one of the twins. Famine, the Black Rider of Apocalypse stood to face her as he recovered from his fall. She glared into the Rider's eyes. Under the cowl of his black hood, the Rider sent chills down Aléshai's spine. It was she who took the first swing.

The Black Rider responded with a parry. He remembered fighting her in the palace of the Golden Kingdom. Her style had not varied. Famine also thought back on the time that he and his brothers had attacked the planet Talsûrŏn. In fact, the Order of the MorningStar Talsûrŏn originated there. The reason they were named this was because the planet was one of the last stars to appear before dawn broke on Névorn. Aléshai was the last warrior to learn from them. The only reason she'd stayed alive is because that is where the Riders had first met her father, Belwin.

Famine never thought that Aléshai would defect and become such a fierce warrior. But as he continued to battle her, he realized how dangerous she really was. It was very difficult for him to keep up with her. Constantly he was on the defense.

Kyliŏn drove his eyes into Hades. The Ashen Rider laughed to himself as he viewed the elf. This was going to be too easy. All he had to do was speak a spell of death and this puny poltroon would fall upon the field.

"Pak ôrthí un rüthír."

The dark clouds covered the sky once again. Thunder resounded and lighting flashed. Kyliŏn held his sword out in front of him. The lightning that was supposed to strike him ran down the blade of his sword. As it finished soaking up the lightning, Kyliŏn whipped his blade around his head and clashed with the Ashen Rider's sword.

Hades was quite surprised. But this would not stop him from winning this debate. Just as Kyliŏn thought he was going to be on the offensive, the Ashen Rider pushed him onto the ground. He brought his sword into the air and directly down into Kyliŏn's left arm. The Prince of Ivŏrus could not move. Hades had him now.

The Ashen Rider drew another sword. He lifted it into the air. As he brought it down upon Kyliŏn's face, Autôw struck the sword and sent it flying across the field. This caught Hades off guard. The General of His Majesty's forces removed the sword from the prince's arm and helped him off the ground. They turned to face Hades.

"Thou fool," he uttered, "How dare you come between me and this waste of space? Now you will both die."

"Bring it on, you dark scoundrel!" Autôw bellowed.

Hades drew another sword. Autôw and Kyliðn rushed him. Two swords to fight against was much more fun than just one. Hades pleasured in the fact that he was going to kill two leaders today. He'd always wanted to destroy a general and an elf. He relished that he got to murder both of them at once.

Jewel started her battle with a sword. But Pestilence was a cunning warrior. He'd held back his greatest skills until now. And what better time was there to use them? She'd thrown her sword aside and drew the knives that had been given her by Sésad after Triaphor's first death. These seemed to work more for her advantage.

The Princess of Orés had come very close to killing Pestilence several times. Rips in his robe could be found all over. She actually sliced open a vein on his arm as well. But the Red Rider continued his ceaseless fight.

Jewel twirled her knives. She spun and stuck her right knife into the Rider's chest. Then, as he ducked, she brought the left knife over his head. She got closer and planted the knife into his right shoulder. Blood spewed from his mouth. He fell to his knees. She'd finished him.

So she thought.

Triaphor, holding on to the Sword of Tântrígðr for dear life, had fought the White Rider in difficulty. War used magic to his advantage as Triaphor used it for his protection. The constant barrage of having to strike and speak ran Triaphor's strength into the ground.

It was just as War had hoped. He wanted Triaphor to grow weak and to falter. By this, he knew that he could kill the Lalrola. If he destroyed the key to the Allies' survival, they would not last long. His blade graced Triaphor on the cheek, giving him a minor cut.

Triaphor doubled his attack, using more effort than before to fight. War was trying his best to take away his energy, but Triaphor knew many different spells that the White Rider didn't.

"Orírgriânús ãirísaél!"

War looked at the prophet in confusion. Suddenly, two Messengers of Jesu appeared, flanking the Lalrola. With bows and arrows, they shot three rounds into War. Six arrows stuck into the White Rider and Triaphor continued his attack. War was able to defend almost as well as before.

But Triaphor's power was growing upon him and War knew. He glanced around him to see how his brothers were faring. Hades seemed to be the only victorious one. He knew he'd have to draw them back to the gates soon.

Aléshai brought her sword down upon the head of Famine. His sword met hers in midair. He was unable to hold it for that long. The Black Rider collapsed under the Talsûrðn Leader's strength. Falling flat on his back, Aléshai put her sword point in his face.

"Give up. Your death is upon you."

As soon as she lifted her sword from its place to strike him dead, she felt an arrow pierce her armor. Though barely entering the skin, it was enough to bring her to the ground. The MorningStar Talsûrõn warrior fell to her knees. She didn't know where the arrow came from, but she saw that Famine was well pleased with this person.

The Warlock of Wyrdrías loomed over Aléshai. As he rode past her, he helped Famine to his feet and looked at Aléshai in disgust. The Talsûrõn Leader returned the gesture. Taking the arrow from her back, she rose swiftly to her feet. The Warlock drew his sword. One on horseback and one on foot. She wasn't sure she could do it, but Aléshai was going to try.

Suddenly, a deep horn blew in the distance. Famine turned his head. He knew the signal and what it meant. His black horse came to him and took him back to the gates. Aléshai and the Warlock began to fight. It ended soon though, for Aléshai—the better swordsman of the two—cut off his feet.

"Stay there. Prophecy spoken by the Prophet Triaphor shall come true this day."

The Warlock had no choice but remain, for his mode of transportation was detached from his body.

Jewel, Kyliõn, Autôw and Triaphor watched as the Riders fell back to their gates. The four joined Aléshai and waited for them to return. Triaphor knew that they were going to come out more deadly then they had the first time. All of them had to be prepared to kill.

The Gate of Daréngir exploded as the Riders of Apocalypse, Sons of Tântrígõr, burst forth. As the stone flew all over the place, each Rider possessed a new weapon. These were the weapons that had been written about in the legends. War, the White Rider, carried the Sword of Ivõrus. This was a thick sword that was supposed to be able to bring him to swift victory. On his head was the crown he'd made out of the Orb of Uthir Áthéris. Hades, the Ashen Rider, possessed a pair of balances in his hand. With these balances and his circlet made of the Orb of Uthir Pañé, unspeakable power to bring death to the masses was at his disposal. Triaphor shivered as he saw this. Famine, the Black Rider, held a massive sword. Unfortunately, this sword didn't kill; it only caused whoever was struck by it, to slowly die of a dreadful disease. The chain mail of the Orb of Uthir Mínyõn had been donned as well. Finally, Pestilence, the Red Rider, held a pair of morning stars in his hand. Aléshai found it ironic that she was going to be fighting him. He also wore his chain mail, made of the Orb of Uthir Cíliõn.

"For Jesu, have strength," Triaphor instructed, "For Jesu, have faith. For Jesu, fight back and fight hard. He will give you the victory. Take it! It's yours!!! This day, the Lord your God will deliver them into our hands. Let us rid this world of their foul stench!! Forward, Leaders of Névorn!!!!"

Aléshai, Triaphor, Jewel, Autôw and Kyliõn ran forth to meet the stank creatures. The MorningStar Talsûrõn warrior struck Pestilence's left morning star directly. The two fought for hours against each other. Aléshai found it difficult and trying to strike against Pestilence now, but nevertheless she availed. She took her sword, named after the planet

Talsûrõn and struck off his legs. Next, she severed his head from his shoulders. Thus the word of Jesu was fulfilled as spoken concerning the Riders of Apocalypse saying,

"When your Day of Reckoning comes, it shall be swift and cold. Those who serve you your death sentence shall not think twice upon your death."

Jewel, Princess of Orés took on the second twin. Famine fought bravely against Jewel, but he could not keep up this time. Even though his sword was much bigger, Jewel's knife work had been doubled by this point. She refused to lose to this foul monster who'd plagued her people for so long. Thinking upon all he'd done to try and thwart her and her father at the Field of Soltran, her anger boiled inside her. She spun round and plunged her knives…

…directly into his stomach.

"No!!!!" she heard a shout.

Hades came racing across the field. He held his brother in his arms.

"Pestilence," he wept, "Pestilence, hear me."

The Lord of Death knew that it was too late. He bitterly wept upon his dead brother's body. War joined his brother's side. Thus the word of Jesu was fulfilled as spoken concerning Famine, The Black Rider of the Riders of Apocalypse saying,

"Many warriors will stab you in your stomach, causing it to rupture and rupture continually. Never will you heal."

Hades closed his brother's eyes. Triaphor came to stand beside Jewel.

"You'll all pay for what you've done to my brothers," Hades glared at them.

He spoke magic of a considerable proportion. With the height of his power being utilized, his circlet glowed a bright white. For miles around, this light could be seen. Triaphor drew the Sword of Tântrígõr and knocked the pair of balances from Hades' hand. Anger flooded him now. Triaphor took Jewel's sword from her sheath as he saw that the White Rider came his way. He back flipped out of her direction, so as not to cause the White Rider to strike her down.

Triaphor, Son of Tahiti, fought his way around War. War was skillful with the Blade of Ivõrus. But Triaphor knew this would not save him from his brother's wrath. Hades eyed the Prince of Orés. When Triaphor nodded, he removed himself from the fight. War gave a questioning glance. Tracing Triaphor's eyes, he turned round to meet with Hades' blade in his gut.

"This was your fault," the Ashen Rider said, "Now the power shall be all mine. Goodbye War, oh scheming brother, King of Ivõrus and Daréngir. May the blood of the Twins of Tântrígõr rest upon your grave."

War's eyes closed and he fell to the ground. He died by the hand of his brother Hades. Thus the word of Jesu was fulfilled as spoken concerning War, The White Rider of the Riders of Apocalypse saying,

"One close to your heart will be the cause of your death."

Hades came forward unto Kyliõn and Autõw, who'd been waiting for him. All three fought violently, but someone had to die. Hades had been fed for centuries by the hatred against his brother. It is what drove him to his very end. Once War had passed on, Hades' strength dissipated. He no longer could fight as well as he once could. No longer did he possess the power to kill at will. Autõw was badly wounded and Kyliõn, Prince of Ivõrus destroyed Hades, once Prince of Ivõrus, Crown Prince of Ivõrus and yea, even Crown Prince of Daréngir. Thus the word of Jesu was fulfilled as spoken concerning

Hades, The Ashen Rider of the Riders of Apocalypse saying,

"Since you have led your twin brothers into your debauchery, you will lose them within the first hour of the battle that will take your life."

When the Warlock of Wyrdrías saw his sons fall upon the battlefield, one by one, his heart failed him. Violent shaking befell him and the footless wizard fell that day in the Plains of Daréngir. Thus the word of Jesu was fulfilled as spoken by the Prophet Triaphor, Son of Tahiti, concerning the Warlock of Wyrdrías saying,

"You will suffer a death most unimaginable. Your powers shall be taken from you and thou shalt be reduced to a man of normalcy. Then, you will travel with us to the land of Apocalypse. There, you will be suffered to watch the death of your Four precious boys. Upon seeing this, your heart will fail you and you shall die. And it will be known amongst the generations that the Warlock of Wyrdrías, the fool who thought it best to help the Riders, perished on their Day of Reckoning."

Triaphor rested his soul. For finally, the Sons of Tântrígõr were dead. They'd reeked havoc upon the nations for thousands of years. It was time for them to rest in the grave. He and his companions would rule Névorn jointly until the Apocalypse occurred. Jewel came to his side, as did Aléshai and Kyliõn. Autôw went to go find the king. The rest of the soldiers of the Army of Jesu relaxed on the Plains of Daréngir.

"Ariyisté Áthéris," Triaphor blessed, "Peace be with you War, once King of Ivõrus and Ruler of Daréngir."

Upon Hades' body he cried,

"Priyigirsé Pañé. Peace be with you Hades, Lord of Death, once Prince of Ivõrus, Crown Prince of Ivõrus and High Prince of Daréngir."

When reaching the twins, he said,

"Cyronisé Cíliõn. Miriyiriasé Mínýõn. Peace be with you Pestilence and Famine, once Princes of Ivõrus, Princes of Daréngir and Twins of Tântrígõr.

Blessings be upon the Four Sons of Tântrígõr who became The Riders of Apocalypse."

Epilogue
Upon Returning Home

It had been many months since Jewel and Triaphor had left Kyliõn and Aléshai at Ivõrus. Many tears were shed that day. Jewel loved Aléshai as a sister and Triaphor and Kyliõn were brothers at heart. It was hard for Triaphor to leave his cousin, but he knew that Prince Kyliõn, now crowned king, would serve her well.

It felt strange leaving the Iristaniquans in their native kingdom. Not many of them were left after the Battle of Daréngir. Even stranger than that was not having Salzahirz with them. The Sultan's body was prepared for burial and the funeral was held in Ivõrus. But all of them knew where he wanted to be laid. In his own land amongst his people. This had been done. Ric cried the most, for Salzahirz had been his friend since they were small children in the palaces of their fathers.

The journey had taken its toll on Ric as well. It was difficult for him to move on. Three days before they reached Orés, the capital city of the Empire of Orés, King Ric of Orés died. Jewel wept bitterly when her father perished. His body was embalmed and they were even now returning it to Orés. They buried him next to Tahiti, Prophet of Jesu in the Grove of Prophets by the south gate. This wasn't custom, but Jesu had commanded Triaphor to do such because of the king's loyalty to Him even when he sinned and was cursed.

Finally, the grey curtain of night fell back and as dawn broke on the 60th day after the Battle of Daréngir, Jewel and Triaphor looked upon a familiar sight. The inside of their home at Menoléon, formerly known as Tortroc. This time a little bundle of joy filled the household.

Triaphor arose this morning and kissed his son on the forehead. He'd missed him terribly when he'd left him in the hands of Tahiti at the Golden Kingdom. Today was a special day. It was the Coronation Ceremony of Triaphor and Jewel. All of their friends would be there. Kyliõn had been chosen to actually place the crown upon Triaphor's head. Aléshai would do the same for Jewel. The Princess of Orés appeared in the doorway.

"How's my baby?" she kissed Triaphor's lips.

"Which one?" Triaphor smiled.

This is the moment they'd both waited for. No, not the crown. All they'd ever wanted in their lifetime was peace. Finally they'd achieved it. Through water, fire, axes, swords, spiders, wicked Princes turned Riders and even a Warlock, they'd fought for this exact moment right here.

Everything lay still. Everything was filled with one tiny word that everyone on Névorn had shed blood for.

Peace.

The End

Please Look Forward to <u>The Great Deception</u>, the next novel in <u>The Riders Of The Apocalypse Series</u>

City Of Orés
Characters, Places & Objects of Importance

People
Jesu, the One & Only God, Creator of Névorn
Sornsé, Evil Demoness, worshipped as a goddess
Prophet Trílautûs, Prophet of Orés
Prophet Sõnércus, Prophet of Orés, Master of Tahiti & Belwin
Prophet Tahiti, Prophet of Orés
Prophet Triaphor, Son of Biora, Lalrola of Prophecy
Princess Jewel, Daughter of King Ric
King Ric, Ruler of Orés
Biora, Wife of Niron
Niron, Husband of Biora
Tântrígõr, King of Ivõrus
War, the White Rider
Hades, the Ashen Rider
Pestilence, the Black Rider
Famine, the Red Rider
Ranglicius, Retired Chief Advisor of The Riders
Tantricus, Chief Advisor of The Riders
Sultan Salzahirz, Ruler of Iristaniq
Datos, Ruler of Tortroc
Autôw, Chief War Councilor
Sésad, Keeper of the Golden Tree
King Asta, Ruler of Ardenôs
Belwin, Prophet of Evil
Queen Aléshai, Daughter of Belwin, Ruler of the MorningStar Talsûrõn
Bryan, Griffin of Aléshai
Spéliskir, Unicorn of Kyliõn
Phôrastérõn the Phoenix, Firebird of Triaphor (given as a gift from Réstôngrír)
The Fire Masters of Réstôngrír
Lord Laúres, Ruler of Réstôngrír
The Dwarves of Gírgéthôr
King Hûram, Ruler of Gírgéthôr
The Eagle Riders of Énrísõr
King Eärísaél, Ruler of Énrísõr
The Secret Sisters of Sérõndín

Lady Síntrînãs, Ruler of Sérõndín
The Giants of Álgrériõn
King Gângror, Ruler of Álgrériõn
The Elves of Ivõrus
Prince Kyliõn, Ruler of the Elves of Ivõrus
The Elders of Magic
Prince Jõniathor, Son of Triaphor
Sorcerer Eléctrasûmõn
The Warlock of Wyrdrías
The MorningStar Talsûrõn

Places
The City of Orés
The City of Tortroc
The City of Ivõrus
The City of Menoléon
The City of Maesõrn
The Kingdom of Iristaniq
The City of Álgrériõn
The Kingdom of Réstôngrír
The Land of Apocalypse
The City of Apocalypse
The Fortress of Daréngir
Mount Tortroc
The Forest Of Death
The Field of Gold
The Field of Soltran
The Golden Kingdom
The Wilderness of Westcott
The Field of Rulers
The Woods of Wyrdrías
The Wastelands of Åbérdeen
The Golden River
The River of Hades
Mount of Eléctrasûmõn

Objects of Importance
The Orb of Uthir Áthéris, orb of King War, the White Rider
The Orb of Uthir Pañé, orb of Prince Hades, the Ashen Rider

The Orb of Uthir Cíliõn, orb of Prince Pestilence, the Black Rider
The Orb of Uthir Mínýõn, orb of Prince Famine, the Red Rider
The Orb of Dimensia^3
The Necklace of Biora
The Necklace of Lalrola
The Sword of Tântrígõr
The Staff of Sõnércus